ALL-AMERICAN ALIEN BOY

The United States as Science Fiction, Science Fiction as a Journey; A Collection

Allen Steele

ACE BOOKS, NEW YORK

This Ace Book contains the complete text of the original trade edition. It has been completely reset in a typeface designed for easy reading, and was printed from new film.

ALL-AMERICAN ALIEN BOY

An Ace Book / published by arrangement with the author

PRINTING HISTORY
Old Earth Books trade edition / 1996
Ace mass-market edition / October 1997

The Putnam Berkley World Wide Web site address is http://www.berkley.com

Make sure to check out *PB Plug*, the science fiction/fantasy newsletter, at http://www.pbplug.com

ISBN: 0-441-00460-1

ACE®
Ace Books are published by The Berkley Publishing Group, a member of Penguin Putnam Inc., 200 Madison Avenue, New York, New York 10016.
ACE and the "A" design are trademarks belonging to Charter Communications, Inc.

PRINTED IN THE UNITED STATES OF AMERICA

10 9 8 7 6 5 4 3 2 1

Praise for Allen Steele and
THE TRANQUILLITY ALTERNATIVE

"A CRACKERJACK HEINLEINIAN PLOT and a lesson in the value of tolerance. *The Tranquillity Alternative* sets us up for a dandy climax on the moon, featuring lots of action, unpredictable plot twists, and a believable alternative history of the post-World War II half-century leading up to the present, all neatly wired with the motivation and actions of well-drawn characters."

—*Washington Post*

"A LEADING YOUNG WRITER OF HARD SCIENCE FICTION . . . a gripping tale."

—*Science Fiction Weekly*

"AN ACTION-PACKED PLOT."

—*Publishers Weekly*

"HIGHLY RECOMMENDED . . . Steele vividly recreates the experience of manned space flight through excellent technical detail."

—*Library Journal*

continued . . .

THE JERICHO ITERATION

Ace Books by Allen Steele

ORBITAL DECAY
CLARKE COUNTY, SPACE
LUNAR DESCENT
LABYRINTH OF NIGHT
THE JERICHO ITERATION
RUDE ASTRONAUTS
THE TRANQUILLITY ALTERNATIVE
ALL-AMERICAN ALIEN BOY

For
Mark Tiedemann
and
Donna Schultz

CONTENTS

INTRODUCTION:
Dispatches From America

Welcome to this, my second collection of short stories.

The first collection, *Rude Astronauts,* is still available as of this writing, either in its original trade paperback and limited hardcover editions from Old Earth Books, or in its mass-market paperback edition from Ace Books. This second volume could be considered a companion set, not only because it collects most of the short fiction I've written since then, but also because it's also a reverse mirror image of the first book.

Rude Astronauts is set mainly in outer space, with a few stories taking place on Earth. In contrast, *All-American Alien Boy* takes place almost entirely in the United States—specifically, the Midwest, the South, and New England. Because all of these stories were published elsewhere, I've included new introductions to each story in an effort to make this volume worth your money. Many are autobiographical in nature, and they attempt to explain the circumstances under which the stories were written. If you really don't care to know the behind-the-scenes stuff, though, then you're heartily invited to skip the introductions and go straight to the stories themselves. Hey, it's a free country: you can read whatever you want, and no one will jump on your case for it. For the time being, at least.

This is a book of SF stories about life in America.

Until 1991, the four novels and most of the short fiction I had written had focused on space exploration in the near future, either set in the "near space" chronology that I began with my first novel, *Orbital Decay,* or in the alternative space cycle that I recently capstoned with *The Tranquillity Alternative.* Many readers liked these stories, and the ones who sent fan mail or whom I met at signings or SF conventions encouraged me to do more of the same. After I finished *Labyrinth of Night,* though, I discovered that I had temporarily run out of things to say about space. I could continue to write exclusively about astronauts and spaceships, but unless I found new territory to explore, I stood a strong chance of rehashing the same things over and over again. Many SF writers have ruined themselves by doing this; the umpteenth volume in a given series may be very popular in terms of sales, but, by then, the author's vision may well have turned stale.

I got interested in writing a more contemporary, down-to-Earth sort of SF. As luck and circumstance would have it, my wife and I had just moved across the country, and I soon discovered that the American heartland in general, and St. Louis in particular, offered just as much fertile ground for SF as did the Moon or Mars. In fact, it was something of a challenge: instead of resorting to my reference library of books on astronomy and space technology for inspiration—a safe but rather overworked pasture—I had to get stories from more immediate surroundings. As it turned out, this was not a difficult task. As I explained in the introduction to *Rude Astronauts,* I've always sought inspiration more from the real world rather than books. Although I was no longer working even part-time as a journalist, St. Louis offered plenty of places upon which I could hang a story, whether it be a waterfront bar, the baseball stadium, or the alley next to a friend's house, and when St. Louis wasn't sufficient inspiration, there was always rural Tennessee, the North Carolina coast, Boston, or New Hampshire.

In hindsight, it's fortunate that most of my adult life has been nomadic. Before moving to St. Louis, I rarely lived in the same place for longer than a year or two at a time. During 1985 alone, I had four different addresses in four different states. It's hard to get a good credit record that way, but all this accumulated road time let me store away impressions and memories that I could later mine for new stories.

Otherwise, none of the stories in this collection are linked to one another (although "Lost in the Shopping Mall" has a little of the same background as my novel, *The Jericho Iteration*). I may have lost a few readers this way, but many others have been nice enough to write cards, letters, and e-mail that have encouraged me to continue this sort of experimentation.

To those readers, I give my most humble thanks.

These stories are quite contemporary. Indeed, some critics may complain that the settings look very much like the present. There are no domed cities or mile-high skyscrapers; you won't find any flying cars, alien embassies, ESP cops, or secret enclaves of renegade computer hackers. The changes I've made are small and usually subtle. A couple of big robots here, a few tiny ones there; a crashed spaceship in Tennessee, a floating city off the North Carolina coast. The imminent extinction of the human race by asteroid collision. Nothing major.

"Is this all that Steele imagines the future is going to be like?" these critics may ask. To them, I reply, "No, it ain't . . . and if you want prediction or prophecy, give your money to someone who reads astrology charts, tarot cards, or chicken entrails, because you'll stand just as good a chance of divining the shape of things to come from them as you will from an SF story.''

Nor is SF about determining the future. The idea, which has become popular in some quarters, that this genre somehow guides the course of human history strikes me as self-aggrandizing at best, even a bit narcissistic. Some great ideas and inventions have doubtless been inspired by SF, but if the world's political leaders, inventors, and scholars studied this literature in hopes of gleaning kernels of truth, then we would be living in domed cities by now. We would also have a permanent base on the Moon, pay taxes to a centralized world government, and commute to work on moving sidewalks. Alternatively, we would live in the radioactive ruins of cities, dine on rodent du jour and pay tithes to roving motorcycle gangs. All of these scenarios were forecast, at one time or another, as the state of affairs by 1996.

If you lead a man into a room, give him a loaded shotgun, blindfold him, twist him around a few times, and then tell him to shoot at a small target you've placed on a wall somewhere in the room, sooner or later he may hit the target (if you keep reloading the gun). When and if he does, would you call it sharpshooting or a lucky guess? This is the way it is with science fiction. Sometimes an SF writer will hit the mark, or get close enough to the bullseye that it seems like prophecy, but even that rare event can only be ascertained through hindsight.

Anyone who believes that science fiction forecasts or predetermines the future is deluding himself. SF isn't about prediction or prophecy. When a good SF story is running on all six cylinders, it holds our own times up to a warped funhouse mirror, in hopes that we can better see and understand our present condition. It certainly isn't about figuring out future events, however, because SF writers make lousy soothsayers, and even the best of us are dead wrong most of the time.

That being the case, why not write stories as close to

home—that is, our present-day circumstance—as possible?

The most common accusation made against SF is that it's escapist literature, mind candy that offers temporary relief from the troubles of day-to-day existence. Yes, well, SF does this, too, and quite successfully at that. There's nothing wrong with escapism, so long as you recognize it for what it is. Fantasy is a necessary component of daily survival, and a little mind candy now and then is a good thing.

Some of these stories are the mind candy of goofy ideas, and some are meat-and-potatoes serious speculation, with a dessert mint left on the side.

The next collection will include stories further out in space and time. There's a handful of "near-space" tales, which I've already published, that were deliberately left out of this volume, and I'll put them in the next book, along with those that are conceived but not yet put on paper. Be patient, please; I'm making this up as I go along.

The title of this book is borrowed from a song written and recorded by Ian Hunter, the former lead singer of Mott the Hoople; it appears on the album of the same name released in 1976 and also on the two-disk compilation *Shades Of Ian Hunter*. This nugget has never been remastered on CD, which means you'll have to search second-hand vinyl stores to find it. That's too bad; it's a great get-happy song.

The title also refers to many of the characters in these stories. To live in America today and not be utterly shell-shocked by all the changes that have occurred within our lifetimes, not to mention the changes just around the corner, means adopting something of an alien mind set. Our present is the future of old-time SF, but it has become an entirely different future than those which were projected by SF writers twenty or thirty years ago.

The people you'll meet in this book aren't world-conquering heros or scientific masterminds. Frank and Jesse James are here, and so is Joseph Pulitzer, but even then, I've tried to bring these historic figures down from their pedestals and make them a little more human than popular history usually allows. By and large, though, the characters are commonplace men or women trying to get by in a world that they didn't make.

Isn't this the way things usually are?

A couple of years ago, Speaker of the House Newt Gingrich went on record decrying "counter-culture values" that are anathema to "normal" Americans. Outside the Washington Beltway, America yawned and shook its collective head, or laughed out loud, and life went on. Speaker Gingrich lives in the past; his "counter-culture" is what every American experiences as part of his or her daily life. He might as well have demanded legislation repealing the laws of gravity. He doesn't have a clue.

That's the rhetoric of reactionary politics. This is fact: nothing stays the same. We're on the verge of the 21st century. We can't go back, and we can't stand still.

No one is normal anymore. We're all American alien boys.

St. Louis, Missouri
July, 1996

ALL-AMERICAN ALIEN BOY

INTRODUCTION:
"Lost in the Shopping Mall"

Linda and I moved to St. Louis in October, 1990, after spending the past five years living in Massachusetts and New Hampshire.

The reasons for this transcontinental migration were both practical and sublime. Although Linda had established a good reputation as a radio announcer in New England, she wanted to pursue her career in a major-market city. Although I loved the Northeast, I was born and raised in Tennessee, and I longed to hear Southern accents again. St. Louis is Linda's home town, so there was also a bit of homesickness involved in the decision to move to the Midwest.

There was also a less obvious reason. For the past three years, we were living in a very small town in southern New Hampshire, renting first one, then another, lakeside cabin on a dirt road out in the middle of nowhere. Although this isolation was conducive to writing, I came to realize that I was getting out of touch with the world. For months on end, my only contact with virtually anyone other than Linda and a few friends came through long-distance phone calls or my post office box. My

knowledge of current affairs was derived solely from
newspapers, magazines, and TV.

It wasn't long before I found myself experiencing future shock. This was driven home to me when I wrote
an article on cell phones for a Massachusetts business
magazine, in which I explained that portable phones were
already being used in England, and it would only be a
matter of time before they were widespread in the United
States. This brave forecast was based on a visit to London
three years earlier, which was when I first saw someone
walking down a sidewalk while talking on a phone. After
I mailed in the piece, the editor called to inform me that
he and half of his friends were already using cell phones,
that these phones were now palm-size and didn't require
bulky shoulder bags, and where the hell had I been for
the last three years?

Clearly, it was time to come down out of the mountains and rub shoulders again with the late 20th century.

So, we moved to St. Louis, where we rented a house
and began searching for a permanent residence. Within
the first week of our arrival, the strange incident occurred
that inspired this story.

Linda and I had gone shopping in the St. Louis Galleria, an enormous shopping mall in the 'burbs not far
from our new house. Indeed, I had almost forgotten how
huge the shopping malls in major cities have become in
the past few years. The Galleria had recently been expanded, and its upper and lower levels seemed to go on
for miles.

Linda and I became separated. While she went into a
ladies' fashion boutique, I wandered over to Waldenbooks. I thought she knew where I was, but she didn't,
and when I went back to where I had last seen her, she
had already left to try to find me. She went one way, I
went the other, and it wasn't until an hour had passed
that we found each other again.

As I began to search for her, I came to the uncomfortable realization that I had not only lost track of my wife, but also my own location. Here I was, a 32-year-old man wearing bib overalls and old sneakers, looking every bit the hapless hillbilly from the sticks, wandering helplessly in this sprawling mall, with no real idea of where I was or even how to get out. No doors, no windows, just seemingly endless rows of shops . . .

And, of course, teenagers hanging out everywhere.

I had forgotten how much teenagers congregate in shopping malls and the reasons why they do.

Several years earlier, when I was a staff reporter for *Worcester Magazine,* the weekly alternative newspaper in Worcester, Massachusetts, I wrote a story about a recent chain of teenage suicides in the nearby town of Leominster. Seven kids from Leominster High had killed themselves within less than eighteen months, and no adult had ever figured out why. It was the most depressing piece I had ever done, mainly because it brought back memories of a close friend who committed suicide a year after we graduated from high school. Like the parents of these kids, their teachers, and the cops who investigated the suicides, I couldn't ferret out the reasons either. Despite wild rumors of satanic cults and suicide pacts, everything I learned about them told me that they had all been normal, middle-class kids living in a normal, middle-class town.

The only concrete thing I learned about the kids in Leominster was that they frequently hung out in the town shopping mall . . . because, like so many other teens in so many other places, there was no other place for them to go.

A year later, during a trip to Austin for the annual Armadillocon SF convention, I was among a group of SF authors who were given a tour of the labs at MCC, a microelectronics research firm that deals with advanced cybertech development. During the tour, one of the things we were shown was a demo program for a prototype VR shopping mall . . . and damned if it didn't look almost exactly like the St. Louis Galleria.

Didn't see any teenagers. But there weren't any doors or windows there, either.

I don't think shopping malls lead teenagers to kill themselves, nor do I believe that widespread use of virtual reality will, either. The reasons for suicide go much deeper than that. You can get lost in cyberspace, however, just as easily as you can in a shopping mall.

LOST IN THE SHOPPING MALL

The day after Rebecca DiMiola became lost in the shopping mall, Joe Bass caught the TWA morning flight from Boston to St. Louis. He could have just as easily found her while sitting in CybeServe's corporate headquarters in Framingham, but that wasn't the way he did things. Especially not when children were involved; kids were always the toughest ones to track down, and Bass intuitively needed to meet Rebecca face to face before he could hope to bring her home.

The company's senior sales representative in St. Louis met Bass at the gate when the plane arrived at Lambert International. He was a big-boned midwesterner with the obligatory salesman's mustache and a mouth that seemed to be charged by solar cells; he said hardly anything until after he escorted Bass out to the short-term parking lot, but as soon as they were alone in the car he began to talk nonstop—quickly, nervously, less as conversation than as a constant drone, as if the hot summer sun had energized his vocal cords:

"We don't know how it could have happened . . . the family had all the usual fail-safes installed in the default directory . . . her father had even put a one-hour timer on the system, but you know kids today, they can crack anything if you leave 'em alone long enough. . . .''

"They do," Bass said. He absently caressed the aluminum briefcase laid across his knees that contained his portable system. The sales rep had stowed his carry-on bag in the trunk, but the computer had never left his hands since he had walked off the jet.

"Yeah, yeah, I hear you . . . caught my own kid downloading beta-test games from one of the IBM boards last year . . . locked him out of the computer for six months, that taught him a lesson . . . but the strange thing is, there haven't been any major purchases except for a pair of sneakers from The Athlete's Foot, and that was in the first fifteen minutes of entry . . . she hasn't done anything since then . . . hey, you want a cigarette?''

"No," Bass said. "Don't smoke." He watched the traffic rushing past them on the inner belt. He had never been in St. Louis before, but it looked much the same as Cincinnati, Minneapolis, Cleveland, Houston, Los Angeles, or any other city where CybeServe had previously sent him: exit ramps leading to cookie-cutter suburbs and high-rise business districts, electronic billboards and dead animals lining the shoulders of the highway.

"Good for you . . . ought to give it up myself . . . anyway, the hard copy of the initial search is on the back seat, if you want to look at it . . . of course, you've probably seen it already, I dunno . . . hey, uh, we're not in any trouble for this with the home office, are we? . . . I mean, all we did was follow the service order, give the customer what he wanted . . . y'know, we're sympathetic to what's happened to the little girl, but we can't be blamed if something goes wrong, right?. . . . oh, and hey, I've snagged a couple of tickets for the Cards game tonight at Busch Stadium, if you want to unwind later on . . . right behind home plate, and the Mets are in town, so maybe we could grab us a couple of brewskis and. . . ."

Bass looked away from the passing scenery and turned his gaze toward the sales rep. Even though the salesman had told Bass his name at least three times since they met at the airport, Bass couldn't remember it. There were large sweat stains beneath the armpits of the salesman's shirt, he talked too much, and he was trying to squirm out of any culpability, real or imagined, he had for the situation: those were the lasting impressions Bass had of him. The name didn't matter.

"Do me a favor," Bass said. "Just shut up and take me where I gotta go. Okay?"

The salesman's face reddened and his mouth trembled beneath his Burt Reynolds mustache, but at least he stopped talking. He stared straight ahead as he put a little more shoe leather against the metal, whipping the Ford through the noonday traffic as he mentally updated his résumé, just in case things didn't work out for the better. Bass gratefully lay back against the headrest and shut his eyes, taking temporary comfort in the uneasy silence within the Ford.

Soon he would be meeting Rebecca. That's when the job would begin.

The DiMiola residence was located in Clayton, one of the more upscale suburbs of St. Louis County: large houses on small lots, arranged along tidy streets near mini-malls, trendy restaurants, and small parks. The homes in Rebecca's neighborhood had neat half-acre yards shaded by oak and elm trees; parked in the driveways were late-model BMWs, Mazdas, and Volvos, all beige or red or charcoal-gray. A couple of middle-aged ladies in florescent jogging suits, their pinched faces shadowed by sun visors, pigeon-walked down the sidewalk. Bass counted at least three cop cars as they drove through the side streets, and police helicopters constantly prowled the azure sky. American apartheid: the urban combat zones in the north county, where cops and black street gangs waged war every night, were located in a different space-time continuum entirely. Here, the only African-American to be seen was an old man, sweltering in the summer heat as he pushed a mower around somebody else's lawn.

The salesman pulled into the driveway of a two-story neo-Colonial home; he seemed to want to come inside, but Bass wouldn't let him get out of the car. Instead, Bass picked up his case and climbed out of the Ford, asking the salesman to take his carry-on bag to the hotel—he would call a cab once he was through. The salesman looked both chastized and relieved; he murmured something from the common phrasebook of senior sales representatives—"good luck," or "break a leg," or "rightaroonie, good buddy"—before Bass slammed the car door shut. Bass waited until the Ford backed out of the driveway and disappeared down the street before he turned and strode up the front walk to the door.

As he pressed the doorbell, he heard the familiar click-and-whirr of a hidden security camera rotating to focus on him. He didn't look around or move but simply stood in front of the door, gazing at the archaic brass knocker. After a few moments, the electronic lock buzzed, then the door was opened from within.

The woman who answered the bell looked like a younger version of the two joggers he had seen a few minutes ago: artificially blonde and slender, aristocratic but somehow graceless, as if her fading early-forties beauty had been purchased from the cosmetics counter at Lord & Taylor, her regal bearing the result of late-night readings from Miss Manners. She wore a bright-orange jogging suit—apparently the uniform of choice for the housewives of Clayton—and she didn't smile as she peered through the half-open door, but studied Bass for a moment before she spoke.

"Oh," she said, feigning polite surprise. "You must be from the computer company."

As if he hadn't already been scanned by the door camera. It was easy to imagine how she saw him: a pudgy little man with a receding hairline and a soft stomach, wearing an off-the-rack business suit from J. C. Penney and old shoes from Sears. Definitely not Clayton material.

"Yes, ma'am," he replied. "Joseph Bass, from the CybeServe Corporation." He put down his computer, pulled his card case from the inside pocket of his coat, and extended one of his business cards to her. "I'm here to see Rebecca DiMiola."

"I see . . ." She took the card and glanced at it, matching the holograph against his face. When she looked up again, her narrow gaze darted back and forth past him, as if scanning the sidewalk beyond her front lawn to see if anyone was watching. Then she tucked the card into a pocket, opened the door a little wider and stepped out of the way. "Please come in, Mr. Bass."

"Thank you, ma'am." He wiped his feet on the doormat—stenciled The DiMiolas, with an embroidered picture of a golden retriever sitting in a country meadow—then walked into the front hallway. Everything in sight was marble, china, Irish glass and Brazilian mahogany, with not so much as a dustbunny in sight. Nice house. "You must be. . . ."

"Ms. DiMiola. Evangeline DiMiola." She held out her hand, palm down; Bass put down his briefcase and grasped it. The skin of her palm was very soft and smooth; she had never held anything harder than the handle of a tennis racket. The handshake was brief and perfunctory. "I'm so glad you could come so quickly, Mr. . . . what did you say your name was, again?"

"Bass. Joseph Bass." She smiled very slightly, then eased the door shut behind him. "Is Mr. DiMiola here?"

Her smile faded as she stepped back, folding her arms

together. "My husband is out of town," she said. "He's in Japan on business. He. . . ." Her gaze travelled to the floor, studying the Indian carpet beneath their feet, as she murmured something indistinct.

"I'm sorry, Ms. DiMiola," Bass said. "I didn't catch that."

Evangeline DiMiola looked up again; for a moment, there was a pleading look in her eyes. "He doesn't know what's happened to Rebecca," she repeated. "He hasn't called since two, three days ago. I didn't want him to know, because if he did, he might. . . ."

Again, her voice trailed off, and her gaze wandered. "Get upset?" Bass finished.

"Yes. He might get upset." She took a deep breath and closed her eyes for a moment, apparently recollecting herself. When she looked at him once more, her gaze was again hard and direct. "When I spoke to someone from your company on the phone, they said that they would send someone to help, but I wasn't sure what they meant. Can you tell me what you do, Mr. Bass?" She frowned a little. "Are you some sort of technician?"

She could have been asking if he were a plumber or a licensed electrician. "I'm a consultant for the company," he said. "A cybernetics psychologist . . . sort of a computer shrink."

"Ohhhh . . . I see." Evangeline DiMiola tried to look worldwise, but at the same time she seemed to flinch at the word "shrink." Bass wondered how much time she herself had spent in therapy, spending a hundred dollars an hour to deal with upper-class anxiety.

"If you want to know my credentials," he went on, "I've been employed by CybeServe for the last three years, handling situations much like your own." Again, the slightest flinch and frown. "Before that, I was a research associate at M.I.T.'s artificial intelligence lab, after I received my doctorate in psychology from Vanderbilt and did my clinicals at Baptist Hospital in Nashville. I've also done some consultant work for IBM and Toshiba, and. . . ."

"Okay, okay. I understand." Ms. DiMiola impatiently waved her hand. "What I want to know is, can you fix my daughter?"

Not help. Not cure. Not even talk to . . . she had said fix, as if she were discussing a washing machine with a broken rotor or a car that had inconveniently blown a radiator gasket. She seemed to realize the gaffe as soon as she had uttered it; her face reddened beneath the Estée Lauder makeup, yet her eyes became challenging, daring him to make something of it. He was the serviceman, here to deal with an appliance that failed to perform according to its warranty specifications.

Which, in a sense, was the truth.

Bass said nothing; he dispassionately waited for her to go on. He had been in this situation before; he knew what she would inevitably say, as certainly as if this whole conversation had been flow charted and logic diagrammed. "I want . . ." Evangeline DiMiola began, then paused to reconsider her words. "I would like for you to see my daughter." A deep breath. "To see if you can make her speak to me again."

Bass still didn't respond. He waited for the only word he wanted from her.

She knew what he wanted; her mouth trembled slightly as she spoke. "Please," she almost whispered.

"Certainly, Ms. DiMiola," he said. Then he picked up his briefcase and took a single step off the foyer carpet. Entering her nice house was a little victory, and he allowed her a little smile as a consolation prize. "Now, if you'll take me to her, please . . . ?"

Evangeline DiMiola escorted Joe Bass across the chandeliered first-floor hall and up the winding main staircase to the second floor of her house, but before they went to see Rebecca, he asked if he could see the girl's room.

She hesitated for a moment, then silently nodded and led him to a bedroom next to the stairway.

Rebecca DiMiola had not lived the first fifteen years of her life in poverty. She slept on a queen-sized four-poster that was covered with a down comforter and a large assortment of stuffed animals. She had her own high-definition TV, complete with Sega box and cable hookup; on her desk was an Apple computer and a videophone; in a cabinet was a CD stereo system. Posters of rock idols and famous young teenage TV stars were thumbtacked to the eggshell-white walls, and in an open closet were hung new clothes: silk party dresses, stylish school outfits, sweatshirts, and prefaded Levis 502 jeans. On the bookshelf next to her bed were copies of everything from *Charlotte's Web* to Kitty Kelly exposés to trade-paperback comic books; on top of the shelf was a glass jar filled with loose change, mostly nickels and dimes.

"She's an only child, you know," her mother said as Bass stood in the center of the bedroom, taking everything in. "She almost had a younger brother once, but . . . well, there was an accident, so she's the only kid we have."

"Kid," he whispered under his breath. Wonderful word, that. Formerly used to describe an adolescent goat. Bass walked over to the dresser. Beneath the glass top were a couple of dozen photos, ranging from baby pictures to recent snapshots. He stopped and looked down at them. Rebecca had been a bright, shining little girl who had gone many places and done many things. Here, she rode a pony at summer camp in the Ozarks. There, she played in the surf at Maui. She posed next to a beefeater at the gates of Buckingham Palace, looked through the eyepiece of a large telescope in a great observatory, stood on her head in front of the White House—always smiling, waving, full of adolescent joy. A princess from Missouri.

"Maybe we spoiled her a little too much, you know." Her mother's voice came from a distance behind him. "Whenever she wanted something, all she had to do was ask. Perhaps that's spoiling her, but . . . God, if you have the money, why not? At least she's not like her friend Rosie . . . her parents were hippies, raised the kid on some godawful commune in Tennessee where they only ate brown rice and tofu. . . ."

But something changed as Rebecca grew older; Bass could see it in the later photos. In her transition from childhood to her teenage years, Rebecca's smile gradually faded, lapsing into a sullen stare. She lost her pixie figure and got fat, then lost all the weight again and became anorexic. Her breasts grew; when she was thirteen, she tried to hide them beneath baggy sweaters, but two years later, she had taken to midriff sweaters in winter and tight T-shirts in summer. She changed her hair color from blonde to mousy brown and back to blonde again, gradually letting it grow down past her shoulders. And she stopped going to Hawaii and England and Washington, D.C.; most of the recent pictures were taken in other people's houses.

"We tried to send her off to boarding school," Evangeline DiMiola continued, "but she lasted only a couple of months before she was thrown out. We put her in Country Day . . . good school, best in the city . . . but even then her grades didn't improve. And I didn't like . . . y'know, the other sort of kids she was hanging out with. From the south side, you know. . . ."

Recognizable in two of the older pictures was a younger Evangeline DiMiola, before the shopping trips got to her, but in none of the photos was anyone who could be her father. And after childhood, Rebecca had almost always been alone when her picture had been taken, as if she had demanded that someone shoot a photo or had used a camera's timer to issue a blurry self-portrait. In one shot, she was flipping the bird at the camera; in another, she was sitting on her bed, wearing only her underwear bra and panties, a can of malt liquor cradled in her lap. In that picture, she looked less like a princess than a drunken ghost.

"When did she start using computers?" Bass asked.

"Hmmm? . . . oh, computers." Evangeline DiMiola awoke from her reverie. "When she was about nine, ten, I guess . . . her father bought her one after she used his to do a science project for her fourth grade class. She's had one ever since." Her condescending tone returned, this time mixed with ill-disguised bafflement. "She's always been good with computers, God knows why. I mean, when I was her age, I didn't know what an . . . ah, a Pentium was, or what an eighty-megawhatsis was. Why does a little girl need to know . . . ?"

"When did you and your husband buy the VR system from us, Ms. DiMiola?"

She shut up and stared at him. When she spoke again, her voice had become as glacial as her eyes. "About six months ago, Mr. Bass," she said. "That's when Mr. DiMiola had the spare bedroom turned into a . . ."

The rest of the sentence was bitten off by another dark frown. "A dataroom," Bass finished.

"Yes. The dataroom. Down the hall." Evangeline's mouth had become a thin, dense line of lipstick. "Donald . . . my husband . . . gave it to her for Christmas last year. She tried all the other services . . . the games, the tours, stuff like that . . . but she really got attached to the Gallerie Virtual. Pretty soon, that's all she wanted to do when she was home. Go hang out in the mall."

Her eyes narrowed as she glared at him. "It's still covered by the warranty, you know. I checked it before I called your company. Besides your airfare, I don't believe we owe you for. . . ."

"No. You don't." Bass turned away from the dresser, away from the dusty mosaic of Rebecca's life. He walked toward the door, not wanting to look at her mother's face.

"It'll be covered in the final statement. Now, if you'll take me to your daughter, please . . ."

He was ready to go shopping.

The dataroom was located just down the hall from Rebecca's bedroom; Bass wondered if it had originally been intended to be the nursery for the baby brother who had been lost in miscarriage. Its walls and ceiling were lined with white foam-padded Naugahyde, which covered the magnetic sensors; if there had once been windows, they were now bricked over and invisible behind the padding. The room was completely bare of furnishings, except for a single leather-upholstered armchair near the VR terminal, which was built into the right wall.

The dataroom was sound proof, climate-controlled, clean, and odor-free, and it resembled a padded cell in an insane asylum.

Rebecca DiMiola sat cross-legged on the carpeted floor on the opposite side of the room from the empty chair. Her datagloved hands rested loosely in her lap, and her posture might have suggested zen meditation were it not for her slumped shoulders and bent spine; instead, she looked frail and exhausted, as if she had hiked miles through a desert only to arrive at a dry oasis.

Bass walked slowly around the girl, studying her. Most of her face was hidden by the black HMD that covered her head except for her nose, mouth, and the lank blond hair that spilled out from beneath the back of the helmet. The orange Spandex datasuit she wore, normally skintight on most people, was slack at her chest and shoulders—she was a very skinny young woman—but it was her mouth, devoid of expression, that caught his attention.

Bass squatted in front of her, gazing at the opaque mask of her face. "Rebecca," he said, "can you hear me?"

"It's no good," her mother immediately said from the

doorway behind him. "I've tried talking to her, begging her, yelling at her, but she won't. . . ."

Bass glared over his shoulder at Evangeline DiMiola; the woman instantly shut up. His gaze shifted to the VR terminal; green LEDs on the panel told him that the room was still in operation. "You didn't try to unplug her, did you?" he asked quietly. "You didn't push the reset button or reboot the program, or otherwise try to break the link?"

For a second, Ms. DiMiola's expression became hostile. "Of course I didn't!" she snapped. "What do you think I am, stupid? I may not know much about these things, Mr. Bass, but I've read the newspaper stories. I know what can happen if someone's in . . . what do you call it, VR shock . . . and they're suddenly unplugged. I can read, you know. . . ."

Bass stared silently at Evangeline DiMiola until her voice trailed off. She sagged against the door frame, suddenly appearing much older than her vanity and cosmetics normally permitted. For the first time since he entered her home, she looked like a scared, middle-aged woman, trying to understand something that her pampered, sheltered life had never allowed her to contemplate.

"Please," she whispered. "Just do something about my baby."

Bass looked away from her, back at Rebecca's still, hollow face. God help him, how many other kids had he seen like this? Gary in Houston, crouched on a mountain of gold in Smaug's underground lair, lost in a Tolkien fantasy. Crissy in Minneapolis, standing at the edge of an improbably high cliff on Ganymede, entranced by the vision of Jupiter rising above the icy horizon. David, poor David, sitting cross-legged much like Rebecca here, except in a black and featureless void, so flat-lined that, in the end, the only recourse was to unplug him, leaving the seventeen-year-old institutionalized for the rest of his life.

And then there had been Geoff, and Akheem, and Mike, and Dorothea, and Jane. . . .

At first, when he had started working for CybeServe, he had thought them to be tragic anomalies, freak accidents that occurred from time to time. But he had been doing this for three years now, and he knew that there was no shortage of Rebeccas, and he was tired of seeing them. So much pain for so little reason, and his reserve of sympathy was finite. Perhaps this would be the last case he would handle for the company. Let someone else shoulder the responsibility. He was exhausted.

She'll be the last one, he told himself, perfectly aware that this was not the first time he had made this promise to himself.

Bass took a deep breath and slowly let it out, never taking his eyes away from Rebecca's face. "Please leave us," he said at last. "Rebecca and I have to be alone by ourselves for a little while."

Evangeline hesitated. For a moment, Bass thought she was going to argue with him, but then he heard the door close, and he was alone with the girl.

Bass opened his briefcase and prepared to make the jaunt. His gear was strictly industrial, with none of the consumer-friendly frills of home-market VR equipment: datagloves for his hands, a Snoopy-helmet HMD with a built-in headset mike, a pair of overweight goggles, all hardwired to the portable computer nestled within the foam padding of the briefcase. He used a roll of tape to strap thin sensor cables to his arms and legs. Once he used another cable to interface his computer to the dataroom's terminal through their serial ports, he ran a quick systems test to make sure that the link was solid and that his telepresence program was loaded. Then he jaunted into the Gallerie Virtual.

He was standing in the mezzanine of a vast, enclosed shopping mall. Summer sunlight spread its warm rays through ceiling skylights, casting unnatural, too-straight shadows from benches, potted trees, and incidental post-modern sculptures. Luminescent signboards glowed above the wide doorways and awnings of artificial shops, displaying the bright logos of a thousand corporations, marching away into infinity: Timex, Waldenbooks, J. Crew, Banana Republic, Babbage's, Camelot Music, Victoria's Secret, The Gap, Toys 'R' Us, Hallmark, Brooks Brothers . . . an endless corridor of different tastes and interests, materialism rendered pixilated, three-dimensional phantoms of free enterprise.

But the Gallerie Virtual was completely vacant, despite the allure of bright lights and readily available products. Computer-generated beings usually strode through the mall—adults, teenagers, small children—to give the illusion that the mall was occupied and being used by many people. It was even possible to select a function that allowed the visitor to see the other CybeServe subscribers who were currently logged into the Gallerie, permitting somebody in San Francisco to go shopping with a friend who lived in Boston.

Both features were elective, though, and Rebecca had evidently toggled them off. This was a bad sign. Bass glanced up at the row of icons displayed in a red border just above his range of vision—SELECT, VIEW, CREDIT, BUY, HELP and EXIT—and raised his right hand to point at HELP. A pulldown menu was superimposed over the scenery, listing a variety of mall services. He touched the one labeled OTHER, opening a second box on top of the first, then spoke aloud. "CybeServe security override," he said. "Bass, Joseph Peter, code Tango Mary Romeo three-zero-eight-six-niner, backslash six-nine-eight."

Another window, bordered in silver and labeled AUTHORIZED USERS ONLY, was laid over the first two boxes. He moved his finger to the line marked USER TRACE. "DiMiola, Rebecca," he said. "Account num-

ber six-three-six-eight-one-nine-zero-zero-one-seven-two-
five-three, expiration date two-slash-nine nine. Execute,
please.''

A message bar appeared at the bottom of his line of
sight, blocking out the tiled floor of the mezzanine: ''No
Trace Found. Security override initiated 6-12-98 3:47
PM.''

''Negate override,'' he said. ''Execute backup trace.''

The message changed instantly: ''Override negated.
No backup trace located for DiMiola, Rebecca.''

''Damn,'' Bass muttered. He was afraid of this. Just
as the local sales rep had intimated, Rebecca had managed to crack the security codes that prevented unau-
thorized users from accessing the Gallerie Virtual's
default codes. It happened on occasion, usually when
some would-be cyberpunk attempted to go on a shopping
spree using someone else's credit number. In this instance, though, Rebecca had overridden the mall's tracer,
which allowed a CybeServe investigator to track an individual's past and present movements through the Gallerie. Then, to make matters worse, she had also
instructed the computer to eliminate the backup file of
her movements.

This didn't look good. Bass closed the silver window,
then fingered the menu item that listed Rebecca's purchases during this run and her remaining credit line; as
he had been told by the sales rep, she only purchased a
pair of running shoes from the Athlete's Foot before she
disappeared. As an afterthought, he moused the VIEW
window, and found that the shoes in question were an
expensive pair of men's Nikes, size 10. The shipping
order stated that they were to be sent to Donald A.
DiMiola, in care of the address of a St. Louis office complex. No, this didn't look good at all. The only purchase
Rebecca made in the Gallerie Virtual was a pair of running shoes for her father, to be sent to his office instead
of his home . . . then she vanished, carefully instructing

the mall to delete her footprints behind her.

The message was more subtle than a handwritten suicide note, but the intent was just as blatant.

There was only one way left to find her. Bass exited the menu, took a deep breath, then began his long walk through the shopping mall.

The search for Rebecca DiMiola took many hours. Even walking in place, pantomiming an endless stroll through the Gallerie Virtual by raising his feet and putting them down on the real-life floor of the dataroom where they had just left a moment before, while the mall itself unravelled before him step by step, was eventually fatiguing. A couple of times he sat down and rested; the second time, he took off his shoes and briefly massaged his aching feet, then he continued his journey in his socks.

Bass never removed his helmet and goggles, though; to do so would have meant removing himself from telepresence, and he didn't want to do that. He had to keep himself locked within Rebecca's world, this obscene and infinite teenage universe of simulated stores and fake water sculptures and digital trees. Without the convenience of a trace-pattern, his only hope was to keep walking.

Once, he heard the door of the dataroom open and he felt Evangeline DiMiola's presence behind him. He said nothing, though, and, after a few moments, he heard the door shut once again.

When Gary had run away into a role-playing program and Bass had gone in to find him, he been able to play the riddle game with Gollum and thereby gain a hint as to where the boy had gone, eventually locating him within the dragon's cavern. Finding Gary had been easy, as long as the person trying to find him was familiar with *The Hobbit*. With Rebecca, though, there were no twisted subterraneans to give him vital information. All he could do was follow a sourceless, banal river of consumerism.

He was not entirely without clues, however. He had

been in her bedroom, had seen the things she collected in real life. It was a small hunch, but it helped to narrow the focus of his search.

She had stuffed animals on her bad, so he visited the toy stores and walked up the long vacant aisles, passing shelves of plastic guns and games and dolls, until he found the section that contained images of Winnie the Pooh and Mickey Mouse and Bugs Bunny and a hundred different kinds of bears. There was nobody here, so he exited Toys 'R' Us and went across the mezzanine to another teen-style clothing store, where he strode through aisles of party skirts and jumpsuits and hosiery until there was nothing left to see. Then he kept walking until he found another music store—his third since he entered the mall. He went inside and wandered past the bins of CDs that contained the latest hits by the latest bands, and when Rebecca wasn't to be found there, either, he left Discount Records and kept walking until something else caught his eye.

The trick was in thinking like a teenager, so he ignored the more upscale and conservative clothiers, and the places that offered fine-art reproductions and household gadgets. He passed the Museum Store and L. L. Bean and Bausch & Lomb, because there was little in them that would catch the fancy of a fifteen-year-old girl. But, at the same time, he had to remember that she was lonely and intelligent, a girl who had spent most of her years by herself. She knew computers and high-end electronics, so he visited Radio Shack and Babbages. She was into photography, so he went to places that sold cameras. So on through the mall, until he covered dozens of stores that carried all these items, randomly hitting places like Walgreen's and Spencer's Gifts on the odd chance that she might wander into them.

He also remembered that she had a lot of books on her bedside shelf. She liked to read, so he went into every bookstore he found—Waldenbooks, B. Dalton's, Bor-

ders—until, four hours and thirty-seven minutes after he
began the search, the hunch paid off, and Joe Bass finally
found Rebecca DiMiola.

She was hiding in the back of Mark's Books, hiding in
the children's section. As in real-life, her VR image was
seated cross-legged on the floor, but this was the only tie
to reality. Her telepresence was much more beautiful: her
figure was fuller, her hair longer and more curly. She
was wearing an old-fashioned gingham skirt that made
her vaguely resemble an older Alice from the Lewis Car-
roll novels. Fairy-tale innocence combined with some
teen magazine version of physical perfection, as much of
a disguise as her mother's makeup and haute monde man-
nerisms.

Rebecca was staring straight at a row of Dr. Seuss
books on the bottom shelf, her hands folded together in
her lap. As soon as he spotted her, Bass dodged behind
a rack of books so that he couldn't be seen. He opened
the security window on his menu and activated a real-
time tracer, just in case she attempted to run away. Then
he stepped out from behind the rack.

"Rebecca?" he said. "Rebecca DiMiola?"

She was visibly startled by the sound of his voice; her
unchanging face jerked around toward him, and at the
same moment she made as though to rise, her hands moving from her lap to push against the floor. But her real-
life body had not eaten or slept for almost a full day; she
was too weak to run off. Instead, she fell backward, half
collapsing on the floor of the bookstore.

"Hey, hey," he said gently. "Better watch yourself.
You can still get hurt in here."

Bass took a step forward, holding out his hands to help
her up, but Rebecca scuttled backward, avoiding him.
"Who are you?" she demanded. "What are you doing
here?"

Although her simulated face was incapable of chang-ing expression, her voice, electronically filtered in his headset, was tinged with fear and anger. Bass was aware of how she saw him; his telepresence was much the same as his real self, except that he had preprogrammed it to soften the lines of his face and shorten his height, lending himself the image of a kindly Dutch uncle. He could have programmed himself to resemble anyone from Santa Claus to Mickey Mouse—with very young children, he often did just that—but in this instance, he wanted her to see him much as he really existed. Honesty was the key to everything, whether they were in virtual reality or, hopefully, when they emerged from cyberspace.

"I'm Joe," he said. "I work for the mall. Your mom asked me to come in here and find you." He allowed himself a chuckle; all emotions he chose to display had to be verbal. "You're a hard lady to find, Rebecca."

"My mother . . . ?" She remained still on the floor. "She sent you after me? Oh, gaawd. . . ."

Bass took another step forward, bending over with one hand outstretched. "Here. Let me help you up and we can talk about. . . ."

"Keep away from me!" Her voice became a high-pitched yell as she found the strength to scramble to her knees. "Get any closer and I'm outta here!"

From a seemingly vast distance away, Bass heard the door of the dataroom softly open once again, felt a cool draft of fresh air. Although he couldn't see her, he knew that Evangeline DiMiola had to be standing in the open doorway. Yet her daughter didn't react; either she was unaware of her mother's intrusion, or she had chosen to ignore her . . . and Bass himself couldn't risk acknowledging the woman's untimely arrival.

Bass shrugged and let his hand drop to his side. "Okay. Fair enough. I'll stay right here." He squatted, resting his arms on his knees. "Y'know, Rebecca, your mom is worried about you. . . ."

"Uh-huh, sure. Like, she's really torn up, right?" She

was crouched on her knees and hands, like a sprinter ready to bolt at the starting gun. In her present state of agitation, she might not treadmill-run either, but charge straight into the wall of the dataroom, possibly injuring herself. "What's the matter, she think I might crash her credit rating?"

He sighed and pantomimed scratching behind his ear. "No . . . no, I think she's really concerned about you, kiddo."

She laughed sullenly. "If you know that bitch the way I know her," she said, "you'd know how stupid that sounds." She paused. "And don't call me a kid. I really hate it when people call me that."

Bass heard a sharp intake of breath from the doorway. For an instant, he was afraid that Evangeline DiMiola would say something that would break the spell . . .

Then the door shut, a little more loudly this time, and once more the two of them were alone.

"Sorry," he said. "I won't do that again." He sighed loudly enough for Rebecca to hear him. "Look, I'll make a deal with you. I won't try to grab you and you won't run away, okay? We're just going to talk. Fair enough?"

A moment of hesitation. "Okay," she said at last, seeming to relax a little. She eased out of her running stance. "Fair enough. Just so long as we talk and that's it."

She sat down on the floor in an ungainly heap, unwittingly allowing the hem of her quaint skirt to fall down around her thighs. She looked down at her lap, then made a pushing motion that caused the skirt to move back into place. "Whoops," she said, her giggle tinged with an uncomforting touch of hysteria. "Can't let you see my virtual panties, can we?"

Bass shrugged again. "Doesn't matter to me, Rebecca. I'm a little too old for you, anyway."

"Beck," she said. Her voice became insistent. "If you're going to call me anything, then call me Beck."

"Becky?"

"No, not Becky . . . Beck." She looked away, her changeless face moving toward the holographic display of Dr. Seuss books. "Only my mom and dad call me Rebecca. I asked them to call me Beck, but they say it sounds like I'm a gang member or something."

"Uh-huh," Bass said slowly. "Sounds like they don't listen to you very much."

"You got it." She reached out and briefly touched the cover of *Green Eggs and Ham*; a window opened in the corner of Bass's screen, listing the book's price, author, page count, plot summation and recommended reading level. "Great book. Can't wait for the movie."

Bass touched a menu key that closed the window. She let out an irritated sigh. "Let's talk about your parents a little. . . ."

"Let's not and say we did." Beck removed her hand from the book. She went silent for a few moments, staring straight at him, before she spoke again. "Look, Jim. . . ."

"Joe."

"Jim, Jack, Joe, whatever you said your name was . . . I know you're supposed to be a shrink or something, but you and I both know you're just a neural net system in Massachusetts, running an AI program." She laughed again, this time more bitterly. "You're pretty good. The dweeb who programmed you did a righteous job, but you couldn't pass a Turing test to save your chips, y'know what I mean?"

"Yeah. I know what you mean." Bass felt for the right pocket of his trousers, fumbled inside while Beck watched him, and found a quarter. He pulled it out, knowing that the coin was invisible to her in cyberspace, then aimed carefully and pitched it straight at her.

She jerked back a little as the unseen coin hit her in the chest. "Whuu? . . . what was that?"

"The quarter I just threw at you," he said mildly.

"How's that for passing a Turing test, Beck?"

"Christ on a crutch. . . ." Her hands searched the lap of her dress until she found the invisible yet tactile coin; she raised her right hand, the non-virtual coin pinched between her thumb and forefinger. "Oh, my gaaawd," she whispered. "You're real! You're in the room!"

"Yep. Sure am. Real as they get." Bass raised his hands and waved them around. "Listen, Beck . . . I hate to tell you this, but this store, this whole mall . . . it isn't real. None of it's real, no more than the stuff you see in the movies is real. Sure, it's a good fake, but. . . ."

"I know it isn't real!" she yelled, her voice shrill with frustration. Her hand lashed toward him and Bass felt a sharp pain as the quarter struck him in the forehead. "Jesus Christ, you think I'm stupid? Of course I know it's not real, gimme a break . . . !"

"Okay, all right." Bass rubbed at his forehead. "That really hurt, you know."

"I'm sorry," she said. "I'm sorry. Didn't mean to hurt you. . . ."

She didn't sound very apologetic, but at least the fact of his real-life presence had been proven to her. It was a good start. "Don't worry about it," he said. "I'll live. Look, Beck, the point is, you're trying to run away inside this thing. That, or maybe you're trying to kill yourself. . . ."

"I'm not trying to kill myself!" she snapped, standing up suddenly as her anger rose again. "Gaawd, I don't have to listen to this shit!"

Bad move. He had rushed her and she was retaliating. Time to backpeddle. Bass didn't rise to his feet; he lowered his voice, struggling to remain easy going and un-confrontational despite her hostility.

"Please, Beck," he said. "I'm sorry. I didn't mean it. Just sit down, okay? We've got a deal, don't we?"

"What deal?" she demanded.

"The deal we just made a minute ago." Joe forced

himself to remain steady. She was on the verge of a breakdown; getting mad at her or being patronizing wouldn't help. "Hey, I just want to talk things through with you, that's all."

Bass silently cursed the present state of cybernetic technology, which only allowed her face to be a mask. It was remarkable how much therapy depended upon seeing the patient's facial expressions; without such subtle clues, he was little better off than a Catholic priest hearing confession from the other side of a screen. If she ran off now, he would be able to trace her wherever she went into cyberspace, now that the computer had re-established a fix on her position, but the opportunity to communicate with her would be lost, and he might not be able to regain her trust again.

"Uh huh. Right." She sounded tired. So many conflicting emotions in so few minutes. "You're just here to help lil' ol' me. . . ."

"Yeah," he said. "I'm here to help lil' ol' you." It was his turn to do a little begging. "C'mon, Beck, give yourself a break. Just sit down again. Please?"

Rebecca hesitated. The crucial moment was here; either she would trust him, or she was gone for good. Bass said nothing. The decision belonged to her alone.

"Okay," she said very quietly. "Maybe we can talk." Then she sat down on the floor again, hugging her knees between her arms.

"Thank you," Bass said. "I'm sorry I offended you."

"That's okay," she said weakly. Her voice sounded choked; he heard a faint sniffle, and her right hand raised to rub against her nose. "No, I . . . I mean, you didn't . . . aw, shit. . . ."

He said nothing, only sat still and waited. "Yeah, maybe I wanted to kill myself," she went on, her voice a dry rasp now. "I mean, not really, but . . . I dunno, I thought maybe if I came in here, stayed in the mall long enough, maybe someone would start to pay attention to me. . . .''

"Like your folks?"

"Yeah, like my parents . . ." Her head bent forward as she rubbed her hands against her face; the sniffling grew louder. "My dumb parents. I mean, my mom . . . my royal bitch mother, she's always with her friends, at the club or out shopping for shit, and when she's home I'm like a piece of furniture she forgot to take to Goodwill or something. . . ."

"And your father? Your dad?"

A harsh, brittle laugh. "Never see him. Haven't seen him in months. He's always away . . . Russia, Germany, Japan, Australia, some stupid country. I try to get him on the phone, but he doesn't call back. Just buys me something instead."

Her mask-like face rose from her hands. "I mean, where do you think this place came from? I thought if I asked for something really expensive, he might notice me . . . but naw, he just paid for it. One more thing for his little girl back home."

"Hmm." Bass nodded his head. "Then how do you really feel about this place? The mall, I mean."

Beck said nothing for a few moments. Her face moved back and forth, up and down, her eyes searching the peripheral view of artificial reality. "I . . . I dunno," she said at last. "I kinda think it sucks." She looked back at him. "You're right, y'know? It looks really dumb, when you stop and think about it. All you do is dress up and buy stuff and shit."

"Uh huh. Know what you mean." Bass carefully scooted closer to her; this time, she didn't move away, not even when he held out his hand.

Instead, she reached and grasped his palm, their gloves encircling one another's in a grip whose warmth could not be simulated by a computer. For several minutes, they simply held onto each other; nothing was said, because nothing needed to be said.

"This place gives me the creeps," she said at last.

"Don't ask me," he replied. "I just work here."

She sniffled and laughed a little. "I've got an idea," Bass said. "Let's get out of this joint, then we can talk about this some more."

"Yeah . . . okay. That sounds good to me." She raised her free hand to an invisible place above her forehead and her fingertips danced in midair. Then she winked from sight, although Bass continued to feel her right hand grasped within his own.

He took a long, deep breath and took one last look around the bookstore before he reached up to the menu bar and touched the EXIT key.

They remained in the dataroom for a little while longer, sitting on the floor across from each other. Rebecca removed her helmet and Bass took off his goggles and headset, so for the first time they saw each other as they really were. They had a conversation, but the girl did most of the talking: she spoke of her frustrations, she got mad a few times, she cried some more, and when she was done, Joe Bass did his best to help her put the pieces back together.

When they were through, he sent Beck to her room to take off the datasuit and take a long shower, advising her to put something in her stomach, then go straight to bed. He gave her his card and told her to call him if she ever needed someone to talk to; Beck smiled, sniffling some more, and bashfully thanked him. Then she left the dataroom, perhaps for the last time.

Bass used a cellular phone to call for a cab and to arrange airline reservations for an earlier flight back to Boston, then he took off his equipment, unjacked his computer from the room's terminal, and began packing them away in his case. When Evangeline DiMiola appeared once again in the doorway, he didn't turn around.

"I just wanted to thank you," she said. She hesitated, then added: "For bringing my daughter back to me."

"I got her out of the mall, Ms. DiMiola," he replied, still not looking at her. "Bringing Beck home is still your problem. You're going to have to work that out with her."

She didn't respond, saying nothing until he had closed the briefcase and stood up. Bass noticed that her eyes were red-rimmed, her makeup was gone. She looked away, visibly embarrassed; her right hand fumbled inside the pocket of her jumpsuit, came out again with a small wad of dollar bills. "That's for your help, Mr. Bass," she said quietly. "Please take it."

Bass looked down at the money and shook his head. "I don't need a tip, ma'am. If you want to do something useful with it, use it to dismantle this room. That's what Beck told me she wants you to do."

She blinked quickly, not quite understanding what he had said. "Beck?" she asked. "My daughter?"

"Yes. Your daughter. She wants to be called Beck." He hesitated. "And if I were you, I'd start listening to her more often . . . or you're going to see me again."

He didn't wait to hear what she had to say. In fact, all he really wanted just then was to get the hell out of her house. Bass stepped around Evangeline DiMiola and walked down the hall, down the stairs, through the foyer, and out the front door, out to where a cab was already waiting by the curb.

As the cab cruised through the leafy suburbs of St. Louis, making its way through the late afternoon traffic to the inner belt and the airport, Bass sat in the back seat and silently watched the houses go by. He thought of all the children he had met: Matt, Angie, Stephen, Raoul, Beth, Karen, Jackson, Jennifer . . . and Rebecca, sometimes called Beck.

She wouldn't be the last case he would handle. As

much as he wished otherwise, Bass knew that there would still be another shopping mall to enter, another lost kid to find. He knew this now; if he had forgotten it before, then he had been reminded.

All the children, all their pain, in all the imaginary worlds. Lost in the shopping mall.

INTRODUCTION:
"Mudzilla's Last Stand"

To borrow a line from Julie Andrews, these are a few of my favorite things.

One of my fondest childhood memories is the sound of stock car races from the Nashville Speedway. I've never been to a stock car race, but only because I never felt like I needed to go. On still summer nights, sitting on the front porch of the hillside house where I grew up, I could clearly hear the rumble of cars from the Speedway many miles away. If I listened closely, I could make out the downshifting gears, the abrupt wham! of collisions, the muted drone of the announcer's voice. It was like old radio drama: you didn't really need to see anything as long as you kept your ears open.

My wife is a lifelong Cardinals fan, so we go to many baseball games in the summer. Although baseball itself is only a minor interest to me, I have great fondness for Busch Stadium. It has the best hot dogs money can buy and the coldest beer on Earth, and Cards fans are the nicest in the league; they'll even applaud when the visiting team makes a good play. I'll happily watch a Cards game, but, for some reason, my real fascination is with the stadium itself.

And then there's Japanese animation, particularly, the kind that involves humongous robots that can stomp Tokyo or Osaka flat in no time. I've got a small collection of Japanese videos—*Macross, Patlabor, Giant Robo,* the terrific *Robot Carnival* anthology—and I've also built a few imported plastic models of the same.

And this is one of my least favorite things: racism.

Americans often vent their frustration at Japan's success in the world economy by claiming that it only managed to accomplish this by ripping off Western technology and ideas. This is a cheap excuse for rednecks, both white and blue-collar, to indulge in yellow peril Jap bashing. American ideas and technology have been exported for sale around the world for several decades. Should you blame another culture if they legally buy our technology at fair market value, then improve upon it through discipline and hard work? If the Japanese make better cars, computers, TVs, VCRs, cameras, and even robots, than the Americans who invented these things in the first place, then whose fault is this?

For the record, I buy American whenever I can, if only for the fact that we need to keep jobs in this country. But economic competition is one thing, and racism is another; it has become too easy to confuse one for the other.

This story is about favorite American pastimes, including bigotry. Most of all, though, it's about big robots with an attitude . . .

MUDZILLA'S LAST STAND

"*Raaaaaa-ooooogawwhhh c'mon down to the Midstate Coliseum this Saturday night for raaaaww power! power! POWER! as Big Muddy Promotions and Fratz Beer present aawwwrrrrggh! Motorama 2000! Fast cars! Funny cars! Bigfoot trucks! Watch 'em skid! Watch 'em crash! Baaaaroooooghh! And featuring for the first time in this area reeearrrrgghh! MUDZILLA-zilla-zilla! Haaawwwwnnnnkkkk! Tickets nineteen-ninety-five for adults, twelve-fifty for children, available at all Big Bee Mart, Discville, and Computix locations! Motorama 2000 featuring Mudzilla, this Saturday night at the Midstate Coliseum! Ahhhrrrreeeeebahhh! BE THERE!*"

Edwin "Eddie Joe" Carlisle; owner, Big Muddy Productions:

Mudzilla? The best idea I ever had and maybe the worst. Drove me bankrupt by the time it went to the Tennessee Speedway, and my lawyers would probably kill me if they knew I was even discussing this with you. Want to guess how many lawsuits I'm still fighting? *(Points to a file cabinet in the corner.)* Enough to fill that cabinet, yes sir.

Well, y'know, what the hell. *(Sighs.)* You've come a long way, son, so you might as well get the story from me and not from one of my competitors. Pull up a rock and lemmee give you the lowdown on what happened with Mudzilla. . . .

Big Muddy Productions, y'see, specializes in arena entertainment. Big-name concerts, demolition derbys, sporting events . . . you name it, we done it. It started out here in St. Louis about twenty years ago as a small company, booking night-club acts and so forth, until we eventually expanded and began working with various sponsors to bring shows to places like Busch Stadium and the St. Louis Arena. Later on, we started booking stuff with the major venues in the Southeast and Midwest. For a while there, we were doing pretty good business, 'specially with rock shows and tractor pulls, things like that.

A couple of years ago, though, the bottom just about fell out of the whole industry. For one thing, the major rock groups all but stopped touring because the overhead costs became too prohibitive and people couldn't afford to spend thirty dollars for cheap-seat tickets . . . and, y'know, who wants to go see a bunch of guys lip-synching a tape, right? All the sports teams had become franchised, so independents like me couldn't afford to bring 'em into town. As for the auto events . . . well, they were still dependable revenue during the summer and fall, but after the big tractor-pull craze of the '80s, the whole blamed thing had started to die off, once the movie stars stopped slumming with the hillbillies and the old-timers wanted to stay home with their families and watch it on TV instead.

'Round about '97, this company was beginning to feel the pinch. Insurance premiums, union payscales, the costs of renting all the equipment, everything from contract riders to paying for ushers and custodial services, not to mention city and state taxes . . . it was just wearing us to the bone. Meanwhile, our gate revenues were taking a steady slide, 'cause we couldn't offer people anything new. *(Shrugs.)* Y'know, to be quite honest, if you've seen a guy jump a motorcycle over ten school buses once, you've seen it a hundred times, right?

Like I said, times were tough, and this company was beginning to hurt, and I don't mean maybe. Now, I knew that we had to find something fresh that would bring people back into the stadiums, but I didn't have a handle on what would work. Hell, if I could have hired Madonna to take on the entire Dallas Cowboys starting lineup on the field under the lights, I would have done it as long as it would make a buck.

At any rate, I was sitting here one day, working the phones and trying to find a fair-to-middlin' country band who wouldn't mind playing intermission during Monster Truck Rally, when my secretary steps in and tells me there's some Jap . . . 'scuse me, a worthy Oriental gentleman . . . waiting to see me in the lobby.

"Tell him to get an appointment," I says, and Bobbie says he doesn't want one, he wants to see me now. "Ask him what he wants to see me about," I says, and she says, "He wants to sell you a robot." Well, that kinda pisses me off, so I say, "Tell him to take a hike, 'cause I got one at home, A CybeServe Butler 3000, and it isn't worth a tinker's damn, can't bring me a cold drink from the refrigerator or nothing."

So she ducks her head out the door and tells him, and she listens for a second, then she comes back to me and says, "He wants to know if your robot is forty-eight feet tall and can demolish an infantry platoon."

And I say, "What?"

"This is the new face of modern warfare . . ."
(CLOSE-UP SHOT of a cylindrical weapons pod as it

opens fire. Anti-tank mortar fires at thirty rounds per minute, smoke blossoming from its narrow shafts, as rockets flash into the pale sky. CAMERA PANS LEFT as the missiles streak across the hot desert toward mobile artillery parked near the horizon; there are distant fireballs, followed seconds later by faint booms, as the artillery units are destroyed.): "The unmanned mobile artillery units that were targeted during this test simulation in the Gobi Desert have been completely destroyed, from a distance of two and a half miles. Were this an actual combat situation, this would be considered a tactical victory. However, you're not watching the work of a mere tank. . . ."

(CAMERA SLOWLY BACKS AWAY from the weapons pod, until it gradually becomes apparent that it is not mounted on top of a tracked vehicle. First, an armorplated shoulder becomes visible, then a glass-canopied head, then the box-like thorax, then the enormous arms, then the wide legs, until finally the entire robot can be seen. As we watch, the enormous machine lifts a foot and takes a step forward.): "This is a semi-autonomous robot, the last word in ground-support combat armor. It is Yuji Corporation's XCA-115A, sometimes known as the Kyojin-1. . . ."

Tazaki Norio; Senior Sales Representative, United States Division, Yuji Corporation:

Yes, Mr. Steele, you may switch on your recorder . . . um, no, we won't need to use the autotranslator. I speak American English quite well, thank you.

Let's start at the beginning, shall we? The Yuji Corporation had been working on the development of the XCA-115s since the late '80s, and we produced the first two prototypes in 1998. To understand why we would want to build these machines, you must realize that my country has had a long-standing fascination with robots. In Japan, we've had animated cartoon adventures about giant robots for many years now, so it would only follow that the generation of engineers and scientists who had grown up watching shows like *Macross* and *Patlabor* might actually want to build these things, just as your country's space scientists were influenced by watching *Star Trek*.

Among other things, the Yuji Corporation has been a world leader in industrial robotics since the 1970s, and many of our products have seen extensive military applications. The company foresaw some possible value in developing man-piloted combat robots, so it devoted considerable time and expense to designing and building two prototypes of the XCA-115 Kyojin. The intent was to produce a large, bipedal vehicle that could be used for two major purposes . . . first, as an all-terrain mobile weapons platform, specifically for tactical ground warfare, and second, as an urban police vehicle, specifically for use in riot situations. We believed that if such a machine could be built and successfully demonstrated, the company would have a product that could be marketed overseas as the leading edge of 21st century munitions technology.

As I said, the Yuji Corporation spent considerable time, money, and resources on the Kyojin's R&D, so it didn't . . . ah, how do you say? . . . go down well with the company's directors when the two prototypes were field-tested and it was discovered that they didn't perform very well in real-life situations.

First, one of the XCA-115's . . . specifically, the Kyojin-1 . . . was tested in a mock combat scenario, simulating a ground war in the Middle East. As you saw in the promotional film, it operated superbly as an aggressor. However, in a defensive mode, it . . . ah, how shall we say? . . . it stuck out like a sore thumb. Anything that tall tends to stand out on the battlefield, making itself an in-

viting target for enemy aircraft and artillery. Even with
on-board electronic countermeasures, any pilot or gunner
who had good eyesight could easily aim his weapons at
the robot and . . . er, blow it away. Also, the robot's die-
sel motors consumed an enormous amount of fuel and it
required almost constant maintenance, so a small convoy
was necessary to supply and service even one robot, and
such a convoy is especially vulnerable in a real combat
situation.

So then we took the second XCA-115, the Kyojin-2,
and refitted it with tear-gas launchers instead of ballistic
weapons. We tested it in Osaka, where there had been a
great deal of streetgang violence in one of the city's worst
slums. We put it in the service of the Osaka police force,
on a trial basis, and at first they were very proud to have
it. Showed it off to the press and so forth. Then it was
sent into a riot situation, and . . . *(coughs)* pardon me . . .
um, it didn't do very well there either. . . .

How? Well . . . *(coughs again)* excuse me . . . the Kyo-
jin-2 was a bit too cumbersome for an urban environment. It tended to fall over things like vending machines,
trash cans, cars. Had problems walking around buildings.
Stepped on things . . . no, no people, but it did crush quite
a few parked motorbikes.

And instead of being intimidated by its size, the gangs
. . . well, to be quite honest, they laughed at it. The tear
gas didn't faze them, because they had already learned
how to wear goggles and masks when the police fired
gas cartridges at them, and then they took to the rooftops
and threw objects at the pilot's cockpit, or even jumped
out of windows onto the robot's shoulders, where they
would tear off the antennas and break the cameras. The
unfortunate pilot suffered a cut on his forehead when his
canopy was shattered by a brick, and he swore he'd never
drive one of these things again.

(Sighs.) It was most embarrassing. After the test, the
Osaka police declined our further assistance . . . in fact,

they asked us to remove the Kyojin from the city. And, of course, we had to pay for all the vehicles it stepped on. Many people in the company suffered haji . . . lost face, you might say. Several executives had to quit their jobs, many more were demoted. Mr. Yuji himself had to apologize to the Osaka city government.

When it was all over, the company decided to abandon the project entirely and leave this sort of thing to manga books and TV . . . but the board of directors decided that we had to recoup our losses, and the only way to do that was to sell the two XCA-115 prototypes to whomever would purchase them.

As a result, I was asked to find an American buyer, at least for the Kyojin-1, which had suffered the lesser amount of damage. *(Shrugs.)* This was not very easy, because the Pentagon had no interest in the XCA-115, nor did any of your country's police departments . . . everyone had seen the news media's film of the Osaka riot. For a time, I thought they could be sold to Hollywood, but everyone at the studios with whom I spoke said that giant robot movies were . . . um, I believe the word is passé. Besides, they told me, Industrial Light & Magic could do the same thing using miniature models.

No one in America seemed to be interested. I had almost given up hope when I turned on my TV late one night and saw . . . *(Smiles.)* Yes, I saw my first tractor-pull. I watched this and I thought, ''Wouldn't it be interesting if . . . ?''

(VIDEOTAPE CLIP of a river barge docked at an industrial pier on the Mississippi River; a bridge crane is unloading an enormous cargo container onto a flatbed truck, while several dozen people watch from nearby.):
''A small crowd gathered this afternoon to watch the anticipated arrival of St. Louis's newest attraction . . . a giant Japanese combat robot. And although bystanders saw

nothing of the robot itself, expectations are already running high. . . ."

(A YOUNG BUSINESSMAN, speaking to the microphone): "I can't wait to see it. This is gonna be one heck of a thing, I can tell you that . . ."

(CLIP from the promotional video of the XCA-115): "The robot, known as the XCA-115 Kyojin-1, or 'giant' in Japanese, was recently purchased from the Yuji Corporation by St. Louis arena promotor Big Muddy Productions. It is expected to be making its debut six weeks from now at Busch Stadium during Monster Truck Rally 2000. . . ."

(EDDIE JOE CARLISLE to microphone): "We're really proud to be bringing the Kyojin to audiences here in St. Louis and other venues in the South and Midwest. It's a unique, one-of-a-kind machine, and we know the fans will get their money's worth when they see this big guy in action. . . ."

(REPORTER on screen): "Although Big Muddy Productions is not allowing anyone to see the Kyojin-1 until its first appearance at Monster Truck Rally, the company promises a show to rival the Cardinals' opening day game for popularity. For News Channel Five, this is Laura Summer. . . ."

Donnie Hale; former driver of the XCA-115:

There were quite a few professional drivers who wanted to take a crack at riding the robot. *(Laughs.)* Hell, not just drivers either, but everyone you could imagine, once word got out that Big Muddy was lookin' for an American to take the stick. Test pilots, bulldozer and fork lift operators, computer freaks. And lots of danger nuts, rambos and bungee-cord jumpers and so forth. Everyone who wanted to sit in the pilot's seat wrote letters and made phone calls to Eddie Joe. Shit, they had to hire another secretary, just to answer the mail and handle the phones.

But Eddie knew he wanted a stock-car driver, so he called up maybe a dozen guys who had worked for him before and asked us to come to St. Louis to do interviews. I lived nearby, out in Booneville, so I said, "Sure, what the fuck," and drove into the city. And, y'know, to make a long story short, he gave me the job.

What . . . ? Why did he pick me? *(Smiles.)* Well, first thing Eddie asks me, he says, "Donnie, are you still married?" And I say, "Ed, the missus left me six months ago for a college professor and took the kids with her, you know that." Then he says, "Is your health insurance paid up?" And I say, "Hey, man, I've been in and out of the hospital three zillion times in the last ten years. My doctor just bought himself a place on Fire Island from all the business I've given him and I've even started dating his receptionist. Allstate gets the first check I cut each month. What the fuck do you think?" So he nods and says, "Are you sure you can handle a fifty-foot robot that could cream your car by just farting on it?" And I said, "Yes, if you pay me." And then he just grins and says, "You're my boy."

Well, next thing I know, I'm on a plane to Tokyo, where I spent the next month out there in Yuji's VR simulators, learning how to handle the system. The company's U.S. sales rep, Tazi, took me out there, even played the first few rounds against me . . . sumbitch, even one of their salesmen was able to kick my ass at first, it was so weird. Y'know, sort of like learning how to steer with your feet and shift-and-clutch with your hands . . . and the guys running the simulators really rode me hard, making sure I got it straight.

But anyway, I pretty much got the hang of things by the time I was ready to come home. Eddie himself picked me up at the airport and, even though I was jetlagged like crazy, he drove me straight to his office. "I got a present for you," he says when we get there. "Something that'll put your name up in the bright lights.''

Then he gives me a box with a red ribbon tied around it, and when I open it up, inside's this silver one-piece crashsuit . . . big Old Glory patch on the back, my name stitched on the front, all sorts of sponsor patches on the thing. Looked tight enough for me to need a truss just to get in it. And right on top is a big, white cowboy hat with a lil' green dinosaur patch on the front, and a word printed on it . . . ''Mudzilla.''

I look at this and the first thing I say is, ''Mudzilla? What kind of name is that?'' And he just smiles and says, ''You don't really expect me to call it a Jap name, do you?''

''It's coming . . . !''

(CLOSE-UP of an immense mechanical boot crushing a Honda Civic: slow-motion shot of its top being pulverized, window glass shattering, hood and trunk hatches kicking open, doors blowing off their hinges. Heavy-metal soundtrack, slowly rising.): ''It's big . . . !''

(MEDIUM SHOT of two enormous fists pulling a bridge-cable, slowly hauling an exhaust-fuming, rubber-peeling Peterbilt tractor-trailer rig backward through rising dust.): ''It's dangerous . . . !''

(DISTANT SHOT through nocturnal fog and hazy half-light, as a shadowy behemoth slowly marches toward the camera, then stops and raises its menacing claws toward the night sky.): ''And it doesn't pay parking tickets . . . !''

(ZOOM IN on the juggernaut as an array of spotlights flash on, exposing every sleek and frightening inch of its fuselage, until the camera centers on the chestplate beneath the cockpit, which has been painted with the picture of a tyrannosaurus holding a Confederate flag, as the music reaches a screaming crescendo.): ''Mudzilla is here!''

(Ten-second FREEZE-FRAME for local ad insert.)

• •

Eddie Joe Carlisle:

We saturated ads on all the local TV and radio stations for four straight weeks, getting everyone primed for Mudzilla's debut at the Monster Truck Rally. It cost us a bundle, almost as much as the 'bot itself . . . well, maybe I shouldn't talk about that . . . anyway, by the time we were through, every man, woman, and yard monkey in three states knew about Mudzilla. It wasn't just a show, it was a news event . . . and, boy, did it pay off.

There's exactly 54,224 seats in Busch Stadium, and we sold out every blessed one of them. Shit, the day of the show, there were scalpers out on the sidewalk hawking tickets for a hundred bucks a pop, and that was for the nosebleed section. We had the mayor and the whole city council shoved into the home plate section, plus some local celebs you've never heard of, all schmoozing away, and meanwhile there's jokers trying to crash the gate out front, helicopters up in the sky, TV people going apeshit in the press box . . . *(Sighs.)* Jeez, it was a goddamn circus. And I loved every minute of it.

We started off low-key. The national anthem. Everyone stands up and sits down. Then we put on an hour and a half of the same-ol' same-ol'—some funny-car stuff, a big-rig tractor-pull, a little ten-car demolition derby—just enough to whet everyone's appetite, sell some more hot dogs and beer. A lounge act out of Nashville, the Five Dudes, did a quick set during intermission while everyone went to the pot . . . and then, just when people were beginning to get bored, we broke out the big guns.

We dimmed the arena lights and put on some loud rock music . . . uh, yeah, ''We Will Rock You'' by Queen, if I remember right . . . we had it blasting out of every loudspeaker in the place, and getting everyone to clap their hands and stomp their feet, like Wham wham WHAM! Wham wham WHAM!, just awesome . . . and meanwhile, the big gates out in left field open up and out comes the tractor-trailer rig with this giant American flag draped over the back, and it arrives in the center of the field and stops, right in the middle of the floodlights, and the cheerleaders run out to surround it.

And then, right as the music peaked and everyone in the stadium was on the verge of going nuts, the girls pulled off the tarp. . . .

(Grins.) And Mudzilla stood up for the first time in America.

"Okay, we're back again . . . Sir Douglas and the Big Boner, here with the Morning Mania on KPSR. The subject is last night's Monster Truck Rally at Busch Stadium and the world premiere of Mudzilla, and we're ready to take your calls . . . yes, sir, you're on the air. . . ."

"Uh, yeah . . . uh, hey Doug man, this is Ray Jay out in Wentzville. . . ."

"Oh, jeez, Ray Jay walks among us again. . . ."

"Hey, Big Boner, man!"

"Good morning, Ray Jay out in Wentzville. Were you at the stadium for the show last night?"

"Aw, hell yeah, dude! Mudzilla was a really [bleep] . . . I mean, like, it was total [bleep] awesome . . . !"

"Watch your language. Umm, yeah, so I've heard, but can you give us your exact impressions?"

"Oh, yeah . . . sorry, man . . . I mean, it was so big, I couldn't stand it. I mean, I never seen anything like it. Y'know, like, when it started firing its guns, man. . . ."

"They weren't using live rounds, were they, Rayster?"

"Aw, no way, man, it was just . . . y'know, blanks, I think it was. But I thought I was gonna drop a load in my pants when they let go. Y'know, boom! boom! boom . . . !"

"Good thing you weren't wearing any underwear, right, Ray?"

"Yeah, Boner, it was maximum [bleep] cool!"

"Okay, Ray Jay, we'll let you go back to your bong now . . . yes, ma'am, you're on the air."

"Yes, Doug . . . I was there last night with my two children . . . that's Marcie, age ten, and Wendell, age twelve. . . ."

"Yes, ma'am. The family that plays together, stays together . . ."

"Especially if they're playing with each other, heh heh. . . ."

"I don't think that was called for, Mr. Boner. We're a decent family. . . ."

"Out for a night with fifty-two thousand screaming beer drinkers at the truck pull, uh-huh . . . so how did your kids like Mudzilla?"

"Well . . . they liked it just fine, but that's what bothers me. It's one thing to have a giant robot do a tug-of-war with a bigfoot truck, but . . . well, you know, I think it sends the wrong message to young people to have them see it destroying school buses. . . ."

"Uh-huh, I see. . . ."

"It's not the sort of proper role model for children these days. . . ."

"No, no, you're right. They might want to grow up to drive fifty-foot Japanese war machines. . . ."

"Hey, teacher! About that last report card. . . ."

"I don't think that's very funny, Mr. Boner. . . ."

"Thank you for calling, ma'am . . . okay, caller on line three, you're on the air."

"I saw Mudzilla last night and, although I don't usually go for this sort of entertainment, I thought it was an excellent display of modern cybernetic technology. . . ."

"Oh my God! He speaks fluent English!"

"Boner! Stop drooling! Your doctor told you about . . . I'm sorry, sir, will you please go on?"

"Uh, sure . . . as I said, I was impressed by the technology and what it could do, even though I have to agree that pulverizing old school buses might have gone a bit too far, considering the current deficiencies in the American school system. . . .''

"Uh-huh, yeah . . .''

"But what irritated me was how Mudzilla was painted with corporate logos. I'm aware that this is standard with stock cars, to have them bearing sponsor's names on them, but to see this highly . . . uh, advanced machine . . . um, carrying the names of American companies that are directly responsible for third-world poverty. . . .''

"I got it! Next time, instead of school buses, we should have Mudzilla stomp across college professors from Washington University . . . !''

"Good idea, Boner. I'm sure that will really go over well at the next faculty meeting . . . we're going to cut for a station break, then the Morning Mania will be back with more discussion of Mudzilla, here on KPSR, St. Louis. . . .''

Donnie Hale:

We did three more appearances at Busch Stadium, just enough to get some national media attention, and when the novelty began to wear out with the locals, we took the show on the road. After the first show, Eddie Joe had already begun to get offers from all over the country . . . there was a promoter in Los Angeles who was willing to lease a C-141B Starlifter to haul Mudzilla out for a gig at Dodgers Stadium, f'rinstance . . . but he wanted to keep the 'bot in the southern and midwestern states for the time being.

Hmm? Yeah, I thought it was kinda peculiar. We could have been hitting the big time. "Let's work out the bugs before we go big-time,'' that's what he told me. "I wanna be low-key for a while.'' Didn't make sense but, hell, he was the boss, right?

Anyway, there were plenty of bugs left to work out of the system. Mudzilla was a pretty sophisticated piece of work, but it wasn't perfect. Grit would get into the hand-unit actuators, so they'd lose dexterity, and we had a real bitch of a time keeping the primary engine manifolds from overheating during the really hot days. During one show in Little Rock, the right hip-mount froze up entirely, right in the middle of the show, so we had to shut it down and jimmy the thing right there in the middle of the racetrack. And one time in Memphis, my helmet decided to go on the fritz while I was trying to haul a bus, which meant I had to lose the VR and switch to manual override . . . royal pain in the ass, lemme tell you.

But we kept on doing it, y'know, and for a while there it was pretty hot shit. Barnstorming from town to town, four support trucks with Mudzilla lashed down on the back of the big-ass GMC Aero Astro. Sometimes we'd roll into a city to find kids in their hopped-up cars standing on the side of the highway, just waiting for us to arrive. Got a couple of motel chains to put us up for free during the tour, in exchange for adding their logos onto the robot . . . *(Laughs.)* Man, we had so many sponsors for motor oil, soda pop, candy bars and shit, Mudzilla started to look like a walking billboard.

It was a tough job, though, keeping the show fresh. When everyone sees TV news about how Mudzilla stomped a school bus in one place or dragged a bigfoot backward in another, they're not so surprised when you do the same thing again. So we had to keep coming up with new stuff. I might learn how to pick up a Toyota and drop-kick it halfway across a stadium . . . Eddie always made sure it was a Japanese car I demo'd . . . and it was a show-stopper in Bowling Green, but three dates later in Jacksonville and it's already old news. On the other hand, we were never able to fire Mudzilla's cannons except for dud rounds, because if we had opened up, we might have leveled the stadium. So we had to dream up more stuff all the time. Did we tug-of-war two Peterbilts in Atlanta? Okay, then let's do three in Birmingham, and so forth.

But we were doing pretty well, all the same. We dragged trucks and stepped on school buses and did crazy shit like that all over eight states, and for eighteen months it looked like the gravy train would never end. I had my own fan club for a while . . . and, y'know, there were lots of lil' girls out there on the road who were willing to drop their pants for the guy who drove Mudzilla. *(Snickers.)* I couldn't complain. It beat hell out of the demolition derby, I'll tell you that.

What I didn't know, and neither did anyone else, was that everything wasn't right at the front office. I knew that Eddie Joe had laid out major bucks for the robot and Yuji was supposed to be getting a regular cut of the action, but I thought that end of things was pretty much settled. Y'know, me and the road crew were getting paid every two weeks, and we were getting dividends from ticket sales and T-shirts and all that shit, so it never occurred to me that, deep down inside, Big Muddy Productions might not have been able to make all the ends meet.

(Shakes his head.) That was my big mistake, trusting him as much as I did. Turned out that Eddie wasn't able to keep his fingers out of the cookie jar, so to speak . . . and when push finally came to shove, the Japs sent the repo man.

"Here comes the ultimate weapon . . . Mudzilla!"
(CLOSE-UP on a toy Mudzilla being pushed by a child's hand through a tabletop racetrack. Lights flash and electronic noises erupt as it knocks model cars out of its way and tramples miniature buildings.): "It's mean! It's strong! It's the indomiatable king of the demolition derby . . . until now!"
(EXTREME CLOSE-up as another child pushes for-

ward an almost identical robot, this one painted with the Rising Sun flag.): "Look out . . . now there's two combat robots! Mudzilla's arch-nemesis from Japan, Kyojin-2!"

(MEDIUM SHOT as the two toys are slammed into each other, beating each other with their plastic fists.): "Which will survive the Battle of the Giants . . . Mudzilla or Kyojin-2? Only you can decide!"

(CLOSE-UP shot of two adolescent boys, howling delightedly at the camera): "We're into Mudzilla!"

(DISPLAY SHOT of the two toy robots.): "The Mudzilla and Kyojin-2 action figures, from War Toy. Batteries sold separately."

Tazaki Norio:

The terms of the agreement made between my company and Big Muddy Productions were that Eddie Joe Carlisle would pay us five hundred thousand dollars as the initial down-payment for the XCA-115, plus ten percent of the gross gate receipts for each appearance it made in the United States. It bothered us a little when he renamed the robot Mudzilla and began to use it for subtle . . . um, I believe the popular term is Jap-bashing . . . but as long as Yuji was being paid for our product, it was only a minor nuisance.

However, Mr. Carlisle did not adhere to the terms of our agreement. After we received the initial sum, we received another payment of about one hundred thousand dollars, which represented ten percent of the gate receipts from Mudzilla's first appearance in St. Louis . . . but after that, the checks gradually began to get smaller and more infrequent, until in early 2001 they ceased to arrive altogether.

Although he told us that Mudzilla was only doing a few shows outside Missouri, we knew that the Kyojin-1 was constantly touring the southern and midwestern states, and this led us to the unfortunate conclusion that

Mr. Carlisle was cheating us. First, our lawyers contacted Mr. Carlisle and requested that he send us the complete financial records of each of Mudzilla's performances. He told us that he would do so, but these records were never sent. This forced us to demand an audit of his records by our accountants and legal counsel, to which he reluctantly complied. When the audit showed that he was in arrears by ... ah, a considerable sum of money ... we demanded that he cease using the XCA-115 for live performances and return our property to us.

However, Mr. Carlisle continued to be uncooperative. First, he filed under Chapter 11 of the federal bankruptcy laws, which shielded him from his creditors while he continued to stay in business. This meant that we could not immediately repossess the XCA-115. In the meantime, he continued to tour Mudzilla, which added further insult to injury. Although my company's attorneys continued to pursue the matter in court, we were aware that it could take months, if not years, to resolve the matter. Not only that, but considering the amount of damage being suffered by the XCA-115 each night, what we would finally receive in the end was a machine that had been battered to uselessness, plus the assets of a bankrupt company.

(Smiles.) However, we were not entirely without recourse. By this time the other XCA-115 prototype, the Kyojin-2, had been successfully repaired and substantially upgraded by our engineering team. We had already been considering using it for much the same entertainment purposes as Mr. Carlisle had so successfully done with Mudzilla ... in fact, we had already contacted a different promoter in Tennessee about representing Kyojin-2.

When I informed Mr. Yoji of Mr. Carlisle's intentions, he gave me a simple directive. "Teach the gaijin some manners," he said. "And you must do it personally." *(Pauses.)* And I knew exactly what he meant.

• •

"Gaaaawwwrrrggghhh! Get down to the Tennessee Speedway this Friday night for the bawwwrrrroooog-gahhh grudge match of the century as Harpeth River Productions in conjunction with the Yuji Corporation and Pizza Trough presents raaagghhh Mudzilla versus Kyojin-2! Oooorrawwwhhhh mighty fists of pure power POWER collide for the first time anywhere for ONE NIGHT ONLY! haaaawwwwwnnnkk with special guests, the Dobermann Clowns! Tickets ten-ninety-five for adults, five-ninety-five for children, available at all Granny's General Store, Video Wiz, and Com Tix locations! Gaarrrraaooogghhh! The ultimate BATTLE OF THE CENTURY this Friday night at the Speedway har-rruuuuummmmm! BE THERE!"

Eddie Joe Carlisle:

Yeah, I fell for it . . .

(Sighs and shakes his head.) Like a damn fool, I fell for it. When I heard that they were gonna use the other robot, I should have never sent Mudzilla down to Nashville. Shit, I should have been trying to protect my meal ticket instead . . .

Why did I? *(Laughs.)* Hell's bells, boy, do I look like the sort of guy who runs away from a fight? If I hadn't gone down there, I would have been called a wussie. I would have been the laughing stock of the whole industry. Not only that, but Kyojin-2 would have been called the champion, and before you know it Mudzilla would have been playing the Buttfuck County Fair.

I couldn't let that happen, no sir . . . so I called the guy at Harpeth River Productions and I said, "Sam, my robot can beat your robot with one arm strapped behind its back." Damn lil' Nashville yuppie says to me, "Eddie Joe, that isn't necessary, but if you want a blindfold during the show, just let me know and I'll be happy to give you one.''

(Sighs.) Well, maybe I didn't do the wise thing by taking Mudzilla down to Nashville . . . but I didn't ask for no blindfold, neither. Not even when the shit hit the fan.

''Tonight was a scene of incredible violence at the Tennessee Speedway as two rival combat robots, the world-famous Mudzilla and its Japanese twin, Kyojin-2, fought each other before a sell-out crowd. And in the end. . . .''

(VIDEOTAPE CLIP, shot from the distance: the two robots face to face in the middle of a dusty racetrack beneath harsh white floodlights. They are battering each other with their fists, pieces of metal breaking off as nearby ground crew members run for cover, until Kyojin-2 unexpectantly slams its right fist straight into Mudzilla's chest and the huge machine topples backward onto the ground.): ''There was only one left standing . . . Kyojin-2. But even then, it was not over . . .''

(Camera ZOOMS IN upon the fallen Mudzilla: the transparent canopy opens and the pilot, looking bewildered but unhurt, is helped out of the cockpit by two other men. They have barely cleared the area before Kyojin-2 begins to stamp upon Mudzilla. The sounds of angry shouting and booing can be heard from the bleachers.): ''Kyojin-2 waited until Mudzilla's driver, Donnie Hale, had been safely evacuated from his robot, before Kyojin's unidentified driver reduced Mudzilla to a pile of junk. Yet despite the destruction of their favorite and the apparent unsportsmanlike conduct of the challenger, fans were not disappointed. . . .''

(CLOSE-UP of an audience member, a bearded young man wearing a Cat cap): ''Hey, I hated to see Mudzilla get defeated and all that, but at least he went out in a blaze of fire. It was one hell of a show!''

(MEDIUM SHOT of the TV reporter, standing in front

of the race track): "The owner of Mudzilla, Big Muddy Productions president Eddie Joe Carlisle, was on hand for the fight, but refused to comment on the outcome. However, a spokesperson for the Yuji Corporation, the owner of Kyojin-2, issued a brief statement saying that this was the only appearance its machine would make in the United States, and that their robot would soon be returned to the company's headquarters in Japan, where it would be permanently retired. So it looks like robot fighting has both begun and ended, here at the Tennessee Speedway. This is Lynn Kaufmann, on the scene for Eyewitness Thirty."

Donnie Hale:

When I was told, just before I climbed into Mudzilla for the last time, that the driver of the Kyojin was going to be none other than Tazaki Norio, I knew I was going to get ripped out there. He had helped train me, and he had been the one who had come up with the idea of selling Mudzilla to Eddie Joe in the first place, so I knew he had to . . . y'know, save face by defeating it as well.

With me, it was just a job. I gave it my best shot, don't get me wrong . . . but Tazi had something to prove, and you just can't defeat a man who's determined like that. Maybe that's how we're always getting the Japanese wrong, when you stop and think about it. At least I'm grateful to him for letting me get out of the cockpit before he trashed Mudzilla once and for all. He just wanted to make sure Eddie Joe couldn't keep rippin' his company off, that's all, even if it meant destroying their own machine.

I'm out of the game for good now . . . back to demolition derby and all that. Yuji invited me to come back to Japan, because it's building a second generation of the XCA series and it wanted me to help train new drivers, but I said no, thanks anyway. Ridin' that monster once was enough.

Hmm? How do I feel about it now? *(Grins.)* Man, I wouldn't have missed it for the world. Custer didn't survive Little Big Horn, after all . . .

But me? Hell . . . I was there for Mudzilla's last stand and lived to tell the tale!

INTRODUCTION:
"Hunting Wabbit"

Ask any author what he or she thinks about critics (or reviewers, if you want to split hairs), and you'll usually receive a diplomatic response. Buy that author a drink and ask them again, though, and you'll probably hear a horror story or two, even from writers who are widely considered to be critics' darlings. If you should ever find yourself in the company of three or more authors at once, casually raise the subject and watch what happens.

Writers and critics exist in a co-dependent relationship. Although all authors dread bad reviews, the best wordsmiths know that there is something to be learned from logical criticism that is polite and well stated, because it can help them to sharpen their skills and to avoid repeating mistakes. The best critics know this, and they strive to perfect their craft just as much as authors fine-tune their art. When the relationship is at its best, a mutual symbiosis develops; if there is rivalry, then at least it's friendly. No hard feelings, just professionals doing their jobs.

Unfortunately, there are quite a few bad critics out there, too: the failed authors who bear personal grudges against successful ones; the unethical hacks who will knowingly lie about a book's content (or, at very least, neglect to mention pertinent details that would undermine their argument); and the self-styled curmudgeons with hidden agendas and poison pens, slamming everything in sight with the not-so-secret intent of furthering their own reputations at the expense of someone else's.

This story came out of my experiences with bad critics, plus one or two horror stories that have been told to me by other authors. I won't relate the details behind the happenstance that inspired this story, because doing so would simply gratify the culprit and ennoble the crime. It's also my attempt to do an end-of-the-world story. Every SF writer is entitled to one, at least, and this is mine. I took the British approach of focusing global events through the actions of a small group of people in one location, in this case a waterfront bar in St. Louis. "Hunting Wabbit," however, was mainly written as a protest against hack reviewers. So it's appropriate that its most negative reponse came from just the sort of person I was writing about.

Scott Edelman wanted a story from me for his then-new magazine, *Science Fiction Age*, so I wrote "Hunting Wabbit" for him. At the time, there had been much media attention given to recent estimates made by American astronomers Eugene and Caroline Shoemaker (later the co-discoverers of the Shoemaker-Levy Comet, which struck Jupiter in the summer of 1994) that placed the odds of catastrophic collision between Earth and an Apollo asteroid within the next fifty years as being about 1 in 60,000. I had already written about asteroid collisions in my novel *Clarke County, Space*, but this story gave me the chance to dig more thoroughly into the subject.

Scott had built a large inventory of stories by the time he accepted my piece, so "Hunting Wabbit" had to wait almost a year before it saw print. In the meantime, Arthur

C. Clarke beat me to press by having his own asteroid collision story, "The Hammer of God," published in *Time* about five months earlier.

This happens in the SF genre from time to time, particularly because SF writers tend to read the same non-fiction magazines in search of ideas. Two authors simultaneously get the same notion, and one writer inevitably gets the advantage of faster publication. I scooped Michael Crichton on the idea of dinosaur cloning with my novella "Trembling Earth," which was published in *Asimov's Science Fiction* about six weeks before *Jurassic Park* hit the bookstores. There's a number of similarities between the two stories, but I'd be a jerk if I claimed that Crichton swiped his novel from my novella.

In this instance, there were no hard feelings on either side. Arthur is a friend and colleague, and all's fair in love and publishing. Sometimes you get the scoop, and sometimes you get scooped. Besides, Dr. Clarke later paid me back by giving me the title for another story in this collection (and that's a tale for another introduction).

Shortly after publication of "Hunting Wabbit" in *Science Fiction Age*, the short-fiction reviewer of a monthly trade magazine in the SF field noticed the similarities between our two stories. Only a fool wouldn't have realized that the publication times between the two stories were so close that "Hunting Wabbit" could not have been written, submitted, sold, typeset, and printed so quickly after "The Hammer of God" saw publication in *Time* . . . and it's highly doubtful that this reviewer was unaware that the average lead-time of fiction magazines is six months, and sometimes even longer.

This didn't stop him, however, from insinuating that I had ripped off the core idea of Arthur's story, even though the stories had little else in common. No outright accusation of plagiarism; just enough to suggest that I threw down my issue of *Time* and dashed straight to the keyboard to scratch off this story.

And then he had the gall to rhetorically ask what I had against critics.

Sir, you know who you are; only jurisprudence keeps me from revealing your name. Someone may blow the whistle on you one day, but it won't be me. For the time being, you're safe. Although I sometimes write violent fiction, I'm not a violent man. I don't own a gun, nor have I ever seriously contemplated murder.

But you never know what the next guy may do.

HUNTING WABBIT

I stood in the alley beside Casey's Bar & Grill for a few minutes, giving myself one last chance to decide whether or not I really wanted to kill the wabbit.

It wasn't a hard decision, so I pulled the Smith & Wesson .38 out of the pocket of my leather jacket and double-checked the cylinder. I had fired the revolver three times on my way downtown—twice over the heads of a rioting crowd when I had abandoned my car in a gridlock at the Vandeventer Overpass on Route 40, and once while I was hiking the rest of the way through the city, in the general vicinity of someone who had charged out of another alley eight blocks from here with a tire-iron in his hand—so there were three rounds left in the chamber. It would only take one bullet to knock off the bastard, though, so I wasn't worried about running out of ammo.

I closed the cylinder, put the pistol back in my pocket, took a deep breath, and walked out of the alley. A stiff, cool breeze was coming off the Mississippi, rushing through the narrow cobblestoned streets of the water-front. Above the low brick buildings of Leclede's Landing, the silver crescent of Gateway Arch reflected the moonlight. Further away, on the other side of Memorial Drive, I could hear the sounds of a city in turmoil: scattered gunfire, police and ambulance sirens, car horns battling with one another.

Downtown St. Louis was going to hell, but, remarkably enough, the waterfront was actually rather peaceful. One might have thought it wouldn't be this way, considering that Leclede's Landing is mostly one bar and nightclub snuggled against another, packed together in refurbished antebellum warehouses. On this night, though, most of the bars were closed; considering how many churches I had seen open for services on my way down here, most of the Landing's regulars were rediscovering religion tonight. As the old saying goes, there's no atheists in foxholes. Or at ground zero.

I stopped on the sidewalk, pausing once again to look up at the night sky, searching for my own killer, and everyone else's. Of course, I couldn't see anything except the Moon; the glare of the city lights blotted out the stars, rendering the night sky dark and inert. Nonetheless, it was quickly approaching, careening out of deep space at fifty-thousand miles per hour like God's own shithammer. . . .

Enough. It was payback time for that pesky wabbit. The amber glow of the neon Budweiser sign hanging in the window of Casey's Bar & Grill was as warm as vengeance. Through the window, I saw a half-dozen people huddled over the bar at the opposite end of the room, vague shadows against the pale light of the TV set on the wall above the cash register. I couldn't tell for certain if one of them was my quarry, but I knew he was in there.

I walked to the door, but just before I grasped the handle, I remembered the magazine curled up within the inside pocket of my jacket. Of course. Can't forget that. I pulled out the magazine, unfolded it, glanced at the cover with its cheesy clip-art. *Scrivener—The St. Louis Literary Review*. The wabbit's wittle carrot. I turned the pages until I found the book review section, then I tucked the open magazine beneath my left armpit and opened the door.

No one noticed me as I walked in; their attention was fully drawn to the TV. It was switched to CNN, where yet another talking head—probably a government official, someone from the White House or the Pentagon or NASA—was being interviewed by the anchorman. The finale for the human race was upon us, and it was even going to be shown on TV. I vaguely wondered what David Letterman's gag writers were doing tonight. Compiling a Top Ten list of things to do before the end of the world.

Personally, I had already made my own Number One choice. Go downtown and kill the wabbit. And there he was . . .

A familiar figure squatted on the middle barstool. Big fat guy, wearing a threadbare tweed jacket and extra-large Wrangler jeans, his greying blond hair pulled back in a just-past-trendy ponytail. I couldn't see his face, but I knew what it looked like: unkempt beard, wire-rimmed glasses, cynical eyes. If the information I had been given was correct, he was probably plowed on vodka martinis, just as he was every night in this dump. I only hoped he wouldn't be too zooed to understand what was about to happen to him.

I strode through the seedy barroom until I stopped behind the fat man. I could have done it blindfolded, just homed in on his stale-vinegar sweat. Everyone standing around the bar, including the sallow-looking bartender on the other side of the beat-up oak counter, looked up as I approached, but the fat man sitting in the middle didn't notice my arrival. Not until I pulled the magazine out from under my arm and dropped it directly in front of him.

"Wabbit," I said, "your time has come."

As I pulled the .38 out of my pocket and poked its barrel against the back of his thick neck, George T. Wabbit slowly turned his head to look at me.

How shall I begin? Let's flip a coin. Heads, I'll first tell you about the end of the world. Tails, I'll explain why I decided to go downtown to kill the wabbit. Trust me, I won't cheat. Here's the flip. . . .

Abe Lincoln wins. The end of the world comes first. Poetic justice, that; George Wabbit was always a tail-end sort of person.

There's a class of asteroids that occasionally cross Earth's orbit while circling the sun. They're called Apollo asteroids, and once every now and then one of them comes very close to colliding with our planet. These near-collisions have occurred several times in recent history. In 1989, for instance, a rock about a half-mile in diameter missed Earth by less than 500,000 miles; if it had arrived only six hours earlier, it would have nailed us. Another one, this one only thirty feet in diameter, came within 106,000 miles of Earth in 1991. And then there was the slightly larger asteroid that grazed the upper atmosphere above the Grand Tetons in 1972.

These instances led astronomers to begin seriously charting Apollo asteroids, and what they discovered was quite disturbing. Given the number of impact craters found on Earth—more than one hundred and eighty by 1991—and the number of similar craters located on the Moon, it was judged that the chances of an asteroid striking the earth within the next fifty years were about one in sixty thousand. For comparison's sake, it was also determined that one's chances of being accidentally electrocuted were figured to be one in five thousand, and of dying from a gunshot wound, were one in two thousand.

That's not all. Some Apollo asteroids are mighty large. Many paleontologists believed that a collision between

Earth and a medium-size asteroid had been responsible for the extinction of the dinosaurs. If a similar ''dinosaur killer'' were to strike Earth, then all the combined effects—earthquakes, tsunamis, a drastic drop of the global temperature caused by sunlight being blotted out by debris being thrown into the atmosphere by the explosive impact, subsequent worldwide crop failures because of the prolonged winter and the acid rain that would follow, a possible shift in Earth's magnetic field, and more of the same happy stuff—could easily spell dee-double oh-em for mankind.

While the politically correct were still arguing over whether the global populace should instead be called humankind, personkind, or womynkind, a few other people who knew shitfire when they smelled it began to watch the skies. They also argued that the human species should engage in preventive measures: establishing satellites that would act as first-warning sentries, using SDI technology to build a just-in-case orbital defense system, maybe paying a little more attention to this sort of thing, just for a change.

To most people, though, this scenario sounded too much like a bad science fiction movie. Like, y'know, the one with Sean Connery and Natalie Wood. In the United States, after several public hearings on the matter, the members of Congress grudgingly sprinkled a little extra money on NASA for additional research before they returned their attention to their re-election bids. One in sixty thousand in the next fifty . . . hey, that's not so bad. That's better odds than the Washington Post finding out that I've been taking illegal campaign contributions or that I used to smoke pot while I was in college. Now these are things to be concerned about.

So the matter dropped out of the newspapers again, and we recommenced to worrying about bombs in Iraq and the South American rain forests and whether Michael Jackson would record another album, or if Princess Di

would find a steady boyfriend now that she was through
with Chuck . . . and all of a sudden, one nice day in April,
the astronomers at the Kitt Peak observatory in Arizona,
while training the telescope at the Pleiades constellation,
accidentally saw something large and nonreflective occult
the stars.

Phone calls and faxes were hurriedly sent to other observatories across the northern hemisphere, and tele-
scopes from California to Mexico to England to Russia
were hastily realigned toward the same celestial coordinates. The news was confirmed within the next twenty-
four hours. Just as positive as my chances of flipping a
penny and having it come up heads, that one-in-sixty-
thousand probability had come true; the mother of all
Apollo asteroids, a massive rock more than six miles in
diameter, was hauling craggy butt out of deep space and
heading straight for Earth.

An asteroid that big would weigh in excess of one
trillion tons; when it connected with Earth at seventy
times the speed of sound, the released energy of the impact would be the equivalent of five billion atomic
bombs. And, at a mean distance of approximately one
million miles, this particular hunk of rock was less than
twenty hours away from collision, with an estimated
point of impact being somewhere in the middle of the
Pacific Ocean.

Someone at one of the observatories that confirmed the
sighting leaked the news to the Associated Press. Within
an hour, AP printers across the world were ringing five
bells, and by midafternoon in the midwestern United
States the story had broken on virtually every TV and
radio station. Today's episode of *All My Children* was
preempted; how's that for importance? Planet Earth was
in for one lousy day.

And we were about to find out, for certain, what killed
the dinosaurs.

                        •   •

Okay, that's the big picture. Now to tell you about the wabbit. . . .

I was at home in the 'burbs, struggling my way through a short story for *Ellery Queen's Mystery Magazine* when my ex-wife phoned to tell me the awful news. She was total hysterics, alternately begging me to attend Mass with her at St. Whatshisname's or to rush over and jump her bones one last time before the New Madrid Fault got the hiccups. However, I had no intention of either groveling before the Almighty, who had never paid any attention to me, or boffing my ex, for much the same reason. After I suggested that she should have sex with her second husband instead but I still loved her anyway— okay, so I lied—I hastily hung up the phone and ran into the den to switch on the TV.

Dan Rather, looking even more unhinged than usual, confirmed what Joan had just told me. The weather forecast for tomorrow morning called for exceptionally heavy precipitation, with a long-range forecast calling for mass extinction.

Y'know, the mind works in funny ways. It's like, when you find out someone very close to you has suddenly died, you immediately begin to worry about whether you should buy some new shoes for the funeral. Trivialities come to the forefront of your attention because, at the most basic emotional level, you're not ready to accept the horror of what you've just learned.

In this case, upon finding out that the human race had just been given its layoff notice from the universe, my first irrational thought was: Damn, now I'll never get The National Book Award.

While Dan-O blathered about how the Defense Department was hastily trying to load nuclear warheads aboard some NASA rockets at Cape Canaveral as a last-ditch attempt to deflect the asteroid from its present trajectory—and all the usual network experts were saying fat chance, for this or that reason—I wandered over to my vanity shelf and began to look over my life's work.

Every author has a vanity shelf. It's the place where he or she proudly displays copies of his or her published work, just in case Norman Mailer stops by and wants to talk shop. Mine was reasonably large: four novels, in both hardcover and paperback, plus a couple of dozen short stories printed in everything from *The Missouri Review* to one of Martin Greenberg's anthologies to a few issues of *Analog* and *Asimov's*. Two of the novels were science fiction, one was horror, and the latest book was a political thriller with high-lit pretensions. No major awards, but the revenues had been sufficient to keep me in semi-permanent retirement from advertising. As I half-listened to the parade of colonels, astronomers, White House spokesmen, Jerry Pournelle and Pat Robertson, all giving their unwanted opinions on what doomsday meant to them, I found myself fingering the dusty spines of my books, remembering all the nights that had gone into the creation of each work.

It had been more than a career. It had been a life, and a pretty good one at that. I had no regrets over what I had done with my thirty-four years. . . .

Except one.

I had never gotten even with George T. Wabbit.

George T. Wabbit was the publisher, editor, and major contributor of *Scrivener,* a rather pretentious title for what was essentially a low-circulation journal of literary viscidity. I had it on good information from a mutual acquaintance that Wabbit was a failed writer, a wannabe who had done all the usual workshops and university courses, had written short stories and novels and poems and screenplays, but had been unable to get his work published in any professional venue save the "Humor In Uniform" column of *Reader's Digest*. Some people simply keep on trying until they either get it right or give up completely and content themselves with reading, but poor George had been driven bugfuck by his envy and spite for virtually any author who had been successful in the craft.

Using inherited money, he had started the quarterly *Scrivener* as, in his own words, "a new ballpark for alternative literary expression." Meaning, because he couldn't win in the big-league stadiums, he scratched out shorter baselines in his own minor-league diamond. No strikes or outs for the local heroes, but plenty of spitballs for the visiting team.

Self-publishing is often an acceptable recourse—I've read stories in the small press that beat the shit out of anything Knopf put out last month—but Wabbit chose to use *Scrivener* as a blunt instrument. Although much of the magazine was taken up by unreadable short stories written by other local wannabes who had become part of his clique (sample titles: " 'I'm Home!' She Cried to Her Dog" and "Splatter Orgasm, Version 3.5"), it was mostly devoted to reviews of books published by established authors, again those who lived in the St. Louis area.

These reviews were usually written by Wabbit himself. They were, by and large, attacks upon anyone whose work had been published, with the exception of a small handful of authors who had met "higher literary standards," meaning (a) that he wished to kiss their ass, (b) that they were sufficiently obscure as to pose no threat to Wabbit's ego, or (c) that they had once been nice to him by granting him an interview for his rag. It was Wabbit's conceit that, because he and his cronies couldn't be published, any writer who was successful or whose works were popular had "sold out" to the conspiratorial forces of big-time publishing, and thus needed to be exposed as a fraud. In truth, *Scrivener* was a grandiose exercise in sour grapes, the means by which he either wished to gain some sort of low-rent respectability or badger those authors he secretly envied.

I first met Wabbit after I had read from my first novel,

Highway Star, at the St. Louis County Library, shortly after the book was published. The reading had been sparsely attended by retirees and bored teenagers who had slammed the door on the way out, so when he grandly introduced himself to me as "another slave in the litr'y vineyard" and asked me if I wanted to have a beer, I was ready for a stroke, because there's nothing worse than reading aloud to a dead audience.

He seemed like a nice guy, if a little pompous, so I accepted the invitation. He said he knew of a quiet little place—"It's outside walking distance," he said. "Can I give you a lift?"—so I left my car in the library parking lot. Two writers, going out for an afternoon beer. Where's the harm?

I had assumed that he intended to go somewhere nearby. What I didn't realize, until he suddenly got on the interstate, was that his "quiet little place" was all the way downtown . . . Casey's Bar & Grill, in fact. But I didn't say anything, figuring that he would take me back to the library once we had a beer or two. But once we actually got to the bar and we had settled down at a table with a couple of Budweisers, Wabbit eschewed the small talk and cut straight to the chase.

Because he was being actively censored by all the major publishers, he proclaimed, and because the editors within the New York literary elite were obviously unaware of his genius, he needed to collaborate with someone who—although he had admittedly been successful in finding a supportive publisher—obviously needed some polishing before he realized his full potential.

Uh-huh, I said.

Then he began to tell me all the flaws he had perceived in *Highway Star*. There weren't many. Just the plot, the theme, the characters, the setting, the beginning, the middle, and the end. But I still had the potential to become a truly great author, said my new friend Maxwell Perkins, if only I worked closely with a more talented person who could guide me toward the one true light.

Uh-huh, I said.

Well, says Wabbit, who by now was beginning to more closely resemble a boa constrictor than a bunny, I have a proposal. I will give you the plot of a truly incredible novel, titled *Reflections in a Time-Warped Pond* . . . d'ya like it? . . . anyway, you will write it for me, and I will do the final editing. We will then put both our names on the book . . . naturally, my name will appear first on the cover . . . sell it to your publisher, and split the advance and royalties on a 50-50 basis. Of course, I would be entitled to all of the subsidiary sales . . . book club rights, foreign translations, movie options . . . because it was my idea in the first place.

Uh-huh, I said.

Wabbit warmed to the subject. The story was about a time traveller from A.D. 3600 who journeyed back through the fourth dimension to 1995, where he intended to seduce one of his own ancestors, his great-to-the-umpteenth-power grandmother with whom the time traveller had fallen in love after glimpsing her picture in an old family album. Once they had met and had sex a few times, the two of them would travel across the country to Washington, D.C., fleeing FBI and CIA agents who wanted the time machine, where they would then assassinate Dan Quayle, whom everyone in the far future knew was directly responsible for. . . .

Uh-uh, I said, holding up my hand. No way. Won't work.

Wabbit looked irritated. Why not? he demanded. It's the perfect plot.

Yeah, I said, but it needs a different title. We should call it . . . um, how about *Blow It Out Your Ass*?

And then I rose from the table, walked out of the bar, and hailed a cab to take me back to the library. Cost me fifteen bucks for the return trip, but it was worth every penny to get away from him.

I thought that was the end of the matter, but it wasn't. Two months later, the latest issue of *Scrivener* appeared in my mailbox. No note was attached, but it was obviously Wabbit's calling-card; it featured a very long review of *Highway Star*, written by the scorned would-be collaborator himself, which savaged my novel with the delight that only a jealous mind can summon. Three pages of misinterpretations, innuendo, and outright contempt, never once mentioning the fact that we had ever met, let alone the shifty deal into which he had attempted to sucker me. He was canny enough to stop just short of breaking libel laws, though, knowing well that one can't successfully sue over a matter of artistic opinion.

There are two facts about literary criticism that many readers seldom realize. The first is that reviews are often written for reasons that have nothing to do with the published work itself.

Does the critic wish to impress someone else with his ability to praise or kill a novel? Does the critic want to gain or reaffirm membership in a literary clique? Does the critic want to sleep with the author or/and the author's spouse, editor, literary agent, publicist, or cover artist? Does the critic have a personal vendetta against any one of the above?

These questions are rarely posed. The truth is, anyone can be a critic. It doesn't take special training or academic credentials, just basic literacy, typing skills, and the willingness to accept a lot of free books sent in the mail from publishers. Honesty is optional.

Not all reviewers are buttheads, to be sure. Many are worth reading. On occasion, an author finds one who is worth paying attention to, even when the dude is slamming your own work, because you may learn something that will help you sharpen your next novel. But like the bully who used to shake you down in the playground for lunch money or the thug who keyed your car in the parking lot, it's the butthead-type you remember the most.

The second fact is that there's no reasonable means by which the author can reply to a bad review.

Most magazines will not publish rebuttal letters sent by aggrieved authors. In the very few that do, the editor or the reviewer is often allowed the final word through a parenthetical response at the end of the author's letter, one which usually ridicules the writer for complaining about his treatment. Never mind that the author may have spent years painstakingly researching and writing the book and the critic skimmed it while sitting on the pot ... the reviewer is given the final word, and the author ends up looking like a schmuck for complaining.

Wabbit's essay irritated me, to be sure, but there was nothing I could do about it. I eventually got over it, though, dismissing it as cheap revenge by a loser. *Highway Star* did well in the bookstores and most of the other reviews were kind, so I soon forgot about Wabbit again. Then, a year later, my second novel was published, and a shorter yet no less vicious review of it was published in *Scrivener*. It was also penned by that pesky wabbit, but this time he also sent a copy to my publisher.

And this was the way it continued for the next four years. I published another novel and several short stories, and each time anything appearing under my byline was published, Wabbit sank his claws into the work. Every time a review appeared, copies of *Scrivener* were sent both to myself and to my editors, not only to vex me but also as a blatant attempt to sabotage my career.

Wabbit's words didn't harm my career. My editors knew that he was a crank with a grudge and therefore didn't take him seriously, and the few other authors I knew in the St. Louis area were aware that he held nothing but contempt for published writers, particularly those who were in the region. A couple of them, Chris Lasky and Sarah Jean Storrow, had also been victimized by Wabbit's rag; through correspondence and phone conversations and occasional get-togethers, both commiserated with me.

And then the *Scrivener* review of my fourth novel, *The Lamb Lies Down on Broadway*, was published.

It wasn't a review. Not exactly. Just three Polaroid snapshots, printed at the beginning of the *Scrivener's* book review page . . .

The day after the latest issue hit the local magazine racks, Chris called me and asked if I wanted to go have a couple of beers. He had seen the pictures and figured that I needed to get drunk. I said no, he said yes; Chris is bigger than I am, so I told him that I'd meet him that night down on Delmar Boulevard.

"He's a eunuch," Chris said to me over drinks at Blueberry Hill. His two crime novels, *Arch Enemies* and *Good Friday*, had also been given the so-called "Wabbit Test," which was now the title of George's review column. The wabbit had lived, but Chris's books had been given an abortion. Some test. "I wouldn't get mad at him. Just pity the poor fuck. It's the only way he can get back at you and me."

"I'd like to do more than pity him." I had already tucked in a couple of Bloody Marys, so I was feeling good and pissed off. "Fact is, I'd like to murder the asshole."

"Ignore him."

"You ignore you. Did you see that picture? He. . . ."

"Yeah, I know, I saw it." Chris took another swig from his beer. "Y'know, he hangs out every night at some beer joint down by the river. . . ."

"Casey's Bar & Grill."

"That's the place." Chris nodded his head as he signaled the waiter for another round. "We could always go down there later. Take him out in the alley and give him writing lessons. First-person perspective on pain and suffering . . . maybe it'll help change his mind about what he writes about us."

"Good idea. Let's go." Hell, it wasn't a bad idea. I was sick of receiving the bastard's quarterly hate mail. And this last bit. . . .

I started to push back my chair, but Lasky caught my wrist and pulled me back. "Forget it, kid," he said. "I was just joking . . . and you couldn't change his mind even if it was the end of the world. Now gimme your keys and have another drink."

That was three months ago. Now it was the end of the world, and I was ready to see if the wabbit was ready to change his mind.

Either that, or I'd blow it all over the floor of Casey's Bar & Grill.

Problem was, I wasn't the first person to get the same idea.

Before Wabbit could say anything, before I even had the chance to thumb back the hammer of my Smith & Wesson, I heard the unmistakable metallic click of a revolver cocking behind me.

Then another gun was cocked, this time from on the other side of Wabbit. . . .

And then a third, now a little further down the bar. . . .

Then a fourth gun was chambered, again from behind me.

Cannon to the left of me, cannon to my right. From the corner of my eye, I glanced first one way, then the other. Four gun barrels were aimed straight at me.

I damn near shit a brick. The bartender had already thrown himself to the floor, and if Wabbit hadn't been under my own gun, he might have done the same. My first thought was that the sumbitch had actually thought to hire bodyguards for his last night on the town, but—astonishingly enough—I could see that his own face was blanched, his eyes wide with fear, sweat matting his hair against his forehead.

Then a familiar voice came from behind the third gun.

"Hold it, guys. I know him. He's one of us. . . ."

"Chris?" I gasped. "Is that you, buddy?"

"It's me," Lasky said. "Now lower your pistol and let's discuss this little coincidence."

I pulled my finger away from the trigger and slowly relaxed the hammer. Around me, I heard the other guns doing the same thing. The bartender, a skinny college kid, reluctantly reappeared from behind the bar. Wabbit, however, didn't look either relieved nor smug about his mistake. He closed his eyes and took a long, deep breath as his trembling hands closed around the beer mug in front of him, but he didn't say a word.

That gave me a little bit of satisfaction, but I didn't say anything. Instead, I took the gun away from Wabbit's neck and lowered it to my side, then I looked at the people sitting on the barstools around us. Over there, two stools down from Wabbit, was Chris Lasky, placing his Colt on the polished bartop and picking up his beer.

And seated between him and Wabbit, wearing an L. L. Bean parka which effectively disguised her feminine physique, was Sarah Jean Storrow. The Pulitzer-nominated author of *Twilight Forest* gave me a sweet smile as she rested her own gun on the counter, carefully keeping it out of Wabbit's reach. She looked like your favorite liberal-arts college professor, if your favorite liberal-arts college professor carried a rod into a waterfront dive.

"Ray Oppenheimer," someone behind me said, and I turned around to see an older man with a white beard standing behind me, holding a beer in one hand and a Colt revolver in the other. "Glad to meet you. Loved your last book."

"Sure . . . um, thanks." Raymond Alec Oppenheimer, whom I had never met but whom I knew by reputation. Lived in Collinsville, Illinois, just over on the other side of the Big Muddy. Author of *The Last Words of Sitting Bull, The Prairie Schooner,* and a couple of other noteworthy Old West historical novels that I hadn't read. He nodded once, keeping his narrow eyes trained on Wabbit.

"I'm Gary Tyson," a longhaired '60s throwback behind Ray spoke up. He shifted the Glock .45 into his left hand as he extended his right hand to me. "I haven't read your stuff, but I hear it's pretty good."

"Um . . . yeah, okay." I shook his hand, then it dawned on me. "Hey, aren't you G. P. Tyson? The guy who wrote . . . ah, what was it? . . . *I Slept with J. Edgar Hoover?*"

"C'est moi," he said, grinning widely.

I pumped his hand more vigorously. I had heard of him, too; he lived out in St. Charles. "Glad to meet you," I said. "That was a fun novel. I really liked the bit when the hippies kidnapped Elvis from Graceland and smuggled him to Woodstock. . . ."

What was I saying? Was this an ABA convention or a chapter meeting of the NRA? "What the hell are you guys doing here?" I nearly shouted. "I mean, why are you . . . ?"

Everyone broke up. Everyone, that is, except the bartender and George T. Wabbit, both of whom looked as if they couldn't wait for the asteroid to strike. Wabbit was staring straight ahead at the row of liquor bottles on the shelf, his fleshy lower lip trembling ever so slightly.

The bartender's eyes were racing back and forth, trying to watch all of us at the same time. "I think. . . ." he began weakly, then he cleared his throat and tried again. "I think I need to get another keg from the cooler." He nervously pointed behind him. "I mean, y'all might be thirsty after . . . I mean, when you've. . . ."

"Get out of here, kid," Ray Oppenheimer growled, his inflection somewhere between John Wayne and Clint Eastwood. "We won't leave you a mess, I promise." The kid still looked uncertain. "G'wan now," Ray said. "Git. . . ."

The bartender glanced once more at Wabbit. "Sorry, George," he whispered, and then he abandoned his post, heading not for the cooler but for the fire exit. Everyone ignored his leavetaking except George. One of his feet stepped down from the rungs of his barstool . . .

"Not you, buddy." Chris placed his right hand over his gun as his voice dropped menacingly, and Wabbit froze solid. "We're not done with you yet."

Now it dawned upon me, the truth hitting me with the fierce clarity that usually comes only when an unanticipated twist occurs in a storyline, late at night when the creative subconscious delivers a bonus. Five writers, all living in the same general vicinity, had come to the same place at the same time, each with murder in their hearts. None of them had much in common except for one thing: all had been reviled and insulted, lambasted and roasted, their works denegrated and held up for public ridicule, by this one man.

And now, quite unexpectedly, the opportunity had come for revenge. Public order had broken down, and the law was a joke. Civilization was coming to a closure; by tomorrow, our books would be burned as firewood against the long ice age at the end of history. Throughout the world, countless other scores were being settled. It was the night of wicked bad karma, of taking care of business, of giving the Devil his due, of settling old bills.

The night when a long-dormant, unsatisfied ache for revenge would finally be satisfied.

Chris, Sarah, Ray, Gary, myself—each of us had suffered petty sniping from someone whose only justification had been his own envy, our novels and stories disembowelled for the sake of cheap thrills and the vicarious pleasure of other failures and would-be writers, with no acceptable course of rebuttal except for private grousing. . . .

And now it was payback time.

Of course, Wabbit had never thought it would come to this. Not daring to meet our eyes, he stared straight at the mirrored wall on the other side of the stool, until I turned my head and looked straight at his reflection. For a few moments our eyes met—the first time we had seen each other, face to face, since that last encounter in this same barroom—and I was satisfied to catch a glimpse of his naked fear before he glanced away.

No one said anything. We waited for him to speak. When he finally opened his mouth, I could almost hear the crack of his dry throat. "I didn't think," he said slowly, "that you'd take it so personally."

Each of us glanced at one another, but no one said a word. "I mean," he went on, speaking a little more quickly now, "it wasn't about any of you, was it? I was just writing about your books, not about you yourselves. It was just about the words you had put on pages, that's all it was about. A little honest criticism, right?"

"Honest criticism. Hmmm. . . ." Chris tapped a forefinger against his beer mug. "When you wrote that review of *Arch Enemies*, you said that my main character, Joshua Sparrow, was . . . how did you say it? . . . yeah, now I remember. 'He's obviously destined to be another tiresome continuing hero, a detective who will reappear in countless sequels as the author rewrites the same story again and again, á la fellow hacks like Brett Halliday and Mickey Spillane.' Isn't that what you said, George?"

Wabbit reluctantly nodded his head. "But Sparrow died at the end of *Arch Enemies*," Chris said quietly. "He was shot to death by his girlfriend, so how could he reappear in a sequel? If you had bothered to finish the book before you wrote your honest criticism, you would have known this."

"I was just trying to make a general point!" Wabbit snapped back. "I didn't mean Sparrow in particular! What I meant was . . . um. . . ."

"The sort of thing I write?" Chris asked. His fingers drummed the bartop next to his gun. "And, by the way, what did you mean when you called my second novel 'another redundant episode in the Joshua Sparrow series?" Sparrow was dead; how could he be in *Good Friday?*"

Wabbit didn't reply.

Now Sarah Storrow spoke up. "I greatly appreciated the candor of your remarks regarding *Twilight Forest*," she said, not looking up from her folded hands. "Especially the part when you claimed that the suicide of the protagonist's daughter was . . . well, I believe you said that it was hopelessly clichéd and contrived, with barely any more emotion given to the scene than if I had been blowing my nose."

"I thought it seemed that way," Wabbit began. "She hanged herself in her mother's closet, so that seemed like it wasn't. . . ."

He glanced at her, and although she was still staring at her hands, he saw the look on her face. His words trailed off.

"Dramatic enough?" she finished. "Not realistic to you? If she had . . . oh, say, doused herself in gasoline and immolated herself in front of City Hall, would you have considered that original enough for your esteemed tastes?"

He nervously licked his lips "There could have been more . . . catharsis."

"Catharsis. I see." Sarah's hands clenched together until her knuckles went white. "If you had bothered to read the afterword, Mr. Wabbit," she said, now looking straight at him, "you would have known that the character's demise was based upon the suicide of my own daughter, and that's exactly the way it happened. Like the novel's protagonist, I was the one who found her. It took me three years to write that single chapter, sir . . . and only a scoundrel who had not finished reading my novel before writing a review wouldn't have known that."

Wabbit winced, but he said nothing. He couldn't bring

himself to meet her gaze. I wouldn't have wanted to look at her either.

"When you published the review of *The Prairie Schooner*," Ray Oppenheimer began as he picked up his beer and took a sip, "you accused me of being sloppy with my research of the settlement of Missouri. Since your publication accepted letters from its readers, I wrote you one that rebutted your comments, point by point, with all the appropriate references. Why didn't you print my letter, Georgie-boy?"

"I lost the letter, that's all. . . ."

Oppenheimer shook his head. "Uh-uh. That's not good enough, son. I sent that same letter to you three times . . . the third time by registered mail, for which I received a return slip. Of course, you printed the letters which agreed with your review, but I guess those weren't lost."

"And there were two of them!" Wabbit retorted.

"Uh-huh. That there were . . . and both were sent by folks who regularly contributed articles and stories to *Scrivener*. Each of 'em saying much the same thing. Hell of a coincidence. . . ."

Ray shrugged as he set the mug back on the counter, just loudly enough to make Wabbit flinch. "Course now, you're no history expert, so I can't fault you on your not knowing some things . . . but were you really sure about things when you claimed that there weren't any Jews in Missouri during the 1800s? If so, I ought to show you my great-grandfather's diary. It was one of my main sources for the book. He was a rabbi right here in St. Louis, back in the 1880s. Y'know, I recall mentioning that in my own afterword, too."

"I'm not anti-Semitic!" Wabbit insisted. For the first time, he dared to look someone straight in the eye. "Whatever you want to make of it, pal, I wasn't trying to put down Jews!"

Ray opened his hands. "I didn't say you were," he

said easily. "I'm just saying that you're anti-writer. That's all."

" 'Scuse me," Gary Tyson said, raising a hand, "but I got something I want to say on that point."

Oppenheimer yielded the floor to Tyson. He leaned forward against the bar, staring at Wabbit. "Do you remember that piece you wrote about my book?"

"But there was nothing factual about it!" Wabbit shot back. "It was a farce . . . !"

"Sure it was farcical." Tyson's face was almost bland. "It was meant to be a farce. Elvis performing at Woodstock? Marilyn having an affair with Pope Paul? The Apollo 11 astronauts dropping acid on the way to the Moon? Timothy Leary running for president against Nixon in '68? Only an idiot would have thought it was a true-life recounting of the facts. It was straight-out surrealistic fantasy. Every other critic who read the book got the joke. Even if they hated the book, at least they judged it on its own merits. *The New York Times* blasted it, but at least they treated it fairly."

He jabbed a finger at Wabbit. "But you know what this dickless wonder did instead? He deliberately misrepresented the book as a factual novel, claiming that I had tried to write narrative journalism like Mailer's *The Armies of the Night* . . . and then critiqued the book on those lines!"

"It was a matter of opinion." Wabbit's voice rose as a defensive whine. "There's nothing you can have against me on that count. I call 'em as I see 'em, that's all. . . ."

"No," Tyson retorted, "you call 'em as you want to see 'em. There's a difference. You deliberately ignore the author's intentions and pass judgment according to whatever paradigm you see fit at the time. As long as you're the dude who comes out ahead. . . ."

"Okay! Okay! I give up! What am I supposed to do, for Chrissakes?" Wabbit threw up his hands in what we were supposed to see as a helpless gesture. "Come over to your house with my review and ask for your opinion? Ask you what you meant to say when you wrote this paragraph or that? Get written permission to write about your books? I'm a critic, for the love of god!''

For a few moments, no one replied.

''No,'' I said finally. ''You're not expected to do any of those things, and we've never asked you to do them. All you're expected to do, George, is to be an honest man. . . .''

Now it was my turn.

I leaned over his shoulder and picked up the copy of *Scrivener* I had dropped in front of him when I first walked into the bar. ''When you did this,'' I asked, ''what did you intend to prove?''

At the top of the page, printed in customary boldface type, were the title of my fourth book, my name, the book's publisher, its price and its ISBN number. All the usual stuff. Except the review had no words after that . . . only three snapshot photos. The first photo showed a copy of *The Lamb Lies Down on Broadway* lying on the ground in someone's backyard.

The second photo showed the same book, except this time it had been ripped to shreds. The pages, each methodically torn out of the book's saddle-stitched binding, lay in a dismal pile on the ground. A pile of worthless trash, except that the dustjacket had carefully been placed next to the heap so that the title and the author's name were legible.

The third photo showed a man—shot from only the waist down, but it was unmistakably Wabbit himself, judging from the size of his gut—standing in front of the pile. The camera had skillfully been placed so that no obscenity laws were broken, but even without seeing the man's dick, the stream of fluid ejecting from the open fly of his trousers onto the pages clearly showed what was going on.

No words were necessary.

Wabbit looked at the pictures for a few moments . . .
then a strange giggle began to rise from the back of his
throat. Cold hatred surged within me even as he self-
consciously clamped a hand over his mouth and squeezed
his eyes shut. As if on its own volition, my right hand
began to raise the gun to his neck. . . .

Then I caught a glimpse of Chris, saw him shaking his
head, and I lowered the gun again.

"Speak up, George," I said softly. "I couldn't hear
you."

George Wabbit somehow managed to put a clamp on
his laughter. He silently stared at the photos for another
minute, then he angrily shoved the magazine away. "Oh,
for Chrissakes!" he snapped. "You know it was a joke,
just as I know this is a joke! You guys aren't murderers,
you're writers . . . !"

I shut my eyes. After a few seconds, the hammering
in my skull slowed down enough that I could speak
again. "You may be right," I said slowly. "I'm not a
killer, and I don't think the others are, either. But let me
ask you this. . . ."

I sat down on the barstool next to him, still holding
the magazine before him. "What's the difference between ripping apart a book, pissing on it, and taking pictures of the event for publication . . . and burning it in
public? In fact, why not get hold of a lot of copies and
burn them in a bonfire? They used to do that a lot in
Nazi Germany. . . ."

"Aw, c'mon. . . ."

"No, I mean it. And it doesn't stop with the Nazis.
We've had it here in America, too. Books being taken
out of libraries and torched, city councils and school
boards banning everything from *Huckleberry Finn* to
Tropic of Cancer to *Slaughterhouse-Five.* . . ."

"I wasn't suggesting that it be banned!"

"No," I said, "but the intent was much the same. Tell
me, what's the difference between what you did to my

novel and what the Nazis did to anything that wasn't judged to be proper Aryan literature?''

Wabbit's jaw trembled. For a few moments his lips shuddered as he tried to force a reply. If he was trying to say something—''It was just a joke,'' or ''I'm not a facist,'' or even ''It's a free country, I can do whatever I like''—I didn't wait for it.

''And to answer something you said before,'' I went on, ''yeah, I'm a writer, and I'm proud of it. My books are my children. They're a part of me, not something I bang out for money or cheap fame. They may not be perfect. Some have faults and blemishes, I'll admit that, but they're still my kids. And when someone insults my children. . . .''

''When someone lies about them,'' Chris interrupted.

''When someone makes them out to be something they ain't,'' Ray added.

''When someone plays jokes at their expense,'' said Gary.

''When someone attempts to harm them,'' Sarah whispered in a voice as chill as the night itself. . . .

I raised the gun in my hand and placed it against the back of the wabbit's head. ''Then we tend to get really pissed off,'' I murmured as my finger slipped within the trigger guard.

Wabbit closed his eyes, his mouth hanging open. There was the sudden stench of urine as he whizzed again . . . not on my book this time, but in his pants.

It might have been a good joke, but no one was laughing.

If this were a work of fiction, I might have ended it any number of ways. I shot him in the head and his brains were splattered all over the counter. We forced him out to the alley, leaned him up against the wall, and gave him the Gary Gilmore treatment. Or, even more elaborately, and this is the one I particularly liked, we made

him strip buck-naked, marched him out of the bar and
down the Landing to the Missouri side of the Eads
Bridge, where the Metro Link light-rail system crosses
the Mississippi into Illinois, where we gave him a sporting chance to cross the bridge on foot before the train
came through . . . and, of course, we had timed it so that
he had a choice between trying to outrun an oncoming
train or surviving a jump from the bridge.

We did none of the above.

Instead, I removed the gun from his head and, one at
a time, we turned away from the bar and silently walked
out of Casey's. He was right on one thing; we were writers, not killers, despite our guns and our anger. Not even
at this time, not even in this place. We had made our
point, and he would remember it, even though by this
time next week he would be starving to death in the dark
and the cold.

Killing him would have been pointless. What we had
done to him was worse than homicide. So we just left
him there, alone with himself. I was the last to leave, and
I didn't look back when I strode out of Casey's Bar &
Grill.

Chris's Bronco was parked only a half block away; he
had a full tank of gas, so we piled inside. My house was
closest and I had plenty of beer in the fridge, and I knew
some oddball ways through the back streets that would
take us there without having to use the swamped high-
ways. It took us a while; we had to dodge burning buildings and rioters and half-assed police blockades, but
finally we made our way to my place.

I don't know what we were thinking when we made
the trip, because hardly anyone spoke to each other during the long drive, except for me giving Chris the proper
directions. Chris and I were loners, but the other guys
had families; they were undoubtedly worried about them.
But we had almost murdered someone tonight, and I

think we all needed time to be apart, even if it was huddled together in the back of an overweight Ford or camping out in someone's house.

At any rate, you know the rest of the story. NASA and the Pentagon succeeded; three Titan-4 missiles, each carrying multi-megaton nuclear warheads, were launched from Cape Canaveral. Along with the nukes launched by the Russians, they detonated near the asteroid and managed to deflect its trajectory. The asteroid missed Earth by about two hundred thousand miles—too damn close— and by four a.m. the five of us who had stood sleepless watch during the night caught the final word on CNN.

The world was safe again . . . sort of. In the end, hundreds of thousands of lives had been lost in the panic. The combined cost of property damage soared into the trillions of dollars. A couple of governments toppled. Some people were given new reasons to believe in God; others blessed the Air Force, NASA, Glavkosmos, and their local congressmen.

So be it. We picked up the pieces and went from there. Three months later, we were again wondering whether Michael Jackson would make another record or if Princess Di would ever find another boyfriend. A year later, when the inevitable ABC made-for-TV movie about the event was aired, it bombed in the ratings because NBC chose the same night to broadcast the L.A. Law reunion special.

And no one ever heard from George T. Wabbit again.

No more issues of *Scrivener* were published. I was told that he had left town; someone else said that he had joined some religious cult and was now selling flowers on a street corner in San Antonio, or maybe it was San Francisco. Another person said that he was now working for David Duke in Louisiana, trying to get all my novels removed from the bookstores there. And, six years later, after I received the National Book Award for best short-story collection of the year, I was informed that he had been in the audience, booing very loudly when I walked onto the podium to accept the prize.

Who knows the truth? And who cares?

The wabbit was dead. I'm not sure if he had ever been alive in the first place.

INTRODUCTION:
"Riders in the Sky"

"Ladies love outlaws," or so the song goes, but Waylon Jennings only got it half-right.

We all love outlaws, but only as long as their crimes aren't atrocious, they don't hurt anyone we personally know, and they stay away from our doorsteps. Billy the Kid and Al Capone were sociopathic monsters who murdered many people in cold blood, but they've been enshrined in American folklore. By contrast, Jeffery Dahmer was inarguably a sick bastard; when he was killed in prison by another psychotic, no one minded much at all.

That's the point Oliver Stone missed when he made *Natural Born Killers*, an otherwise brilliant movie; he depicted his cross-country serial killers as media heroes. For an outlaw to become a populist hero, he must defy authority, which the common man sees as a mutual enemy, while sparing the lives of innocents. Stone's couple simply killed at random, at whim, and it doesn't work that way. If an outlaw can pull off this Robin Hood hat trick, then the local citizenry will hail him while overlooking the fact that he's a true enemy of the people.

That's how John Gotti, the New York City crime lord, got away with it as long as he did before the FBI finally nailed him. He was a Mafia thug with a bad haircut, but every summer he threw one hell of a block party in Queens. Gotti understood the value of good P.R.

The James-Younger Gang is a good example.

I've always been a fan of Frank and Jesse James. You can't grow up in the South without becoming such, because native-born Southerners are raised in the shadow of the Civil War and the James Brothers' careers were a direct result of the collapse of the Confederacy. Yes, the James-Younger Gang killed quite a number of people, some of them innocent bystanders or lawmen trying to do their jobs. But they were also, for their time, high-tech criminals. They invented the art of train robbery, and, in one instance, they even issued a press release while committing a crime, arguably making them the world's first media-friendly outlaws.

Because I also love dirigibles and blimps and have a fondness for writing alternative history stories, it was only a matter of time before I matched the two together.

When I found out during Magicon, the 1992 World Science Fiction Convention in Orlando, Florida, that Mike Resnick was putting together an anthology titled *Alternative Outlaws*, I begged him for the chance to write a story that had been lingering in my mind for a couple of years. Mike graciously agreed to let me submit this story, whereupon I forgot about the assignment for the next six months while I wrote a novel, until Mike phoned me to remind me of my obligation.

As it turned out, I didn't understand the exact parameters of *Alternative Outlaws*, which was about historical outlaws who turn lawmen, and vice-versa, and instead wrote a story about historical outlaws who behave the same as they did in real life, but take advantage of then-nonexistent technology. Mike accepted the story anyway, which was just as well. No self-respecting Tennessean living in Missouri would ever let Jesse James wear a tin star. Just doesn't fit.

The James-Younger Gang robberies depicted in this story are entirely factual in terms of locations, dates, and casualties. Only the circumstances have been changed. As for the Colt revolver Jesse uses in the first scene . . . it's on display in the Missouri State History Museum. I went to see it before I wrote this story.

Kind of made me want to go stick up Waldenbooks. Okay, lady, empty the cash register, nice and slow . . . oh yeah, and toss me the new Stephen King novel while you're at it.

RIDERS IN THE SKY

St. Louis, Missouri: August 30, 1874.

The Missouri Pacific airship *Ulysses S. Grant* hovers beside the tall, wrought-iron mooring tower, its grey canvas envelope rippling slightly in the morning breeze wafting off the Mississippi River. A packet steamer cruising downstream toots its horn twice as it passes the aerodrome; a small crowd, dressed in meeting clothes for Sunday services at the nearby Episcopal church, gathers at the outer edge of the dusty field to watch the weekly launch of the skyship.

At the bottom of the lowered gangway beneath the gondola, a uniformed conductor, Emmett Riley, snaps the tickets of the last few passengers to board the craft. Wealthy cattlemen, bankers, grain speculators—they're the only ones who can afford the extravagance of a $30 ticket to Kansas City. Some seem to think they're boarding a Pullman coach: a burly gentleman with muttonchop sideburns is puffing on a fat cigar as he extends his ticket to the conductor. Without a word, Riley snatches the stogie from the other man's mouth, drops it to the ground, and stamps it out under his shoe.

"Positively no smoking allowed, sir," Riley says. "In fact, I must relieve you of you matches before you can board."

The businessman protests, loudly proclaiming his God-given right to smoke wherever he God-damned well pleases, but the conductor remains adamant. For the safety of the airship and its passengers, no flammable substances are allowed aboard the *Ulysses S. Grant*. "God-damned Irish," the banker mutters under his breath, but, in the end, he surrenders his tin matchbox to Riley before he stalks up the gangway steps to the passenger cabin just aft of the pilothouse.

The conductor shakes his head as he holds out his hand to the last two passengers in line. "Some people have no common sense whatsoever," he murmurs.

"I quite agree," says one of the men. He's tall and slender, with a dark bushy beard, wearing boots, a bowler hat, and a long linen duster. Riley notes that his eyelids are constantly batting, as if suffering from a nervous tic. He puts down his cloth carpetbag as he digs his ticket out of the pocket of his greatcoat. "One shouldn't be flying if one can't respect simple rules. Isn't that right, Jonathan?"

The other man, older and more heavy-set than his travelling companion, with lighter hair and a trim mustache, grunts distractedly. A horse-drawn buckboard is parked beneath the baggage compartment in the rear of the gondola; he's intently watching the ground crew as they hoist a padlocked strongbox through the open hatch.

The first man coughs. "Jonathan . . . your ticket?"

The second man turns around quickly. "Uh, yeah . . . sure, Tom." He pulls a ticket from the pocket of his duster; his hand trembles slightly as he gives it to the conductor.

The conductor smiles but says nothing as he snaps the ticket. Aeronautics still makes many people nervous; tough as this character looks, his knees are visibly shaking. He watches the two young men, brothers from the looks of them, probably stockmen, as they climb the gangway to the passenger compartment. Riley folds the ticket stubs into his coat pocket and climbs up the stairs, where he cranks up the gangway and shuts the hatch.

A few minutes later, the pilot extends his left arm out his window. "Contact!" he yells as he drops his hand.

Two men standing on either side of the airship grasp the long blades of the port and starboard propellers and yank them down. The twin 200-horsepower internal combustion engines, manufactured in France by the Giffard Sky Ship Company and brought to America aboard steamships, roar to life.

Horses whinny in terror and dance backward as an artificial wind, malodorous with gasoline fumes, rips across the dusty aerodrome, tearing caps off the heads of the other groundmen holding the taut mooring lines. On another hand-signal from the pilot, the mooring tower cable is detached; the men on the ground simultaneously drop their lines and race away from the airship.

For a moment, the dirigible hovers above the aerodrome, severed from all contact with the earth, yet still close enough for its lower rudder to lightly touch the ground. Then the engines are throttled up and the nearby crowd, their eyes stinging from the windswept dust thrown in their faces, gape in awe as the leviathan slowly rises into the sky.

The *Ulysses S. Grant* ascends to its normal cruising altitude of one thousand feet, then the pilot twists the rudder wheel as the copilot steps on the elevator pedals. The mighty airship turns its blunt prow westward and commences its journey across the Missouri plains to Kansas City.

Back in the cabin, most of the fifteen passengers are staring out the bevelled windows, watching as church steeples and the rooftops of five-story buildings recede beneath them. The banker who argued with the conductor about his cigar doubles over in his seat in the front of the cabin and gets violently ill. The conductor snatches up a pail and a wet washrag before he rushes down the aisle to tend to him.

As Riley passes the two men who come aboard last, he notices that, although the one called Jonathan has his eyes tightly shut and is holding fast to his armrests; his brother Tom has pulled a pocket watch from his vest and is studying it.

Riley shakes his head as he pushes the pail beneath the sick passenger. There's always some fool who complains if he's not in Kansas City in eight hours, just as the company broadsheets have promised. Not so long ago, he would have been lucky if he had been on the other side of the state in eight days, let alone eight hours. And only then if his train or stagecoach hadn't been intercepted by highwaymen.

Five hours later, the *Grant* is close to the town of Lexington, following the Missouri River toward Kansas City. It's shortly after one o'clock; the conductor has just cleaned up after a mid-flight lunch of sandwiches and bottled lemonade and has settled down in his seat in the rear of the cabin. Most of the passengers have become bored with watching the passing scenery; despite the omniscient engine roar, some have fallen asleep. The air inside the cabin has become hot and uncomfortable—the passengers have closed their windows against the constant wind and noise—but Riley pays it little mind. In another five hours, the airship will land in Kansas City. Maybe he can catch a few winks before landing . . .

Just then, one of the passengers—Tom, the one who has been carefully studying his watch throughout the journey—suddenly rises from his seat. He picks up his valise with his left hand, grasps the brass ceiling rail with his right hand, and begins to walk toward the back of the cabin. At first the conductor thinks he's heading for the lavatory, a small anteroom next to the galley where the chamberpot is located, but instead he walks past the door.

A few moments later, his companion also stands up. A little less easily than his brother, Jonathan starts to walk the opposite way down the aisle, in the direction of the pilothouse.

Only a couple of the other passengers, drowsy with the heat and noise, take note of their actions, but Riley is astonished. After all, there are placards posted throughout the cabin: *Please! For Your Safety, You Must Remain In Your Seat Unless Escorted By the Conductor!* And, as this man himself observed, those are the rules.

As Tom approaches the rear of the cabin, Riley stands up and steps into the aisle, blocking him before he can go any further. "Excuse me, sir," he says politely, "but you and your kin cannot tour the ship just now. If you'll please . . ."

His voice trails off. For the first time, he sees the man's eyes: blue and cold, not unlike the surface of the Atlantic as he saw it from the deck of the sailship that brought him over from his native Ireland twenty-two years ago, and just as menacing. . . .

In that instant, the passenger's right hand leaves the ceiling rail. It slips beneath the hem of his long coat . . . and then, in a single swift motion, the hand reappears, and clasped within it is a Colt navy revolver.

Riley freezes as he stares down the bore of its seven-inch barrel. Although the click of the hammer is subdued beneath the thrum of the engines, the conductor hears it as clearly as if it were the crack of doom.

"Take me to the baggage compartment," the gunman says softly. "Do it now, y'hear?"

Riley slowly looks up at him. All at once, everything clicks together in his mind. "Oh, sweet Jesus," he whispers. "You're him . . ."

The man scowls at the conductor. "Don't use His name in vain. Not on the Sabbath."

Then the slightest hint of a smile creases the bearded

face. "But if you want," he adds, "you can call me Jesse."

The hijacking of the *Ulysses S. Grant* on August 30, 1874, by Jesse and Frank James marked the beginning of a short yet fascinating part in the history of the American West. The exploits of the outlaws who dared rob airships in flight has been romanticized countless times through novels, TV shows, and movies, albeit wildly inaccurate for the most part.

If one were to believe popular fiction, airship robberies were a constant danger; truth is, only three successful hijackings were committed between 1874 and 1882, although there were a dozen or so unsuccessful attempts. No airship ever crashed or exploded during a hold-up, nor were any beautiful women ever abducted at gunpoint by masked bandits. In fact, women and children were prohibited from riding in airships until 1897.

Nonetheless, both history and fiction agree on one point: it was Frank and Jesse James, along with other members of their gang, who invented airship robbery, and it was the murder of Jesse James that brought the era to a close.

In retrospect, it's only logical that the invention of dirigibles would have naturally led to airship hijackings. New technologies tend to breed criminal activity as a side effect, just as the proliferation of desktop computers has led to computer crime, whether it be by organizations specializing in wire fraud or by teenaged hackers hacking into sensitive databases. In this case, it was the invention of the dirigible in France by Henri Giffard in the 1860's.

Giffard took unsteerable hot-air balloons, developed in the late 1700s by the Montgolfier brothers, and redesigned them as semi-rigid envelopes pumped full of hydrogen. Giffard's early steam engines were too heavy to allow more than one passenger, but with the assistance of the Brazilian inventor Alberto Santos-Dumont, Giffard

married the lighter and more efficient internal-
combustion engine to the earlier models' fuselages, and
thus the modern airship was born.

Giffard's dirigibles were seen only as a novelty in
France, but they were noted with great interest by the
American ambassador, who saw their military potential.
He alerted the United States War Department, and, within
a few months, scientists and generals from America travelled to Paris to watch one of Giffard's ''steerable balloons'' fly circles above the Champs Elyssee and drop
simulated bombs into the Seine River. The Americans
were suitably impressed; the Civil War had just begun,
and the War Department was desperate for a tactical edge
over the Confederate States. On advice of their envoys,
it hastily contracted Giffard to immediately construct two
''sky ships'' for the Union army.

Giffard's dirigibles, the *Boston* and the *Potomac*,
weren't delivered until the war was close to its end, but
they performed well in many ways: reconnaissance mis-
sions above enemy lines, delivering supplies to troops in
hard-to-reach places, taking key officers from one combat
zone to another in less time and with greater security than
even unoccupied rail lines could manage. Although the
Boston exploded in midair during Second Bull Run after
being hit by Confederate mortars, the *Potomac* earned an
indelible place in history as the aircraft that escorted
Abraham Lincoln to Gettysburg; during the flight from
Washington to the battlefield, Lincoln found the peace of
mind to compose his most famous speech on the back of
an envelope.

After the war, popular speculation ran wild about the
possible uses of skyships, ranging from airborne buffalo
hunts in the Dakotas to improbable dime-novels about
Frank Reade's exploits on the Moon. However, the only
private companies that could muster the capital necessary
to develop dirigibles as passenger aircraft were the railroads. They needed a vehicle that could safely transport

people and small cargo across the most dangerous territories in the West, particularly the state of Missouri.

Labeled by the Chicago Times as "The Outlaw's Paradise," the western parts of the state had been overrun by bandits. Like the James and Younger brothers, who were veterans of Quantrill's Raiders, many were former Confederate guerrillas who continued their outlaw lives after the war, often with the aid of Confederate sympathizers among the local citizens. Stage holdups were almost commonplace, and desperados had recently learned how to derail iron horses. Although no one in the rail companies seriously considered replacing locomotives with dirigibles, they realized that dirigibles offered a viable alternative for the gold shipments that frequently needed to be sent to the western settlements . . . and, likewise, there was money to be made from selling seats to well-to-do travellers who wanted "scenic" (that is, safe) passage across the badlands.

In 1872, the Giffard Air Ship Company delivered the first commercial skyship to the Missouri Pacific Railroad: the *Ulysses S. Grant*, two hundred and eighty feet long, complete with a railcar-like passenger cabin and a small baggage compartment. It was scheduled to provide weekly service between St. Louis and Kansas City, weather permitting, Broadside advertisements proclaimed it to be "The Epitome of Grandeur and Comfort, Unstoppable By Neither The Forces Of Man Nor Nature."

As always, one man's hubris is another man's insult, and the man who was insulted was none other than Missouri's most infamous outlaw, Jesse James.

History doesn't record which member of the James-Younger gang came up with the idea of hijacking the *Ulysses S. Grant*. Most of the dime novels of the time said that it was Jesse's brainstorm; in later years, Cole Younger would assert that he was the one who had come up with the scheme. Most historians tend to discount both notions; Younger made many such unverifiable claims to Jesse's fame, and the authors of the "Wide-Awake Library" were the least trustworthy of sources. Conventional wisdom has it that Frank James was the smarter one of the brothers and logically would have been the one who devised the scheme, despite eyewitness accounts of Frank's obvious nervousness during the first hijacking.

As for Frank James himself, he remained laconic on the subject, except once to supply a motive during an interview with a *Kansas City Times* reporter near the end of his life. "If they thought they could fly a skyship named after that sonofabitch Grant over Missouri," he said, "they had another think comin'."

While Frank went into the pilothouse, where he pointed his revolver at the two pilots and demanded that they immediately land the airship, Jesse forced Emmett Riley to lead him into the cargo compartment. There the hapless conductor was tied up with ropes from Frank's bag.

When that was done, Jesse cranked open the cargo hatch. He then pulled out from his valise a long flag made of red and blue-dyed bed sheets, weighted at one end by a small bag of buckshot. As the airship began to descend, Jesse dropped the flag through the hatch. Then he took a seat on the strongbox and patiently waited for the airship to land.

The plan was cunning in both its simplicity and its exquisite timing. The remaining members of the gang— Jim, Bob, and Cole Younger, along with Bill Stiles, Sam Wells, and Clell Miller—had been waiting on the outskirts of Lexington, which the gang already knew from the newspaper stories would be one of the towns the Grant would fly over. Through the same highly detailed accounts, Jesse knew just how fast the dirigible would travel at cruising speed, so he was able to time the journey accurately, using his pocket watch to estimate the air-speed and sighting well-known local landmarks to double check his bearings. The flag was dropped to alert gang members on the ground that he and Frank had taken control of the airship; all they had to do was ride to where the *Grant* finally touched down.

As it turned out, the bandits were already waiting for the Grant when it landed in a cow pasture on the banks of the Missouri, just across the river from Lexington. So deftly was the hijacking handled that the dozing passengers were unaware that a holdup was taking place, and even when the *Grant's* gondola was skirting the treetops, many assumed that the airship, like the locomotives they were more accustomed to riding, was simply stopping to "take on more coal," as one passenger later told a reporter from the *St. Louis Post*.

Meanwhile, a group of Lexington citizens, having spotted the airship's unexpected descent, rode on horseback or in carriages to a bluff across the river from the landing site. There they watched in bafflement as a small group of horsemen grabbed the airship's dangling moorlines, lashed them to trees, then drew their guns and climbed up the lowered gangway into the gondola.

By all reliable accounts, the first airship robbery was peaceful. While Frank held the pilots at bay, and Jesse relieved the baggage compartment of its strongbox, the three Younger brothers made their way through the cabin, taking jewelry, watches, and cash from the startled passengers at gunpoint. The only passenger spared from robbery was one Hiram Taylor, a cattleman whose Virginia accent betrayed him as a Southerner. Upon discovering that he was a Confederate veteran from Lee's army, Bob Younger handed back the silver watch he had just taken.

Less than fifteen minutes after landing, the gang rode off into the forest, having done their job of robbing the airship of $2,000 in gold and currency, plus whatever had been taken from the passengers. They left behind sixteen cowering men, an undamaged dirigible, and a new legend in the annals of history.

As newspaper headlines screamed the story from New York to San Francisco, it wasn't only the Missouri Pacific Railroad that was worried. Three other dirigibles had already been purchased and put into service by other railroad companies, and more had been contracted, all on the assumption that they were untouchable by highwaymen. Now that claim had been put to the test and had failed.

One of the reasons why the James-Younger Gang gained so much notoriety was that the public had little sympathy for the railroads in the first place. The railroads were perceived as being run by greedy carpetbaggers from the East, getting rich at the expense of hard-working Westerners; the fact that the James-Younger Gang killed many men during its railroad hold-ups was conveniently overlooked by the reporters who had lauded Jesse as the "Robin Hood of the Plains."

The additional fact that many of these railroad and bank robberies had not been performed by the James boys, but instead by anonymous bandits claiming to be them, didn't prevent the railroad men from getting alarmed. Although the Missouri legislature had appropriated $10,000 for the hiring of the Pinkerton National Detective Agency solely for the purpose of apprehending the James-Younger gang, the Pinkertons had already been foiled many times in trying to apprehend the James and Younger boys. Eyewitness descriptions of Frank and Jesse James were confused to the point that no reliable drawing of their faces had ever been made, thus allowing the outlaws to walk the streets of Kansas City and St. Louis with impunity. Indeed, on more than one occasion, either Frank or Jesse had shared barroom tables with Pinkerton operatives who were searching for them, and undercover agents who dared to ride into Jesse James' native Clay County to ferret out the gang were often found dead by the roadside. Likewise, no one in the rural Missouri countryside was either disloyal or brave enough to disclose the locations of their hideouts, despite the $2,000 bounty Governor Silas Woodson had placed on their heads.

Within a month of the Grant hijacking, a second dirigible was robbed in flight. The *Andrew Jackson*, operated by the Louisville and Nashville Railroad, was taken over by three masked bandits and forced to land just outside of Bowling Green, Kentucky. Although the modus was virtually identical to the Grant holdup, there was little reason to believe that the James-Younger Gang was responsible for this second assault. However, the *Nashville Banner* did charge Jesse James with the *Andrew Jackson* hijacking, and that unproven allegation was faithfully reprinted in newspapers across the country.

Whether it was the James-Younger Gang or copycats, the railroads took quick measures to prevent a recurrence of the hijackings. Deadbolts were installed on the inside of the pilothouse door, allowing the pilots to lock themselves in their compartment before take-off. Latch-key locks were installed on the cargo compartment hatches, with the key entrusted to the co-pilot.

The Missouri Pacific, fearing a repeat of the August 30 hijacking, hired armed guards to ride in the baggage compartments of the *Ulysses S. Grant* and, several months later, its new airship, the *Prairie Viking*. It also issued two-shot derringers to its conductors. However, the guns were little more than a bluff; on the urgent advice of the Giffard Air Ship Company, neither the guard's rifle nor the derringers were allowed to be kept loaded while in flight. The company was rightfully concerned that a stray bullet within the cabin could pierce the skin of the hydrogen-filled gasbags in the dirigibles' envelope and thus cause an explosion. The railroad counted on that bit of scientific minutiae being lost on the public when it allowed newspaper photographers to shoot pictures of rifle-toting guards posed on the gangway of the *Prairie Viking*; the point was to reassure passengers and to make robbers think twice about hijacking any more airships.

The ruse worked for a while. During the rest of 1874 and early 1875, there were no more successful skyship robberies. In July 1875, two men attempted to rob a Southern Pacific dirigible en route from Austin to San Antonio. They used an axe to break through the hatch of the baggage compartment, only to be confronted by the rifles of two Texas Rangers riding shotgun in the aft hold. The would-be robbers were apprehended without a shot fired, but that wasn't all; in the tradition of Texan justice, the passengers mobbed the bandits as soon as the dirigible safely landed in San Antonio and hauled them to a nearby oak tree, where they were lynched within minutes. The railroad companies made certain that news of the failed hijacking and the grisly fate of the perpetrators was spread wide and far.

For another twelve months, there were no more attempts on dirigibles. Then, on July 7, 1876, the James-Younger Gang struck again. And this time, they got away with one of the most daring robberies in American history.

On that morning, the *Prairie Viking* lifted off from the Kansas City aerodrome and turned southeast; in its locked baggage compartment were two express safes containing $15,000 in gold and currency. As usual, there was an armed guard in the baggage compartment, and the door to the pilot's gondola was locked from within.

It was supposed to be a routine flight to Memphis, Tennessee, yet less than an hour after the skyship departed from Kansas City, three men stood up from their seats, pulled revolvers out of their coat pockets, and calmly informed the conductor and passengers that they were being hijacked.

The conductor, John Blackman, surrendered his derringer on demand but then told the bandits that the baggage compartment was locked and that the only available key was in the pocket of the copilot, who was locked inside the gondola. "Sorry, boys," he said, "but you might as well put away your pistols and sit down. This ship won't land until we reach Memphis."

It was then, according to eyewitnesses, that one of the robbers, later identified as Jim Younger, cocked his revolver and pointed it straight at the ceiling. "I'm not asking you to land, mister," he said, "but if that's the way you want it . . . then we'll land."

Blackman knew exactly what the bandit meant. A single gunshot through the ceiling would cause a hydrogen explosion in the gasbag directly above the cabin, and the *Viking* would go down in a fiery crash. Perhaps it was a suicidal bluff, but Blackman couldn't afford to risk the lives of his passengers by calling it.

While one of the passengers, a Presbyterian minister, began to lead the others in prayer for their lives, the conductor was marched to the aft end of the cabin, where he knocked six times on the hatch, the standard "all clear" signal for the guard within. The guard, Joseph Potts, apparently believed that a lunch pail was going to be passed to him; he unlocked the hatch and pushed it open, but barely had time to raise his unloaded Winchester before Cole Younger thrust a Bowie knife into his chest.

Blackman thought that the bandits' next move would be an attempt to make the pilots land the airship, yet none of the desperados made a move toward the pilothouse. While Jim Younger held the conductor and the hymn-singing passengers at bay, Cole Younger and a new member of the gang, Hobbs Kerry, hauled the overstuffed carpet bags they had carried aboard the *Viking* back to the baggage compartment. Again, a flag was dropped out of the open aft hatch; a few moments later, Kerry and Cole Younger shoved the two safes through the hatch, where they plummeted to the rolling Cooper County countryside a thousand feet below.

What happened next astonished everyone aboard. While the three men took turns keeping the passengers at gunpoint, each bandit pulled large bundles of sewn-together bed sheets out of the bags. Long ropes had been knotted around the corners of the sheets; each of the trio carefully uncoiled the ropes, wrapped them under their chests and around their shoulders, then took the bundles in their arms.

Then, to the horror-stricken cries of Blackman and the passengers, each bandit stepped through the cargo hatch and out into empty space. "See you 'round, square-heads!" Cole Younger was heard to yell before he leaped into oblivion.

Blackman rushed to a window, believing that he would see the three men plummeting to their deaths. Instead, he saw three giant "handkerchiefs" gently wafting downward on the warm summer breeze. Suspended beneath each one was a man, holding onto the ropes, screaming rebel yells that could be heard above the thrum of the engines.

The pious Presbyterian minister muttered a blasphemy as he watched this ungodly sight. Meanwhile, the two men in the pilothouse were wondering what on Earth was going on back in the cabin. Unwilling to disobey company rules, though, they refused to unlock the pilothouse door until they arrived in Memphis some seven hours later; by doing so, they unwittingly allowed the James-Younger Gang to make the best of their getaway.

It wasn't a perfect crime. Jim and Cole Younger landed safely outside Otterville, where they were picked up by the rest of the gang, who by then had already recovered the two safes and hidden them in the woods.

Hobbs Kerry was less fortunate. He got an arm tangled in his ropes, which caused his rudimentary parachute to veer far away from the others. To make matters worse, he broke his left leg upon touchdown. Then, just to prove that bad luck runs in threes, he was discovered hobbling through the bean field of the shotgun-toting farmer who had spied his descent and wasn't about to accept his feeble excuses.

Kerry was hauled in the back of a buckboard to Sedalia, where he was thrown in jail. Suffering considerable pain from his broken leg and scared of being hanged, Hobbs Kerry broke down. He told the entire story to the sheriff and, later, to a reporter from the *Kansas City Times*.

It turned out that Frank James had masterminded the plan. Gaining inspiration from the flight of dandelion seeds, he had persuaded his and Jesse's mother, Zerelda Samuel, to sew together a "sky sock" of old sheets. After Frank himself successfully tested the principle by jumping off a tall Missouri River bluff, he convinced the other members of the gang that they could pull off the robbery.

It had taken nearly a year for the gang to perfect the plan, during which time Jim and Cole Younger proved themselves to be the gang's best jumpers. Although he was willing to leap out of an airship with his brothers, Bob Younger's acrophobia ultimately got the better of him; at the last minute, Jesse decided that Bob would join him as part of the group which would wait outside Otterville for the signal flag. Kerry himself volunteered to substitute for Bob, figuring that he would prove himself to the rest of the gang by taking on the most hazardous part of the mission.

Hobbs Kerry's confession established that the James-Younger Gang was responsible for the robbery of the *Prairie Viking*. Once again, railroad officials seethed while the telegraph wires hummed with the news of the latest exploits of Jesse James and his bunch.

Next time, they quietly swore amongst themselves, we'll get the bastards. No matter what it takes, we will stop them.

And so they did.

On September 7, 1876, exactly two months after the hold-up of the *Prairie Viking*, the Great Northern airship *Jupiter* lifted off from the aerodrome in Des Moines and turned due north toward Minnesota. Although the airship served Minneapolis and St. Paul, it was scheduled to land in the small town of Northfield, about thirty miles south of the Twin Cities, where passengers would board a short-line train to their final destination.

There were two reasons for this oddity. First, the Minneapolis City Council had voted against leasing land to the railroad for the building of an aerodrome. The *Jupiter* itself lived up to its name. The largest skyship of its time, it was four hundred feet long, propelled by two 350-horsepower engines, with passenger seating for up to fifty people. Minneapolis citizens disliked the idea of such a behemoth buzzing over their city and thus had voted down a proposal to build an aerodrome within their county. In this, they were aided by the local steamboat companies, which had foreseen competition from an aerodrome so close to their Mississippi river ports.

Northfield businessmen took advantage of the injunction. Stating that an aerodrome would help boost business in their community, they prevailed upon the townspeople to let the Great Northern Railroad build its dirigible field near the train station. The most prominent beneficiary of the aerodrome was the First National Bank of Northfield, which believed that regular skyship service would help insure the safe arrival and departure of express safes. As a result, the *Jupiter* always carried a large safe in its barrage compartment, often containing as much as

$200,000, from the Northfield bank and those in Minneapolis and St. Paul.

It was too tempting a target for the James-Younger Gang to pass up. Emboldened by the success of the *Prairie Viking* holdup, they made plans to rob the *Jupiter* in just the same way. Unfortunately for them, the Pinkerton Detective Agency had already second-guessed them.

The denouement is well recorded in history, popularized to this day by dozens of novels and movies. Four members of the gang—Clell Miller, Charlie Pitts and Jim and Cole Younger—boarded the skyship in Des Moines, carrying with them the carpetbags containing their parachutes. Frank and Jesse James, along with Bob Younger and Minnesota native Bill Chadwell, had already journeyed north to the drop zone in the forest just south of Northfield, where they would retrieve the safes and rendezvous with the other members once they parachuted to safety.

What no one in the gang realized was that, for the past six weeks, half of the passenger seats in the *Jupiter* had been occupied by Pinkerton agents posing as travelling businessmen, their expenses paid by a conglomerate of railroad companies that wanted to see the robberies halted. Six times already, twenty-five Pinkertons had taken the round-trip flight between Des Moines and Northfield, pretending to read books and newspapers while they suspiciously eyed every person in the cabin.

"It was a long shot," Allan Pinkerton said later, "but it certainly paid off in the end." On that day in early autumn, the patience of his operatives was rewarded.

Shortly before the *Jupiter* began to make its descent for approach and landing in Northfield, Miller, Stiles, and the two Youngers stood up as one. As Cole Younger began to march down the long aisle toward the baggage compartment, the other three men began to spread out through the cabin.

According to eyewitness accounts, Miller and Stiles

made the fatal error that tipped off the Pinkertons; before
Cole gave the prearranged hand signal, they reached into
their jackets and began to pull out their guns. The pistols
barely cleared their pockets before two detectives leaped
to their feet behind each man, pulled out derringers, and
shot both men in the back from a range of less than five
feet.

As Jim and Cole Younger reacted to the gunshots, they
went for their own guns . . . only to find themselves surrounded by nearly a score of Colt revolvers, all aimed
directly at them.

Cole already had his hand on his pistol. According to
popular legend, he whipped it out of his pocket and
pointed it to the ceiling. "How many of you are ready
to go to Hell?" he asked.

The nearest Pinkerton stared at him down the barrel of
his Colt. "We all are, sir," he said evenly, "but you'll
get there first."

Cole Younger looked at him for a minute, then carefully uncocked his gun and dropped it on the seat beside
him. Jim Younger simply sighed and raised his hands.

A thousand feet below, Frank and Jesse realized something had gone wrong in the plan when the *Jupiter*
cruised overhead without a flag being dropped or a safe
falling out of the hatch. They had only begun to climb
into the saddle, though, when three men appeared in the
woods and opened fire upon them; a Northfield sheriff's
posse, patrolling the forest at the behest of the Pinkertons,
had spotted the smoke from their cookfire and had homed
in on them. During the ambush, Bill Chadwell was killed
by a bullet through the chest, while Bob Younger was
severely wounded and left behind.

When the *Jupiter* landed in Northfield, Jim and Cole
Younger were put under arrest. Although they expected
to be hanged, they were put on trial with their brother
Bob and sentenced to life in prison. Photos of the bodies

of the other gang members became the subject of popular postcards.

Out of the entire gang, only Frank and Jesse James escaped. It would be six long years before either of them would be seen again.

In the absence of the James brothers, the world moved on around them as if they had never left.

As usual, a number of bank and train robberies were committed in their name, although it's doubtful that either one of the brothers was responsible. Their notoriety superseded them, so that every cow-town bank stick-up or train derailment by masked men was ascribed to Frank and Jesse James. The reward for their capture, dead or alive, was raised to $5,000, while newspapers made lurid claims of Jesse being spotted during robberies in places as distant as Mexico, Virginia, and South Carolina.

In the meantime, other gangs attempted to emulate the James boys, but none of them mastered the finer nuances of skyjacking. More than once, bandits leaped from airships with homemade parachutes, only to have their arms and legs tangled in the cords or have the chutes themselves rip open; some of these robbers were buried where they were found. Two more were apprehended before they boarded the craft. On one occasion, a gunman was overcome by the passengers, who almost beat him to death until the conductor pried them off the poor man.

Each time, newspapers claimed that Jesse James had been arrested or killed, only to have the truth revealed by positive identification of either the jail prisoners or the bodies in the local morgue. It wasn't until April 3, 1882, that Jesse James turned up again. This time, he couldn't ride or parachute to safety; he was found dead on the floor of the bedroom of his house in St. Joseph, Missouri.

As it turned out, he had been living a quiet existence as Thomas Howard, a wheat speculator who had moved from Nashville, Tennessee, only six months earlier. His killer was a young man named Bob Ford.

According to Ford, Jesse had recently decided to return to airship robbery, and had recruited Bob and his brother Charlie to be members of his new gang. Jesse didn't know that the Ford brothers had already struck a deal with Missouri's new governor, Thomas Crittenden; for the reward of $5,000, Bob Ford had agreed to assassinate Jesse James.

Bob and Charlie Ford had been houseguests of Mr. Howard for the past several days, waiting for their chance to strike. Only that morning, over the breakfast table, Jesse had hinted at his next planned heist, the hijacking of the Union Pacific airship *Abraham Lincoln* out of Omaha, Nebraska. When he walked into the adjacent bedroom to discuss the plan in more detail, Bob and Charlie had followed. When Jesse stood up on a chair to straighten a picture frame, Bob shot him in the back of his head.

Frank James didn't remain at large for very much longer. Six months later, on November 5, he formally surrendered to Governor Crittenden, during a prearranged press conference in the governor's office. As it turned out, Frank James had also been hiding out in Nashville, under the pseudonym of B. J. Woodson. Although he was subsequently brought to trial in Independence, Missouri, for the hijacking of the *Prairie Viking*, the jury, comprised mainly of Confederate sympathizers, acquitted him of all charges.

Frank James lived comfortably for the rest of his life by merchandizing his past. He lectured before packed houses, published his memoirs, and fired the starting gun at many airship races. He died at age 70 on the set of a silent Hollywood movie, *The Great Airship Robbery*, for which he had been hired as a technical advisor.

By then, the age of the skyship was all but over. After the *Liberty* disaster of 1908, when a careless match struck by a pipe-smoking passenger caused the explosion of an airship over Lakehurst, New Jersey, Congress passed laws that prohibited the use of hydrogen in dirigibles. Because of this, the rail companies were forced to resort to helium as the lifting property; this in turn caused fares to rise, because the use of helium meant that fewer pounds could be lifted. In the long run, this spelled the end of the skyship business; airplanes replaced dirigibles as the principal means of air travel before 1915. The railroads retired from the industry, and airship robberies became a cliché left over from the last generation.

The Jesse James House still stands today in St. Joseph, maintained as a state historical landmark. The rooms are carefully preserved just as he left them, including the bedroom in which he was shot from behind by Bob Ford. The chair on which he stood lies in place on the wooden floor, and on the wall above it is the askew picture Mr. Howard was straightening at the moment of his death.

It is a framed lithograph of the sky ship *Prairie Viking*.

INTRODUCTION:
"Whinin' Boy Blues"

There's little to say about this one, really. No great issues to be raised, no scores to be settled. I was out to have fun, period. So it comes down to sources of inspiration.

Mark W. Tiedemann, fellow SF author and one of my best friends, likes throwing parties at his house in St. Louis. On hot summer evenings, he and his partner Donna lay out plates of munchies, put soda in the coolers, warm up the backyard barbecue, and invite a dozen or more buddies over. We grill steaks, drink Cokes, get into long political arguments with Mark's dad, and altogether have a great time.

During one such evening, after having consumed too much potato salad and ribs, Mark and I sat out on the patio and discussed the possible uses of nanotechnology. I forget exactly what was said, but while we were chatting about microrobots being used for jobs such as law enforcement, I remember gazing at the alley behind his house and his next-door neighbor's car port. No real reason why, but the scene stuck in my mind . . .

Later that night, lying in bed, I found myself watching a tiny spider crawling across the bedroom ceiling. One of our dogs was curled up on the end of the bed. Linda came into the room and started getting undressed for bed, and the spider suddenly stopped. Of course, Linda would stop a charging rhino if she took off her clothes in front of it, but, in that instant, it seemed as though the spider was actually studying her.

Spiders. Dogs. Nanotech. An alley. A car port. A ceiling. Something I had read in the paper a couple of weeks ago about a DEA raid on a local drug dealer's apartment . . .

I began to imagine a story, and the more I thought about it the funnier it seemed, and even after Linda kissed me good night and turned off the lights, I was still grinning. The next evening, I wrote this story.

Why ask why?

WHININ' BOY BLUES

I had been on the mission for less than ten minutes before I was eaten by a puppy.

At least, I thought it was a puppy. When the mutt in question is the size of Dogzilla and it's chasing you through an alley, you don't stop to see whether its testicles have dropped yet. As far as I could tell, before its big happy mouth came down around me and swallowed me whole, it was a small black dog with rusty fur running through its mane, dark brown eyes, and wide paws—maybe a cross between a retriever and a German shepherd. Cute little guy, circumstances notwithstanding.

My guess that it was a puppy was based on the supposition that only a pup would bother to run down and eat a spider. I was in the alley for only a few minutes after the drop—off at the curb, following the five other spiders toward the target zone, when the dog suddenly wandered out of a driveway just fifteen feet away, its long red tongue lolling out of its mouth, panting in the noonday heat.

I immediately froze in mid-step. The little shit stopped to raise its left hind leg and squirt some piss on an overflowing garbage can the height of an office building. Savoring the moment, the puppy raised its head and looked away, perhaps checking out the alley to see if there was some other neighborhood dog whose asshole he could sniff.

In that instant, I decided to move. Okay, so it was a dog: big deal. The rest of the team was already climbing the walls of the target house or crawling through cracks in the sill of the basement window, and I couldn't afford to be left behind. My designated entry point, the back door leading out to the car port, was only twenty feet away. All I had to do was duck beneath the rear bumper of the Sunfire parked next to the door, skirt around the left rear tire, and exit from the other side of the wheel-well, then make the climb up the cement stairs to the door frame. After that, the rest was toast.

Sure. Swell idea. But I had barely covered two feet—which, from my perspective, was like making a ten-meter dash on eight legs—when the dog glanced down and spotted me.

I had forgotten what puppies are like; everything looks good to eat before they learn better, and on this sticky hot summer afternoon in St. Louis my buddy Bowser was bored enough to chase anything that moved. Spider? Yeah, eat'um up!

So he charged straight at me.

I tried to escape. Zig-zag run, dead-heat sprint, even a couple of the hopping movements I had practiced in the simulators, but the puppy was on my case before I could make it to the safety of the car, its tags jiggling as I raced for safety. Only twelve feet to go, but the distance now looked as unconquerable as twelve light years . . .

And then the puppy had me in his mouth. Darkness descended as the spider was slurped back on his slippery tongue. I heard the harsh gnash of his teeth as he gnawed on my legs . . . then everything went blank, except for the red menu bar across the top of my screen.

"Jesus," I muttered as I sank back in my couch. "I'm dog food."

"Okay, Roy, you can c'mon out of there," Libby's voice said through my headset. "We've lost visual."

I let out my breath, then reached up with my right glove and clicked the menu tabs which would jack me out of the system. The top half of the sensory deprivation cell unlocked and was rolled back by a couple of techs, and I sat up in the couch, squinting in the harsh light of genuine reality. I peeled off the gloves and dropped them on the seat, then stood up and let one of the techs help me out of the egg.

"Anyone get the license number of that dog?" I asked.

A couple of people in the control room grinned; I couldn't see the reactions of the rest of my team, because they were still in their eggs, driving their own spiders. Libby motioned from behind the glass partition for me to join her at her console. I yanked off the cables and dropped them on the gloves, then walked across the operations pit and up a short flight of stairs to the control room.

"Tough luck," she murmured, not looking up from her keyboard and screens. She was rewinding the tape; in fast-reverse, I got to see the last moments of my life as a garden spider. "If it's any consolation, the rest of the team made it inside."

I glanced at the other controllers hunched over their own consoles. They were tracking the progress of the four other spiders, using both schematic diagrams of the target house and real-time camera images transmitted by the nanocameras. Jeff and Anna had crawled in through the ground-floor windows and were in the bedroom and the living room respectively, while Mike and Harold were scouting the basement.

"Not really," I said. "If that mutt hadn't caught me, I'd have been in the kitchen already." My eyes returned to her console; although the live-action monitor was dark,

I was surprised to see that the rest of the board was still
active. "Jeez Marie," I muttered. "You mean I'm still
alive?"

Libby prodded her bifocals down to the bridge of her
nose. "If you qualify being digested in some pooch's
stomach as living, yeah, you're alive." She pointed to
the status bars. "You lost a couple of legs, but the car-
apace is intact and we're receiving telemetry, so . . ."

She shrugged. "Yeah, you're still in the game." She
finished rewinding the tape. "As for the first question. . . ."

"Morgan, what are you doing up here?"

I looked around, saw the Operation Chief standing in
the back of the room. Phil Cherry was the only other
person in the control center who wasn't busy; he was
running the show, and as such had permission to be his
usual asinine self.

"I was just helping Libby evaluate the mission." I
instinctively reached for the breast pocket of my jumpsuit, groping for my Marlboros, before I remembered that
I had left my cigs in my civvies down in the locker room.
Too bad. Half the reason why I still smoked was because
it bugged Cherry.

"You want an evaluation?" Phil folded his arms
across the front of his suit. Beige business suit, button-
down white cotton shirt, red pinstriped tie, wing-tipped
FBI shoes; either he wore the same outfit every single
day or he had a dozen just like it stashed in his closet.
"A dog ate you . . . how's that for an evaluation? This
mission's been compromised because you couldn't out-
wit a stray mutt. I'm . . ."

"Actually, sir, it's not a stray," Libby said. "I think
we've got a positive I.D. on it."

I looked back around at her console. She had rewound
the tape until she had located the moment when the dog
first spotted me in the alley; in that instant, the metal tags
hanging from its collar had become visible, and she had

used pixel enhancement to zoom in and focus on the engraving on the tags.

"Its license number is number one-one-eight," she said, pointing at a round tag suspended under the puppy's neck. "There's a rabies control tag beneath it, but I can only make out the first three digits . . . see?" She pointed to a smaller, heart-shaped tag which was obscured by the first tag. "Three-one-six . . . that's all I can make out."

"So?" Cherry wasn't impressed. "I don't see what this has to do with anything."

"Let the fingers do the walking." She began to tap instructions into the keyboard. I rested my hands on the back of her chair and bent over to watch her work, but Cherry wasn't done with me yet.

"We needed someone in the kitchen to see who comes in through the door," he said, walking toward us. "You were supposed to be the key man for that position. Now we're going to have to get someone else to cover the kitchen, and if we can't get him in place when the deal goes down . . ."

"I've accessed the city health department records," Libby announced, pointing at a window she had opened on her screen. "Looky what I found."

We looked. The puppy's owner was registered as Coleman, Barry A., address 115 South Baylor: the exact same address as the house we were infiltrating. The puppy's name was Tripper—faintly ironic, considering his owner's occupation.

"I'll be damned," I muttered. "I got eaten by the sumbitch's dog."

"Uh-huh." Libby palmed the trackball to enlarge the dog's image until it filled the screen. "He must put him out during the day when he's gone, then lets him back in when he comes home."

"Poor little bastard," Cherry murmured, his voice a half-whisper as he peered over her shoulder. "No wonder he's hungry enough to eat a spider . . . his master throws him out all day to fend for himself.''

It figured. Cherry was a prick around other human beings, but his heart went out to a lonely puppy wandering around an alley. Maybe he wore a rabies tag himself, hidden beneath his shirt and tie.

"Don't you get it?" Libby asked. "If he's hanging around the back door, then he's waiting for Coleman to come home. Right?"

I slowly nodded my head; Cherry waited for her to go on. "Well," she continued, "if his master puts him outside when he's gone, what does that tell us?"

It took me a couple of seconds to figure it out; Phil beat me to the punch just as I was opening my mouth. "Hell's bells," he said. "He's not housebroken!"

I glanced at the mission timer at the top of Libby's screen. T-minus twenty-seven minutes, fifty-two seconds, and several odd milliseconds remained before Coleman was scheduled to arrive at his house. Local reconnaissance had already informed us that his connection was already parked on the street, waiting for his '99 Monte Carlo to pull into the alley and park behind the derelict Sunfire he kept in the car port for appearance's sake.

"Is the spider still copasetic?" Cherry asked.

"Eighty percent," Libby replied. She closed the window and showed him the graphs I had seen before. "Except for visual, we've still got a good fix. Mobility-wise, two legs are down but the remaining six are still operational. The gastric acids in the dog's . . . in Tripper's . . . stomach don't seem to have had much effect so far."

"Can you override the VR system? Go to straight manual? Lemme see you move the legs."

Libby punched a few keys. Another window opened on her screen: a diagram of my spider, inactive within Tripper's gut. She floated the trackball back and forth; its six remaining legs twitched back and forth. "We've got override, good telemetry. As long as the dog doesn't vomit up the spider, we're . . .''

''That's what I want.''

I realized what they were getting at. ''Oh no,'' I said, shaking my head. ''No way. No fucking way. You can't do this to me . . .''

Libby gave me one of her rare smiles as she glanced over her shoulder at me. ''What goes down,'' she murmured, ''must come . . .''

''Don't do this to me!''

Cherry ignored us as he peered closely at the screen. ''Okay,'' he said, ''I think we're still in the game. Libby, keep tracking the dog. Agitate the legs every now and then, but keep it still until Coleman comes home. Then I want the little guy to have a bad tummy ache right after his master brings him inside. Morgan, go back to your egg and get ready to go on-line.''

''You can't be serious!''

He turned around to clap a hand on my shoulder. ''Link up, agent,'' he said, grinning at me. ''Think of it as service to your country.''

Asshole.

The bureau had been following Barry Coleman for several months now, trying to gather enough evidence against him to convince a federal grand jury to seek an indictment.

Coke, crack, smack, various bathtub hallucinogens and amphetamines, the latest bioengineered fuck-ups like wank and foobah . . . Scary Barry, as he was known on the street, dealt in them all. He was one of the top midwestern operators, brokering dope in and out of St. Louis while carefully maintaining the guise of a middle-class used-car salesman. He almost certainly had ties to the mob, and probably a few connections with the South American drug cartels. A relatively big fish in a relatively small pond, but we hoped that he could lead us to where the sharks hung out.

The problem was, Coleman was no dope himself, despite what he sold. He had maintained a low-profile existence, living in a quiet neighborhood on the city's south side where everyone minded his own business. He didn't have many visitors to his house; he paid his taxes, kept his lawn mowed, even registered his dog. Where he hid his money, God only knew; his bank records didn't announce any hefty deposits or withdrawals, so any larger funds were either laundered through any number of electronic cut-outs on the net or kept in a hole in the ground. He had no criminal record beyond a teenage misdemeanor charge in 1983 for simple possession of marijuana; in the twenty years since, he had been as clean as the whistle no one had ever blown on him. The street told different tales, though, and that's why we were on his case.

The bureau knew that a major deal was going down; a freighter full of raw coke was out in the Gulf right now, sailing under a Dutch flag toward Galveston. Coast Guard, Customs, and the bureau were ready to bring it down as soon as it dropped anchor and Coleman's contacts assured him that the dope was aboard—about ten minutes before we nailed the ship—so that was no problem. Another boatload of dope, though, was just another boatload of dope: what we wanted were the sellers and, most importantly, the buyer, and that was Scary Barry himself.

We knew who, we knew when, we knew how. All we required was taped evidence. After we acquired hard evidence of a cash transaction between him and the seller, all the Attorney General had to do was put her Dolley Madison on the papers and his sleazy ass was ours.

That was the hard part. Normal electronic infiltration had failed so far, because Coleman and his people swept his house and car every day to root out our bugs. Likewise, two of our narcs had already been killed in the line of duty. One of them had been lucky; he had only been shot in the back of the head, his body dumped from a bridge into the Missouri River. Trust me, you don't want to know what happened to the second guy.

And that's where my unit came in. You don't need the details; just pick up the latest issue of *Popular Science* and you'll find out much of the technical stuff, as filtered through the bureau's public affairs office. Nanotech, microrobotics, VR teleoperation, shielded cellular comlinks: every wank's wet dream was at our disposal. We're bad, we're one inch high.

So . . . a half-hour before Scary Barry is supposed to meet with his friends from the cartel, a beat-up lowrider cruises down his street, passing the car his friends are sitting in. The dude in the passenger seat pretends to polish off a sixteen-ounce malt liquor; he tosses the can out the window onto Barry's front lawn. Everyone does it in this neighborhood; the guys in the car don't pay much attention. The can is half-crushed already, so it doesn't roll very far; it lands in the grass near the driveway . . .

And, after a few moments, we crawl out.

Neat, huh? Just wait until a dog upchucks you all over some asshole's nice clean kitchen floor.

Light re-entered my virtual world as the spider landed on the linoleum, its legs curled together into a tight little wad. I had already turned my headset volume down, but the sound of Tripper hurling RoboChunks was enough to make my own stomach roil.

I closed my eyes, thanked God that the nanocyberneticists who had designed the spiders hadn't come up with a way to include olfactory input, and waited for the worst of the vertigo to subside.

"Aw, goddammit, Tripper! Bad dog! Bad, bad dog . . . !"

I opened my eyes again, just in time to see two enormous legs advancing toward me: cuffed denim trousers over a pair of pointy-toed cowboy boots, stopping on either side of the slimy pool in which I lay. A high-pitched canine whine of terror, then a pair of giant hands reached down out of the heavens.

I caught a glimpse of Tripper's hind legs as he was lifted into the sky, then there was the sound of a furry little butt being spanked. "Can't you keep anything down, you little shit? I swear to God . . . !"

Coarse laughter from another room past the kitchen; someone speaking in Spanish. "Hang on a minute, Carlos. Goddamn little shit does this all the time . . . Jesus Christ awmighty . . ."

Another leviathan walked into the kitchen. This one I could see clearly now; to say that he was the biggest Mexican I had ever seen in my life wasn't just a matter of perspective, for he was the size of a Tijuana taxi. "Hey, man, give him to me," he bellowed. "I'll take him home and make enchiladas out of him."

More laughter. Someone else was behind Carlos, but I couldn't see him. The earth trembled as the cowboy boots stomped on either side of Lake Vomito; I heard the metallic rasp of the back screen door being opened, then Tripper's yowl as he was tossed out into the alley.

"Sorry, Tripper," I muttered.

Time to move, before Master came back to clean up the mess. I unfolded the spider's six remaining legs, tapped the floor pedals to get the gyros to set it upright, then pointed the joystick forward. The spider began to wade through the yuck . . .

"Whoa, man, look at that! Tripper ate a spider and it's still alive!"

Great. Carlos the Taxi had spotted me. He was pointing in my direction, his ugly face displaying the greatest surprise he had probably received since he caught Tia Maria giving blow jobs under the table during his birthday party.

"Well, step on it!" the voice of the cowboy boots yelled. "Jeez it's the third one I've had to kill since I got home . . ."

"Whoa, hey man! I'm not stepping in that shit, no way . . . !

No time to wonder what the boots had meant by that remark. I scuttled straight for the bottom of the kitchen counter; the spider picked up speed once it cleared the vomit, but it was still a long three-foot dash until I reached the plywood wall of the counter.

I barely made cover beneath the wainscoting before the cowboy boot stamped down on the inch of open floor I had last occupied.

"Damn! Fuck!"

More laughter. "Time to call the Orkin man . . . !"

"Fuck you!"

The pointed toe slid beneath the edge of the counter and began to scurry back and forth. Activating tiny claws at the ends of the spider's legs, I sank them into the cheap wood and quickly began to crawl up the vertical face of the counter, careful to remain in the shadows. The massive leather toe missed me by half an inch.

"Whatsamatter, Barry? Can't kill a little spider?"

For some reason, Carlos found this to be infinitely hilarious; I listened to his obnoxious guffawing as I groped my way along the dusty wood, praying that the claws wouldn't give way. Yuck it up, fat boy . . . you'll be stamping out license plates in Brushy Mountain by the time I'm done with you.

The cowboy boot slammed around beneath the counter a couple of more times before Coleman gave up. By then, I was already out from under the front of the counter and scaling its side like a miniature rock climber, out of sight for the moment from Barry and Carlos and the unknown third guy. I couldn't see anything, which was good because it meant that they couldn't see me either; on the other hand, now I couldn't hear anything either, even though I maxed the volume on the audio receptors. I was caught in an acoustical dead zone between the soft wood of the counter and the nearby corner of the kitchen wall; the voices of the men in the kitchen were now muffled, their conversation unintelligible to the spider's microscopic ears.

I took the opportunity to report in. "What's going on out there?"

"Bad news," Libby replied. "Units Two and Three are down and out. Jeff and Anna got squashed in the bedroom and living room . . ."

"Aw, hell."

"Yeah. They were spotted and swatted almost as soon as he came home. Their spiders are down for the count. Just our luck to be dealing with an arachnophobe."

I sighed. Things were easier when we handled busts a little further south; down there, people are used to seeing garden spiders. One guy, an arms dealer in Panama City, even allowed one of our mechs to live in a corner of his bedroom for three weeks while we recorded everything he said to his girlfriend. Seems this guy loved spiders; he thought they brought good luck. Only goes to show what happens when you get superstitious; the bureau's only problem was penetrating his house to build a silk web for our agent to hang out in while he monitored chats with his mistress. And people say government work is boring . . .

"What about Four and Five?" I asked.

"Still down in the basement." Libby's voice was exasperated. "On the plus side, they managed to find the guns he's got squirreled away down there . . . might be enough to get him on an unlicensed firearms charge, if nothing else. But . . ."

I heard a hiss and a sharp click through my headset as the comlink was interrupted. "Units Four and Five have been detained by a material buffer at the target egress point," Cherry said. "They're returning to the primary deployment area. Repeat, they're returning to the primary deployment area. Do you copy? Over.''

I shut my eyes and let out my breath. God, I hate it when they go techno on you. "Libby," I said, "is Phil trying to tell me that Mike and Harold can't get out of the basement?''

Another pause, then Libby's voice again: "Roger that, Unit One. It looks like there's one of those long rubber thingies . . . I dunno what you call it . . . stapled to the bottom of the basement door. Whatever it is, they can't get into the house, so we're pulling 'em out.''

Cherry again: "It's in your hands, Morgan. Don't fuck it up again.''

Jerk. Buttface. Meathead. It's guys like him who give narcs such a bad name. "Thanks for the vote of confidence, sir," I said. "I'll keep you posted.''

I got off the comlink and concentrated on climbing. It wasn't easy, scaling a vertical surface with only six legs instead of eight, but I made the traverse across the side of the cabinet to the wall without either slipping or being spotted again.

A line from an old blues number repeated in my head as I worked the pedals and joystick. I soon found myself singing it aloud . . .

"Spider, spider, climbing up the wall . . . when it gets to the top, gonna get its ashes hauled . . . Just a whinin' boy, I don't deny my name . . .''

It took a few minutes, but I finally made it up the wall; from there, I crossed back over to the cabinets, where I scurried across the dusty top, avoiding dustbunnies and old cobwebs woven by my mech's organic counterparts. Another thing my spider couldn't emulate was the ability to walk upside-down across ceilings; it was just a little too heavy to pull that trick.

One out of three ain't bad, though. I found a ledge overlooking the room; from up here, I was able to see the entire kitchen, which from up there looked as vast as the Grand Canyon.

It was like a Sci-Fi Channel rerun of *Land of the Giants*, only a little more stupid. Coleman had wiped up the doggie puke while I was away, so I hadn't missed much. He and the two middlemen remained in the kitchen; they opened cold beers and were hanging around the table. An aluminum attaché case lay on the table between half-filled ashtrays and empty beer cans, unopened but never far from Coleman's hand.

And there, standing directly below me, was Scary Barry himself: early thirties quickly going on forty-five, slight paunch at the waistline, short dark hair receding from a premature bald spot on the crown of his head, wearing jeans, a golf shirt, and his trademark cowboy boots. He leaned against the counter just below me, hanging out by the wallphone. If anything, he looked like an overaged frat boy, some guy who shows up at the neighborhood sports bar to guzzle Bud Light and root for the Blues hockey team. Just to look at him, you'd never think he was responsible, directly or indirectly, for the murders of several men, including a couple of informants. Talk about the banality of evil.

Carlos was a slug. I had seen a half-dozen just like him: another cheap thug from somewhere south of El Paso, marking time in El Norte between deportations and prison terms. But the third guy in the room, the other middleman . . .

He was interesting, now that I could see him clearly: a thin young dude with long brown hair and a beard, a gold earring in his right ear. He was standing between Carlos and Barry, absentmindedly snapping the fingers of his right hand as he swatted it into the palm of his left. The three of them seemed to be waiting for something and were killing time with stupid jokes, but that third guy was just a little too wired. There was something about him that just wasn't right.

I zoomed in on the kid as I reopened the comlink. "Libby, you been catching everything?" I asked.

"Got it."

"Good. See if you can give me a positive I.D. on that kid. He's not someone I recognize."

There was a long pause. While she searched and I waited, the telephone buzzed. A true pro, Coleman wasn't relying on a cordless unit, which could be easily monitored from outside the house. The phone was cross-wired with an audio scrambler resting on the counter behind him. Not that it mattered much; his line was already tapped under court order, and the bureau computers downtown would easily decipher the conversation even as he spoke. He pressed the scramble button, picked up the receiver and listened for a couple of moments.

"Roy?" Libby said just then. "We've got a problem."

"Don't keep me hanging, kiddo. What did you find?"

"That guy? He's with SLPD vice . . . name's Reginald DeCamp, working undercover for the home team. I'll flash you the details. . . ."

A small window opened on my screen, and there was Reg DeCamp's face, rotating in three dimensions: clean-shaven, his hair considerably shorter, but nonetheless the same guy. Detective Reginald L. DeCamp, age 27, presently assigned to vice squad, St. Louis Police Department.

"Oh, shit," I murmured. It happens sometimes in this line of work: the local talent conducts their own independent sting operation and, for one reason or another, either neglects or refuses to coordinate their efforts with the feds. DeCamp had apparently infiltrated this particular buy, hooking up with the Mexican in an effort to take out Coleman, while unwittingly honing in on a bureau operation.

No wonder DeCamp was skittish; he was the inside man in an SLPD vice squad effort to bring down a local dealer. But this wasn't like bringing down a street corner dime-bag operation in Dogtown; he was not only out of his league, he was playing in another ballpark entirely. Give him an A for audacity, a B for balls, and an F for fucking lunacy.

While I was still trying to figure out what to do next, Coleman hung up the phone without saying a word. He turned to the other two men, beaming as if he had just lucked out on the state lottery.

"Gentlemen," he announced as he reached for the attaché case, "our ship's come in. Time to do some business."

Carlos grinned like he was going to have a puppy for lunch. He watched as Coleman pressed a thumb against the case's lock. The case beeped as it unsealed; Coleman raised the lid and stepped back. The green stuff neatly stacked inside sure as hell wasn't Monopoly money.

Carlos put down his beer and picked up a bundle of fifties. "I like this sound," he said as he ran a thumb down the side of the bills. Satisfied with the amount, he picked up another bundle and riffled through it. "Yes, I do like this sound . . ."

DeCamp, or whatever his name was for this ill-timed attempt at a collar, forced a smile; his eyes were locked on the case. He didn't notice how closely Coleman was studying every move he made, but I knew that look.

"Oh, Christ," I murmured. "Barry's onto him."

"You want me to send in the cavalry?"

We had ten agents staked out within a one-block radius of the house, hiding in the backs of phony delivery trucks and utility vehicles. Once I secured evidence of the transaction, all I had to do was give the word and they'd move in. My first impulse was to let the deal go down as planned. As soon as the Mexican took possession of the payola, the bureau would have both him and Coleman by the short hairs, at least in terms of having enough evidence to support a legal search and seizure. The raid could be launched, and even if DeCamp was busted along with the others, we could straighten out matters later.

Yet, as I watched from above, I saw something neither DeCamp nor Carlos could see. Coleman, standing again by the kitchen counter, was surreptitiously sliding open a drawer beneath the countertop.

A Glock .45 automatic, a pink condom stretched tightly down the barrel as a crude but effective silencer, lay within the drawer.

"He's got a gun!" I snapped.

Carlos dropped the last bundle back into the case. "Looks good, amigo," he said, moving to shut the case. "On behalf of my colleagues, I thank you for your business."

"Yeah," said Coleman, still watching DeCamp, "but there's a little matter we need to take care of first . . ."

DeCamp didn't quite realize what was going on. He turned his head to look at Coleman, then glanced back at the Mexican; as he did so, Coleman dropped his right hand into the drawer.

"Hang tight," Libby responded. "We're sending in the posse . . ."

Screw that. There wasn't enough time to wait for back-up. In another moment, DeCamp would be at Coleman's mercy; if Scary Barry didn't kill him on the spot, then he could use him as a hostage when the squad broke down the door. Either way, the operation would be botched and a cop would probably wind up dead on the kitchen floor.

There was only one thing I could do.

I leaped off the top of the cabinet.

Try to understand: although I wasn't actually inside the spider, and therefore wasn't at personal risk by this stunt, in telepresence there isn't much difference between perception and reality. For me, it was as if I just jumped off a sixty-foot cliff, with neither bungee cord above nor air-bag below to break my fall.

"Morgan, what the hell are you . . . ?"

The floor rushed toward me. I think I yelled as I plummeted downward, my six legs spread wide apart in an instinctive, futile attempt to break my fall. At the last moment, I had the presence of mind to switch the spider back into climb mode . . .

Then I landed right where I intended, directly in the middle of the shiny bald spot on top of Coleman's head.

He screamed bloody murder as the spider's sharp little claws sank into his skin. I floored the pedals and jerked the joystick forward. Everything blurred and jerked around as the mech dug in; hair, lights, Carlos and DeCamp just beginning to react . . . and Coleman, howling at the top of his lungs:

"Geddidoffame! Motherfuck goddamn fuck geddidoffame!"

His hands reached up and began clawing at the top of his head. I managed to dodge them for a moment, then a meaty palm the size of Rhode Island slammed down on top of the spider. Everything rocked in the sudden darkness as red warning lights began to flash at the edge of my vision, signaling imminent system crash.

"Hey, what the fuck . . . ?" ican was shouting. "What are you . . . ?"

"Spider! Goddamn fuckin' spider! There's a . . . !"

Still, I managed to hang on. I put the mech in reserve, began scuttling backward across his head, out of the bald spot and deeper into his thin hair. Huge fingers scrabbled at me, trying to grab hold; I could see deep scratches in his scalp, oozing blood in a ragged trail behind me, as Coleman began dancing around the kitchen. There was a crash as he upset the open drawer; I caught a glimpse of the Glock falling out on the floor.

"Ride 'em, cowboy!" Libby yelled.

It might have been funny if it wasn't me riding this particular horse. Coleman's left hand managed to wrap itself around the spider's fuselage; hair and skin ripped away as he struggled to yank me free.

"Motherfuckin' goddamn . . . !"

Through the cage of Coleman's fingers, I could see DeCamp lunging for the gun on the floor. Bewildered, ican was too slow to react; he had barely begun to move before the young cop grabbed the gun and, kneeling on the floor, brought it up to cover the fat man.

No time to think about that now. Libby's voice was meshed in static; warning lights around the periphery of my vision told me that I was about to lose the spider. I retaliated by sinking its claws into Coleman's fingers. Barry, who was now more scared than scary, yowled and let go; I held my breath as I began to drop again.

"Freeze, asshole!" DeCamp shouted.

Coleman wasn't freezing; worked up in a berserk rage, he was already pivoting toward the cop next to him, who was giving all his attention to Carlos. All this I absorbed in a single moment of free fall on my way down to the floor . . .

But I didn't get there. I landed on the nape of Coleman's neck. My gorge started to rise as the spider rolled, end over end, down the fleshy slope . . .

Straight down the back of his shirt collar.

I almost felt sorry for the poor bastard—almost, but not quite—as I sank my claws into the soft flesh between his shoulder blades.

Cherry was good to me. He rewarded my efforts by letting me see Coleman one last time before they sent him down the river.

A couple of cops escorted me to the holding pen in the county jail where he was under lockup. On the way, I walked past the cell where a couple of lawyers were consulting with Carlos the Taxi. Carlos didn't look very happy; considering the fact that he had been videotaped with his mitts all over several hundred grand in drug money, he was probably going to a place where you can't buy your freedom from a local judge. Not easily, anyway.

I brought Tripper with me when I made my visit; the little pup wasn't heartbroken when he saw his former master sitting by himself on a bare bench. The agents who had raided the house had found Tripper's water dish as dry as a stone, the few morsels of food remaining in his bowl several days old and swarming with ants. None of this helped to give me much sympathy for the band-aids plastered on Coleman's head.

Coleman glared at me as I approached the bars. "That's my dog," he muttered.

"Don't worry," I said. "I'll take good care of him while you're gone." I scratched the pup behind the ears for good measure; Tripper yawned, gave a happy little peep, and favored Coleman with that certain go-to-hell look that only abused animals can muster.

Coleman gazed down at the floor and let out his breath, then he stared back up at me. "Well? Who are you? What do you want?"

"Nobody you know," I replied. "At least, not my face . . . but we've been close."

He looked confused. After a moment, he shook his head and gazed back down at the floor again. "I've talked to my lawyer," he muttered. "I've got nothing to say to you, whoever you are."

"Sure you don't. I just thought I'd drop by for a visit . . . see how you were doing and all that."

"Are you a lawyer?"

"Nope."

"Then get the fuck out of here."

"But I thought you might like someone to keep you company," I added.

He glanced up at the dog, then looked down at the floor once more. "I don't care," he murmured. "Take 'em to the pound or something, I don't give a shit . . ."

I shook my head. "Naw," I said, digging my hand into my trouser pocket. "I don't mean old Trips here.

He's going home with me. I've brought someone different . . .''

The timing was perfect. He was just beginning to look
up again when I pulled out the spider and tossed it
through the bars onto the bunk next to him. He was still
screaming as I turned away and began to walk back down
the cellblock.

Okay, so it was a cheap gag. The spider was rubber.
But what's a good job if you can't have a little fun, right?

INTRODUCTION:
"See Rock City"

I have always considered myself to be a Tennessean.

Although I left Nashville at age 19 to live a rather nomadic existence and have lived in my home town for only eleven months since then, and that was more than fourteen years ago, I've never stopped considering myself a Tennessee native. I deliberately retained a Tennessee license plate on two cars while I lived in Missouri, Washington, D.C., and Massachusetts for that reason, until Linda and I moved to New Hampshire and a local cop threatened to fine me for driving with an expired plate.

So why did it take so long, after writing so many stories about places where I'd lived only temporarily, to set a story in the state where I grew up?

It's because my first novel, written while I was in college and unpublished to this day, was largely set in Tennessee. As a result of that novel's failure, I considered Tennessee to be a literary jinx: I could write about anything except my home state. Although Nashville has figured in the background of my first published short story ("Live From the Mars Hotel," included in *Rude Astronauts*) and as a biographical detail for one of my major characters (Mars astronaut W. J. Boggs, in *Labyrinth of Night*), I've been leery about writing about the same place where I spent my early years.

Yet it was inevitable that I write a story set in the Volunteer State. When I finally got around to doing so, though, it was almost by accident.

At least once each summer, Linda and I make a trip to Smithville, a small town on the Cumberland plateau where my family has a country cabin on a ridge overlooking Center Hill Lake. Long before my late father bought the house and added additional rooms and a sundeck, the original structure was a prefab in Oak Ridge, used as military housing during the Manhattan Project. An old friend of my father's, another Nashville attorney, purchased the house as war surplus from the U.S. Army; it was then disassembled and trucked down winding goat-trail roads to this ridge, where it was reassembled. When Linda and I make our summer trips, we use a guest room that may once have been occupied by a physicist who helped to assemble the first atomic bombs.

Anyway, once or twice a year, we visit this ridgetop hideaway. My mother, still going strong at age 76, spends her summers here, and Linda and I stay a week with her at the cabin each year. I bring a spiral notebook and whatever books I'm reading as research for the novel I'm planning to write next. After the evening dinner, once we've cleaned up the kitchen and my mother has gone to bed, I sit at a small table on the screened-in back porch and, under the light of a kerosene lantern and writing in longhand, I work on that novel-in-progress.

This trip was different. It's an eight-hour haul from St. Louis to Smithville, and sometimes the eyes play tricks on you when you're on the road that long. While driving through Kentucky, I happened to glance off to my left . . .

And, just for a moment, I saw a spaceship standing in the middle of a cornfield.

Not just any spaceship. A Delta Clipper, the prototype

of which had just successfully completed its first test-flight in New Mexico, only a few weeks earlier.

I blinked, and it was gone. Just like that. Leaving me to wonder what a spaceship was doing in the middle of a cornfield.

That question bugged me for the rest of the journey, and by the time we arrived in Smithville, I had a new story. That evening, I ignored the research material I had brought with me from St. Louis, sat down behind the back porch table, and began to write.

Two nights later, the story was half-complete, but I still didn't have a title for it, beyond the working title "Spaceship Crash." This is unusual for me, because I often think of a decent title for a story from the moment I start work. During dinner, I explained the story, as best I could, to Linda and my mother, and asked for suggestions.

Mama thought about it for a few moments. "Why don't you call it, 'See Rock City'?" she asked.

"Sounds good," I said.

And here it is. Perhaps it's not the best portrait of my home state that I could offer, but at least I've finally written a story about it. One day, there will be another . . .

SEE ROCK CITY

Junior pulls into the gravel parking lot outside Doc's place and switches off the headlights. He lets the engine run for a few moments, listening to a Nashville country music station as he savors a last toke from the joint he's been smoking since he crossed the DeKalb county line, then he switches off the ignition, stubs out the joint in the ashtray, opens the Camaro's mismatched door, and climbs out.

The night is hot, the air swollen with the kind of mid-summer Tennessee humidity that brings out the cicadas and lightning bugs and causes men to drink long past midnight because they can't sleep. Junior pauses to tuck his sweaty white t-shirt down the front of his jeans and shake his legs a little to make the pants cuffs slide back down over the top of his cowboy boots. A silent flash of heat lightning on the horizon draws his eyes past the parking lot, out to the abandoned cornfield behind the farmhouse where the spaceship squats upon its hydraulic landing gear, listing slightly to one side. It's a moonless night and Doc has turned off the floodlights surrounding the vessel, but Junior can see its vague shape against the treeline, like a giant Dairy Queen ice cream cone turned upside-down in the middle of a farm field.

He spits a big hock on the ground, then the soles of his boots crunch softly against the gravel as he saunters to the door. The front porch lights are off, the shades have been drawn, the little Pepsi Cola sign in the window has been turned around so that it now reads ''Sorry, We're CLOSED,'' but Junior didn't drop out of the eighth grade fifteen years ago before he learned not to believe everything he reads. The door is unlocked; a tin cowbell jangles as he shoves it open and walks in.

Two men are seated at a lunch counter on the far end of the room, silhouetted by the dim glow cast by the fluorescent menu board above the kitchen grill. Between the door and the lunch counter are half a dozen tables, piled chest-high with the detritus of Doc's livelihood for the past twenty months, two weeks, and six days: t-shirts, posters, keyrings, cheap ceramic mugs made in Taiwan, plastic replicas of the spaceship custom-manufactured by a company in Athens, postcards of women in bikinis, and at least fifty different items with rebel flags, Elvis, or that stupid spaceship printed on them. This used to be Doc's living room, but things change.

''Hey, Junior. C'mon in.''

Doc's dry voice, like the creak of old sunburned leather, comes across the darkened room as the two men twist around on the lunch counter stools. ''Have yourself a set, boy. Take a load off.''

''Howdy, Doc.'' Junior walks slowly past mounted dead squirrels holding miniature golf clubs and glass balls that shower fake snow on tiny replicas of the space-ship when you turn them over until he reaches the lunch counter. ''Hot tonight.''

''It's hot, all right.''

''Hotter'n Jesus,'' Junior adds, and immediately re-grets his choice of words when Doc's face, a bit of weatherbeaten burlap framed by long white sideburns, turns stolid and cold. Doc's a good Christian: member of First Calvary Baptist, attends eight o'clock services each and every Sabbath, pays his tithes and all that happy Sunday school horseshit. "Hotter'n the devil," he quickly adds.

"Amen," says the other man seated at the counter, then he belches into his hand. " 'Scuse me."

Doc chooses to ignore the blasphemy, as Junior knew he would. "Need a beer?" he asks as he lowers himself from his stool and begins to walk behind the counter. "We got Bud, Bud Light, Busch, Busch Light, Michelob . . ."

"Michelob will do." Like he's picky about what he drinks; most of the time, Junior settles for Black Label, that he can pick up for three bucks a six at the Piggly Wiggly in McMinnville. He only buys Michelob when he's taking a girl out to the drive-in and he's trying to impress her. Considering that he was invited here because Doc wants him to do a job, though, he might as well splurge. "Tonight's the night for Michelob," he adds, reciting something he once heard on TV.

"Good idea," the third man says, then burps again. He teeters slightly on his stool, his eyes unfocused. "Tonight's the night. I'll have another, Doc."

Doc hesitates, his right hand inside the old Coca-Cola cooler behind the counter as he glares at his companion. For the first time, Junior notices the row of Budweiser cans on the counter in front of the drunk. "You know Howell here, of course," Doc says. "Howell, this is Junior . . ."

"Pleased to meet you." Howell swivels around on his stool to poke his right hand at Junior. Howell looks as if he hasn't had a sober night in twenty years: big, flabby body, unwashed black hair slicked back with too much Barbasol cream, deep creases in the skin at the back of his neck. "I know your daddy, son. What's he doing these days?"

Junior's father, Junior Senior, has been dead for almost three years. He passed away in St. Thomas Hospital in Nashville, his liver shot to hell by Mister Jack Daniels. Junior misses him about as much as he misses his first grade teacher; at least one of them didn't drink whiskey and beat him up for no reason at all. "Nothing much," Junior says, ignoring Howell's hand. "Just laying around as usual."

"Go put something on the jukebox," Doc says as he opens an ice-cold Michelob and places it in front of Junior. He reaches into a coffee can and plucks out a quarter that has been painted red; he pushes it across the counter to Howell. "Anything but Billy Ray Cyrus . . . I'm so sick of him I could spit up."

Howell stares at the store-quarter for a moment before he gets the hint. "I'll put on some Reba MacIntyre," he says, picking up the coin and hauling himself off the stool. "Maybe some Alan Jackson . . ."

"Play that new song of his," Junior says. "Play it twice. I kinda like it." He grins and winks at Doc over the neck of his beer bottle.

Doc only shrugs. "Sit down, boy," he says softly as Howell wanders away, cursing as he stumbles against a table and causes some t-shirts to fall to the unswept floor. "We've got a lot to discuss."

"About your rocket?" Junior hoists himself atop the stool Howell has just vacated. "When you called me, you said you needed a job done on it."

Doc nods as he bends over to rest his arms on the cooler. From across the room they can hear Howell sliding the red quarter into the Wurlitzer's slot and carefully punching a song number into the keypad. "Thank you for making your selection," the jukebox says in a strange feminine voice. "A video is available. If you wish to view it, please deposit twenty-five cents and enter the code number . . . now."

"Fuck the video," Junior says, glancing over his

shoulder at Howell. He's seen it a hundred times already; besides, he knows the holographic screen on the jukebox is busted and Doc is too cheap to get the thing fixed. "Just play the song." In a few moments the room is filled with slide guitars, drums, and twangy keyboards. Junior's left knee begins to twitch in time with the music. He closes his eyes and nods his head with the rhythm. Damn, but he loves this tune . . .

"My spaceship . . ." Doc says.

Junior reopens his eyes. Yeah, right. The rocket out in the back forty. "Last time I looked at it," he says, "it seemed like the paint's getting a little faded out. Kinda peeling around the top of the nose cone and all."

When he bothers to work, Junior paints houses and barns. It's an honest job, and it helps keep him in beer and dope when other work isn't available. "I can mix a little white and grey, maybe get the shade you need to make it look just right, and when that's done I'll shellack it with weatherproofing. It'll last another couple of years before you need it painted again. How's that?"

Doc continues to peer across the counter at him. "That's nice of you to offer," he replies, "but d'ya think I'd really ask you to come all the way out here just to discuss a paint job?"

No, Junior doesn't think he would. For the sort of work he does when he isn't housepainting, nobody meets him late at night, when the lights are low and the only witnesses are crickets and bullfrogs. Not that secrets can't be shared at high noon in the middle of the Smithville town square—a whisper is still a whisper, any time of day—but he's long since accepted the fact that most respectable people don't want to be seen with him. Even if Jesus has forgiven his sins, many people who live around here would just as soon see him return to the county workhouse.

Junior is about to answer when Howell waddles back to the counter. "I put the song on, Junior," he brays, as eager to please as a puppy begging for a Milk Bone. "Alan Jackson twice in a row, just like you said."

Doc winces; Junior grins at his discomfiture. "Go out back and check the dumpster, willya? I don't want the raccoons to go rooting through the trash again . . ."

"I looked at it this evening. It's secured nice and . . ."

"Then look at it again," Doc says. "And take a leak while you're at it . . . something, I don't care. Just leave us alone a few minutes, okay?"

Howell looks wounded; the puppy has been kicked. He starts to argue with Doc—he's the co-owner of this operation, he sold his pig farm and sank his life's savings into that damn rocket, doesn't that give him a say in this matter?—but one look from Junior shuts him up. He wanders away from the counter; a few moments later, Junior hears the back screen door creak open and slam shut.

"Kinda slow, ain't he?" he murmurs.

Doc shakes his head as he glances over his shoulder to make sure that Howell has indeed stepped outside. "No, but he might as well be, considering how much he drinks." His eyes are hard when his gaze returns to Junior. "And don't you be calling Howell slow. He and I have known each other since we were children . . . we've gone through some tough times together before and he's always stuck with me. He's a good man."

Junior says nothing as he polishes off the rest of his Michelob. He has known some good men, too, but most of them are either dead or in jail. Being a good man doesn't mean two shits in this old world; being quick is all that matters and that's why Junior is still drinking beer and getting laid on Saturday night when many good men are lying on their butts in a cold prison cell, waiting for tomorrow morning when they get to return to some god-forsaken interstate median and pick up trash for the State of Tennessee.

And if Doc and Howell are such good Christians, then

why did they invite him out to their little piss-ant tourist trap out on Route 52?

"Talk to me about your rocket, Doc," he says as he pushes his empty bottle across the counter.

The fact of the matter is that there's not much Doc can tell Junior that he doesn't already know. Most of the story is public knowledge already; almost two years ago, it was on the front page of every newspaper in the world, from Taiwan to Athens, plus most of the TV stations.

The rocket parked out in Doc's cornfield is a Delta Clipper, a single-stage-to-orbit spacecraft designed and built by the McDonnell-Douglas Space Systems Company of Huntington Beach, California: no wings, no throwaway boosters, nonmetallic epoxy-graphite fiber hull, low launch and recovery turnaround-time, minimal maintenance schedule, and all that other good shit. About a hundred and thirty feet tall and weighing about twenty thousand pounds, the Delta Clipper is almost the same height (but half the tonnage) of an old DC-8 jetliner and nearly as versatile: it goes up, achieves orbit, delivers its payload, re-enters the atmosphere nose-first, then flops over and lands on its tail where it started, right on the dime with nine cents change.

That's the theory, at any rate. But this particular Delta Clipper had a turn of bad luck.

The ship is christened the *U.S.S. Grissom*—which is kinda ironic, considering it was named after some astronaut who was killed trying to go to the Moon, 'way back before Junior Senior porked the wrong girl and bequeathed Junior upon this lucky world—and it had the distinction of being the sole man-rated ship in the SSTO fleet. Instead of being a pilotless cargo vessel, it was flown by two pilots; its midsection contained a pressurized passenger module. Two years ago last August, the *Grissom* had rendezvoused in orbit with the space station. It had been a routine crew-relief mission—besides the pilot and co-pilot in the flight deck, there were three other astronauts aboard, taking a ride back to Merritt Island from the space station—until something had gone seriously wrong during re-entry.

Exactly what, nobody really knew at the time. Just as the *Grissom* was commencing its aerobraking maneuver over the Atlantic coast, flight controllers at the Johnson Space Center in Texas heard a sharp bang over the comlink, then the pilot shouted something about loss of cabin pressure. Before anyone at JSC could react, the Delta Clipper entered Earth's upper atmosphere, after which there was the loss of signal that occurs when a spacecraft is passing through the ionization layer.

LOS usually ends after nine minutes, but this time twelve minutes elapsed before the JSC controllers reacquired telemetry with the *Grissom*, only to be met with stark silence from the other end of the radio channel. By then they had come to the cold realization that the *Grissom*, albeit still intact, had somehow been knocked dangerously off course. NORAD radar showed that the vessel was somewhere over the southeastern United States, with a new trajectory that would bring it down somewhere in the South.

Although the JSC controllers could raise neither the crew nor the passengers, they still had an uplink with the *Grissom's* navigational computers, and, even if the *Grissom* could not be destroyed by radio signal—as a man-rated spacecraft, it was not equipped with an auto-destruct mechanism—they were capable of overriding the ship's manual control and remote-piloting the vessel to an emergency landing, preferably in a remotely populated area.

And so they did. And that's how, early one morning in mid-August, a spaceship crash-landed in the middle of Doc's cornfield.

None of this had meant jack shit to Junior, who had been serving time in the workhouse on a drunk-driving

charge, but it had been a godsend to Doc, whose corn
crop had been scorched by two straight years of drought
and who was looking for any-damn-way of paying off
his debts that didn't mean waiting for Willie Nelson to
throw a benefit concert on his personal behalf. Even before government officials showed up at his farm, Doc had
set up sawhorses in front of the gate leading to the back
forty and was charging people five bucks a head to take
a close peek at the spaceship that incinerated ten acres
of cornfield.

When the suits from NASA and FAA and DOD and
all the rest arrived, Doc graciously allowed them to come
into his field for free. After the bodies of the two pilots
were removed from the flight deck and the three passengers, unconscious but still alive, were rushed away in
ambulances, Doc put his foot down. His property, his
rocket: no one, but no one—not TV camera crews, not
local reporters, not his Baptist minister, not local residents, nor their children, nor their dogs—got through the
gate without putting five dollars in the kitty.

Even as Doc was bickering with two NASA men and
a U.S. federal marshal in his living room, a slick lawyer
from Dallas who specialized in space law—there actually
is such a thing—called on the phone to offer his services.
Once the lawyer was cut in on a percentage of any money
Doc might make, he informed Doc of his rights. On one
hand, under the U.N. Agreement on the Rescue of Astronauts, the Return of Astronauts, and the Return of Objects Launched into Outer Space, Doc was legally
impelled to surrender the *Grissom* and its crew to the
authorities. However, under Article II of the Convention
on International Liability for Damage Caused by Space
Objects, the United States government had to compensate
him for the loss of his corn field.

What all this meant, the Texas attorney told him, was
that Doc had already cooperated with the government by
allowing them to enter the spacecraft and take away the

dead and injured astronauts. Until NASA found a way to
haul away the *Grissom* and the government ponied up the
money, though, the spacecraft rightfully belonged to him.

Not that the *Grissom* was going to fly away any time
real soon; its fuel tanks had been depleted by the emergency landing and its aft landing gear leg had fractured
during touchdown. Only luck had kept the spacecraft
from going up in smoke itself during the cornfield fire;
the flame retardant that coated its hull had been seriously
eroded during its prolonged re-entry. Not only that, but
when NASA inspectors combed the spacecraft, they
found three small holes in the flight deck, caused by mi-
crometeors that had struck the *Grissom* when the spacecraft accidentally encountered a Perseid meteor shower.
This was what had caused the explosive decompression
that killed the pilots and knocked the vessel off course;
the passengers had survived because their module was
isolated from the flight deck and had its own independent
oxygen supply. It was no small miracle that the *Grissom*
survived re-entry and landed safely, but it would never
fly again on its own power, nor could a spacecraft the
size of the *Grissom* be easily hauled away by either truck
or helicopter. For the time being, it was permanently
grounded in the middle of Doc's corn field.

The government didn't want to handle a messy civil
lawsuit; the circumstances of the crash were embarrassing enough already. Nor did NASA want to foot the bill
for salvaging a useless, unflyable spaceship from somewhere in Tennessee. And nobody wanted to pay for
Doc's ruined farmland. After a few weeks, therefore, Justice Department attorneys reached an out-of-court com-
promise with the farmer: if Doc agreed not to sue NASA
for the loss of his fields, and if he continued to cooperate
with the crash investigation, then Doc could keep what
was left of the *Grissom* after NASA was done with it.

Once NASA inspectors completed their investigation,
an engineering team from McDonnell-Douglas stripped

the vessel of any reusable components; when they were through with the *Grissom*, the SSTO was not much more than an empty hull. But that was okay with Doc, who by now had gone into the tourist trade. Attracted by screaming headlines and breathless TV news reports, people were driving from all over the country to his farm, willing to pay their bucks for a chance to gawk and take snapshots of the spaceship in DeKalb County, Tennessee.

"I can't rightly complain," Doc says as he opens another Michelob and pushes it across the counter to Junior. "Business was pretty good for a while. Howell came in as a partner and helped me run things. I moved everything upstairs and turned this part of the house into a shop. We put in the lunch counter, ordered up a bunch of t-shirts and ashtrays and stuff . . . no, sir, I can't complain."

Junior is only half-interested; three beers and he's got a pretty good buzz going, but he's getting a bit impatient. He knows what the Doc wants, but the old man is rambling, working up his nerve to ask.

"Well, y'know, everything's gotta come to an end sometime." Doc pulls a paper napkin out of a dispenser and absently whisks it across the marble-tone Formica, wiping up the round stains left by the beer bottles. "I guess everyone who really wants to see that thing has come and gone already. I'm in my second summer of running this place, and there's been too many days lately when Howell has sat out by the gate and hasn't collected a dime."

"Yeah, uh-huh . . ."

"Meanwhile, I still owe the bank money, and the bills ain't getting any smaller. Plus the percentage of the take I gotta send that lawyer. And the insurance . . . that's the worst. Premiums just keep getting higher and higher, and I'm not getting anything for it."

Junior knows about insurance. That's part of his line

of work. "It's a bitch, all right," he says. "Damn insurance companies . . . just keep getting richer all the time."

"Sometimes I wish that rocket never landed here."
Doc sighs and looks around the store. "Never believed
in the damn space program anyway . . . waste of time and
money, if you ask me. Now I got a houseful of space
stuff I can't sell and a spaceship out back that no one
wants to see."

"Yeah, uh-huh . . . kind of wish something would happen to it, don't ya?"

Doc doesn't reply. Lost in his thoughts, he toys with
the damp napkin, absently tearing off thin, narrow pieces
and crumpling them into little spitwads. "You ever been
to Rock City, son?" he asks after a little while.

Junior shrugs. Maybe he has, maybe he hasn't; when
he goes somewhere for fun, he's usually stoned on something and doesn't remember it very well afterwards.
"That's up on Lookout Mountain outside Chattanooga,
ain't it? Big ol' place."

"Big ol' place, that's right." Doc continues to strip
the paper napkin as he speaks. "You probably don't remember, being a young man and all, but there was a time
when half the barns in Tennessee had black roofs with
'See Rock City' painted in big red letters across them.
See, the company that owned and operated Rock City
would go to farmers whose barns were facing the high-
ways and make 'em a deal . . . the company would re-
paint their barns for 'em and put up their advertisements
where no one could miss seeing it from the road and, in
return, the farmers would get their barns painted for
free."

"I guess." Junior begins to wonder if that's what Doc
has in mind: hiring him to paint "See Doc's Rocket" on
barn roofs all over the state. Junior hopes that isn't the
case; he really hates painting barns. "I ain't seen many
like that lately."

Doc raises his eyes from the napkin to look straight at

him again. "Why do you think that is? Rock City's still there. You can visit it anytime . . . see four states, check out Mother Goose Village, buy yourself a birdhouse and a pecan pie. Rock City is still in business, but you just don't see too many of those black-and-red barns anymore. So why do you think that is, son?"

Junior hates it when someone calls him son; it reminds him of his drunk old man. The night isn't getting any younger; he could be home in his trailer now, watching an old *Star Trek* rerun on TV and getting wasted. "I don't know why, dad," he says with scornful impudence. "Maybe no one wants to see Rock City anymore."

Doc slowly nods his head. "Or maybe all those old barns burned down," he says very softly.

Junior smiles.

Doc nods again as he looks down at the paper napkin. "These things happen sometimes," he murmurs as he makes another spitball. "Accidents, weird freak things, stuff like that . . . lots of stuff can happen on a farm, nobody ever knows when."

"Sure can." Junior takes a long, slow sip from his beer. "Someone down in Lebanon, his barn went up one night just like that." He snaps his fingers. "Boom, just like a bomb. Burned to the ground in a couple of minutes. Total loss." He shakes his head. "Crying shame."

"I know," Doc says. "That barn belonged to a friend of mine . . . Earl Walker. I believe you know him."

"Never met the man," Junior replies, but he can't keep the grin off his face. "Did the insurance company settle with him okay?"

"Earl did well with his insurance company. They thought it peculiar that someone would want to torch his barn for no apparent reason, but . . ." Doc shrugs. "Well, Earl got his money, and he's using it to move him and his wife down to Florida next month."

"I'd say he got off lucky."

"I'd reckon he did." Doc pauses. "He told me to say

hello to you, next time I saw you . . . but I guess that's kind of stupid, seeing you say you never met the man.''

''I suppose so.'' Junior is still grinning. ''Like I said, I ain't been in Lebanon in months.''

''Guess not. And you haven't been out here for a while, have you?''

''Naw, I ain't been here.'' Junior drains the rest of his beer and wipes his mouth with the back of his hand. ''Fact is, I was in Nashville tonight . . . went in to catch that new Arnold Schwarzenegger movie. Ain't that right?''

Doc doesn't reply. He picks up the three Michelob bottles and carries them out to the back door. Junior hears the screen door swing open and slam shut; while he waits for Doc to return, he pulls another paper napkin out of the dispenser, dabs one end in a small puddle of water Doc missed a few minutes ago, and uses it to wipe down every inch of the counter where he has been sitting. The napkin goes in his back pocket; after that, he is careful not to touch anything in the store.

There're some things they just don't teach a kid in the eighth grade.

When Doc comes back, he's got Howell with him. Howell has a thick roll of money in his pocket: five hundred dollars, split into twenties and fifties. Junior makes him count it out on the Formica, and when he's finished counting Junior picks up the cash and shoves it into a front pocket of his jeans.

''Well, good night, then,'' he says as he stands up from the stool. ''I think it's way past y'all's bedtime, don't you think?''

Neither man answers. Both are staring at the floor, each looking as stupid as only a couple of dumbass hick farmers can look. Ex-farmers, rather; Howell is as thick as the pigs he used to slop, and Doc was never that good at harvesting corn. They should have learned a real money-making skill, like Junior did.

Junior shoulders open the front door and walks to his

car. He drives out of the parking lot and spends the next couple of hours cruising the back roads where the county sheriff never goes. He finishes the joint that was left in the ashtray and listens to country music on the radio, savoring the warm summer breeze and the feel of money in his pocket, and when the night is at its darkest and a cool mist is beginning to rise above the tall grass, he swings back toward Doc's place, where all the lights have now been extinguished and nothing is moving.

Driving another quarter-mile down the road past the rocket farm, Junior finds an old tractor-path off the highway where he can stash his car without it being spotted from the road. The path is nice and dry, so there's no real danger of leaving tire tracks in the dirt, and everything he needs is stashed in the trunk: a pair of old rubber rain boots, some latex dishwashing gloves, and two five-gallon gasoline cans. He switches his cowboy boots for the galoshes and pulls on the gloves, then picks up the gas cans.

'Way off across the abandoned field, the *U.S.S. Grissom* rises above the withered remains of corn stalks. The stars are out tonight; constellations Junior can't name shimmer in the moist midnight heat. Humming his favorite country music hit, Junior begins to wade through the tall wild grass, the gas cans gently bouncing against his knees.

If he gets through with this job soon, maybe he'll get home in time to catch the end of *Star Trek*.

INTRODUCTION:
"2,437 UFOs Over New Hampshire"

Another story set in New Hampshire. There's a couple
of others like it in *Rude Astronauts*, and in some sense
this is a sequel to one of them, "Hapgood's Hoax," in
that it deals with the same subject.

This story had been in the back of my mind for some
time, but it was not until I moved to Missouri that I
actually wrote it. In hindsight, I think that I had to put
some distance between myself and New Hampshire before this story would allow itself to be told. It took Esther
Freisner's invitation to contribute a tale to her "tabloid
SF" anthology, *Alien Made Pregnant by Elvis* (DAW,
1994) to finally prompt me into actually putting it down
on paper.

I'm rather intrigued by accounts of UFO sightings,
landings, or "abductions." Indeed, this interest was
prompted while I was living in Rindge, New Hampshire.
I received a phone call from a person who was sure that
the local "sci-fi writer" would be fascinated by the story
of a UFO crash-landing in a nearby lake some ten years
earlier. As it turns out, there's no shortage of UFO sightings in the Granite State. In fact, if half of the stories are

given credence, then New Hampshire is the Grand Central Station of flying saucers.

Let me make myself clear, at least in an attempt to prevent receiving letters and phone calls from readers who want to call my attention to items such as the Area 51 flying saucer, the Roswell UFO crash, crop circles, cattle mutilations, foo fighters, and so forth. After reading much material from both sides of the issue, with an open mind to all possibilities, I've come to the conclusion that most, if not all, of the "documented" cases of so-called close encounters are total bullshit. They are the result of frauds, rumor mongering, hallucinations, hysteria, unintentional or deliberate misinterpretations of circumstantial events, bad reportage by the news media, and more.

If there is any strange, unexplained phenomenon at work here, then it is psychological rather than extraterrestrial in origin. It is undeniable that the phenomena of UFO belief is quite widespread. Belief is the key word here. The key question—"Do you think UFOs exist?"—has been replaced by another one—"Do you believe in UFOs?"

There's a subtle yet distinct difference between the two. Thinking that UFOs may exist means that the person has weighed the evidence, however intangible or circumstantial it may be, to arrive at a conclusion, either pro or con. But if you take the latter statement, and substitute certain words—"God," "Jesus," "Satan", "hell," "reincarnation," "Scientology," or whatever—for UFOs, then you're working within a different paradigm altogether, the belief in something that you can't tangibly see, touch, or feel. Religious faith, in other words.

Except that UFOs have a certain pseudoscientific cache. All but the most hard-nosed astrophysicists will concur that it's possible that life exists elsewhere in the universe, even though that statement itself is still unproven. So, if you're willing to accept the notion that life may have evolved elsewhere in the galaxy, then you're ready to believe in UFOs . . . if you're not a stickler for irrefutable evidence, that is.

By and large, UFOs have replaced fairies, ghosts, and sightings of long-dead prophets as the leading "evidence" that Some Unknown Force is guiding our lives, intruding now and then in the form of blurred photographs, out-of-the-way landing sites . . . or, on occasion, the individual who is willing to swear that he or she has been inside an alien spaceship (in the middle of the night, on a lonely country road, with no eyewitnesses, etc.). Some of these people sincerely believe this. Some of the others do, too, and they'll tell you the whole shocking story for just $19.99 plus shipping and handling, Visa and Mastercard accepted.

You've already paid good money for this book on the grounds that it's 100% science fiction, and you've now found one story in this volume that is neither hard SF nor purports to be fact. Sorry if you feel cheated, but at least I'm up front about it, which is more than you'll get from Whitley Strieber, Budd Hopkins, and the other guys who have been getting rich off this snake-oil show. In exchange, allow me to give you some free advice:

Remain skeptical. Especially when they ask for your faith and your wallet at the same time.

2,437 UFOS OVER NEW HAMPSHIRE

Giddings is a small town in the southern lakes region of New Hampshire. Located off Route 202 about halfway between Concord and Keene, it's the sort of place that typifies the adage, "Don't blink or you'll miss it." Indeed, most people find the town only by accident; a tourist from Massachusetts or Connecticut might briefly stop there for gas and a Coke on the way to a crafts festival in Bradford or a weekend ski trip in the White Mountains but certainly for no other reason.

To such a visitor, Giddings seems to be just another one of the countless former mill towns scattered throughout rural New England. Near the highway is Tuck's, the Exxon convenience store that sells microwave sandwiches, lottery tickets, and vaguely obscene bumper stickers. That's as much of Giddings as most people see, but if you get off Route 202 and drive down the five miles of the two-lane Main Road toward the town center, you'll pass dense woods and ponds and dairy pastures. Dirt roads branch off Main, leading to nowhere; the woodland surrounds houses both large and small, some dating back to the last century, where beat-up old mailboxes are stuffed with free newspapers and almost every other backyard seems to have a satellite dish.

At the end of Main Road, just past the closed-down paper mill and the small stone bridge that crosses over the Contoocook River, is Giddings Center. There isn't much in the town square. Giddings Market, a grocery and general store. Zack's Pizzaria, a pizza and grinder restaurant. MovieMania, a video rental shop. The tiny U.S. post office. The town hall, which is also home to the three-man police force and the volunteer fire department. At one end of the square is the stolid, windowless Congregational Church; behind it is the town graveyard, whose slate tombstones date back to the Revolutionary War. Bookending the opposite end of the square is the town library, the basement of which serves as a movie theater on Friday and Saturday nights; *Batman Returns* made its Giddings premiere there last weekend, six months after its appearance on HBO. In the middle of the square is a weather-beaten bronze monument to the twelve boys from Giddings who were killed in the Civil War during the First Battle of Manassas; a flag is draped over the monument each Memorial Day, although no one remembers the names of the fallen heroes.

Nothing about Giddings suggests anything odd or unusual, at least to the incurious eye. Yet, if you look a little closer and in just the right places, you may notice a few strange details.

The magazine rack in Giddings Market has all the recent tabloid papers—the *Star*, the *Globe*, the *Sun, Weekly World News, The National Enquirer* and so forth—as well as the current issues of *Fate, UFO Report, UFO Examiner*, and similar magazines. More copies of *Omni* are sold in Giddings than of *Life, Newsweek*, and *TV Guide* combined. New periodicals are delivered each Tuesday by the regional distributor, and most of the weird-science rags are sold out by Thursday.

There's usually someone browsing in front of the shelf.

Don't stare, but look a little more closely; this person is probably wearing a small plastic bracelet around his or her left wrist, its tiny blue LED pulsing once every minute.

The same newspapers and magazines are in the reading room of the town library. Two entire bookcases are devoted to (alleged) non-fiction about UFOs: *Flying Saucers Are Real, Incident At Exeter, Project Blue Book, Chariots of the Gods?, The Bermuda Triangle, In Search of Extraterrestrials, Someone Else Is On The Moon, Communion, Missing Time, Out There*, the entire *Time/Life* ''Mysteries of the Unknown'' series, and much more. There's a perpetual waiting list for *Intruders* by Budd Hopkins; on the other hand, the paperback copy of *UFOs Explained* by Philip J. Klass has been defaced with a single word scrawled across its cover: ''Lies!''

Over at MovieMania, there's an enormous wall of science fiction flicks, most of them about UFOs. The cinematic version of *Communion* is always rented out.

Giddings Mill seems, at first glance, to be abandoned. If you peer closer, though, you can see that the parking lot has been freshly paved. There are always cars parked near the front door; most of them are cream-colored four-wheel-drive Ford Explorers, but one of the vehicles is an ambulance. Look closer at the flat roof between the unused smokestacks, and you'll spot a small grove of parabolic dishes and cellular antennae.

If you could peer through the building's smoked glass window into the high-ceilinged room where the rusted mill equipment used to stand, you would see four men and women sitting behind state-of-the-art electronic consoles, sipping coffee and murmuring into headset mikes as they watch a vast array of television monitors, LCDs, and radar screens. If you're driving down any back road in town and feel the need to pull over on the shoulder to relieve yourself by the roadside, be careful where and how you unzip your fly; the trees contain almost as many TV cameras as bird nests.

The last public place in Giddings remaining open after dark is Zack's Pizzaria, and Zack locks the doors at nine o'clock sharp. When the sun sets behind the hills and the last light of day fades on the Civil War memorial, photosensitive timers bring to life hundreds of sodium-vapor street lights, which bathe the square and all the town roads in a bright yellowish glare. All night long, Ford Explorers from the mill prowl the streets and back roads, stopping occasionally at lonely houses in the woods where the lights stay on until dawn. When this town goes to sleep, it does so with both eyes open.

According to the 1990 federal census, Giddings has a permanent population of 157. At least two-thirds of these people claim to have been abducted by aliens from outer space.

"The last time anyone tallied how many people in this country said they were UFO abductees, it was in the mid-80s, about the time Whitley Strieber's book was on the *New York Times* bestseller list. Back then, it was around fifty or so . . . maybe a couple of hundred, if you count the obvious fruitcakes."

Paul Rucker coughs in his fist as he hands me a thick black pagebinder. Within it are ninety-seven pages of single-spaced computer printout, row after row of names, addresses, and phone numbers. "That's the list of possible abductees we've compiled in the last three years," he says in his soft, Virginia-accented voice. "There's two thousand, four hundred and thirty-seven names in that book . . . and I haven't gotten around to adding the two hundred or so others who have contacted us in the last couple of months."

Paul Rucker doesn't look like a stereotypical UFO nut. Mid-40s, round-figured, balding, wearing horn-rimmed glasses and a navy-blue sweater over khaki trousers, he looks more like an insurance agent or a CPA than a former Air Force intelligence analyst. Yet, as he squats on the seat of a backless ergonomic chair in his red-brick office in the Giddings Mill, he calmly talks of things you and I would consider impossible, absurd, and unbelievable.

"Look at the first name on the list," he says. I flip back to the first page; the top name has been carefully blacked out with Magic Marker, along with the address and phone number. "That's Number One," he says. "I can't tell you his name or where he lives, but he's the one who bought Giddings and made it possible for many of these people to live here."

He smiles in answer to the unspoken yet obvious next question. "If I told you his name, you'd recognize it immediately." He nods toward the list. "Besides, too many people have found out already. Why do you think the list is so long?"

Number One doesn't live in Giddings, but it's because of his wealth and influence that the town has become a sanctuary for UFO abductees. What little is known of him is that he is a millionaire who, during his salad days as a travelling salesman, was kidnapped by aliens while driving alone through Texas. After several years of experiencing the same recurrent nightmares that are symptomatic of other abductees, Number One sought psychiatric help, only to discover that there was an eight-hour gap in his memory, dating back to that road trip through Texas when he thought he had simply fallen asleep behind the wheel.

His quest for an explanation brought him into the small circle of people who had also experienced the "missing time" phenomena. Like Number One, most of them had repressed memories of being taken aboard flying saucers and subjected to humiliating physical examinations by extraterrestrials, horrifying memories that were later unlocked by hypnosis. They lived in constant fear of being kidnapped again, but unlike the former salesman—who, by this time, had amassed a considerable fortune and thus could afford to protect himself—they were virtually powerless against future intrusions.

Altruistic by nature, Number One decided to take matters into his own hands. Cloaking his identity behind a complex network of banks, holding companies, and real estate agencies, he searched for a town that he could transform into a fortress for his fellow abductees. When he found Giddings, it had been bankrupt for several years, rendered penniless by the demise of the local paper mill during the '70s and the wipeout of the state's economy during the recession of the '90s. Most of the houses had been foreclosed and were up for sale, and the town was inhabited by only a few farmers and die-hard oldtimers.

Number One purchased all the available private property in Giddings, including the paper mill, and turned it over to The Astra Trust, the non-profit foundation of which Paul Rucker is the chief executive. There are few clues to Number One's identity; all of the Astra Trust's property in Giddings is owned by a bank in Dallas, Texas, and the annual stipend checks are issued from the same bank. Although the leading suspect is H. Ross Perot, Perot's spokesmen have denied that he is the man behind the Astra Trust.

The Astra Trust is the McArthur Foundation for the UFO set: ninety UFO abductees and their immediate families can live in Giddings, rent-free and with a modest annual stipend, for as long as they feel the need to hide from the aliens. No strings attached; some people stay for only a year or two, others intend to remain in Giddings for the rest of their lives.

"We interview applicants, study their case histories, put them through polygraph tests, and have them undergo medical examinations, including a session with our staff psychologist," Rucker says. "Obviously, with something like this, you're going to get a lot of people who are shamming, not to mention a few outright crackpots, but we've gotten pretty good at weeding out the con artists and fruitcakes. If they're let in, they're part of the community. They'll be protected for as long they want to be here.''

Why doesn't Number One himself live in Giddings? Rucker shrugs. "He doesn't really need to," he says calmly. "I'm not at liberty to discuss his arrangements, but . . . well, let's just say, where he lives now, the aliens are never going to get him.''

"Smile," says Dorothy Taylor. "You're on *Candid Camera.*''

Dorothy—like others in this story, this is not her real name—lives with her six-year-old daughter Nancy and her two attack-trained German Shepards, Rex and Arnie, in a small cottage about a half-mile from the center of town. She is a quiet woman in her early thirties who works as a freelance artist; before she moved to Giddings, she lived in Bowling Green, Kentucky, where she had been an art instructor in the city's public school system.

We're sitting in the living room, drinking coffee as I conduct the interview. She raises her eyes toward the ceiling; I look up, and for the first time notice the fish-eye camera lens positioned in the center of the ceiling, a red LED lamp glowing next to the lens. "It's on all the time," she says, "and there's one in each room except the bath. Plus the two cameras outside . . . one out front by the driveway, one in the backyard near Nancy's swingset.''

Dorothy has been divorced for the past three years; like many of Giddings' abductees, her spouse wrote her off as hopelessly deranged when she began talking about aliens from space kidnapping her. She now has a boy-friend, an art student from Boston who visits her on the weekends. "When we want a little privacy," she says, smiling and blushing a little, "I tape over the lens in the bedroom. No sense in giving the guys at the mill a free show, after all."

The smile fades. "But the tape comes off after nightfall, and I don't care how Alec feels about it." She raises the front of her cotton-print smock; just below her sternum is a small vertical scar. "This is what they left behind after they took me," she says quietly. "I don't want that to happen again."

The near-total lack of privacy in her own home doesn't bother her, no more than the plastic bracelet she and her daughter wear around their wrists. The bracelets contain microtransmitters that relay, via the town's cellular radio network, their whereabouts in Giddings. When Dorothy goes shopping at the grocery, the watchers at the mill know she's there. If Nancy takes the dogs for a walk in the woods, the Mill is constantly tracking her. The signals extend only as far as the town limits, but this doesn't bother Dorothy; she seldom leaves Giddings, and even then only for a few hours . . . and never overnight.

"I spent at least six hours in an alien spaceship in orbit above Earth," she says, quite seriously and without the slightest trace of dementia. "Those were the most terrifying hours of my life. They stripped me naked, took my blood, put . . . things into me." She looks away, falling silent for a few moments. "They raped me," she continues, more quietly now. "I never want to go through that again, and I want to keep my daughter safe from them. That's why we're here. Compared to what could happen . . . well, who cares about a few TV cameras?"

In a spare bedroom is her studio. Most of the incomplete paintings on easels or stacked against the walls are of New England landscapes; she sells them through an agent to hotel chains, for display in lobbies and guest rooms. Several of her oil paintings, though, depict her memories of her ordeal from her point of view. A flying saucer landing in a Kentucky farmfield. An indistinct

group of bulbous-headed, wasp-waisted ETs marching
down a gangway. A similar alien looming over her examination couch, a sharp surgical probe in its six-fingered
hand. A view of Earth as seen through the windows of
a spacecraft in high orbit above the planet.

Are these her private paintings? ''No,'' she says. ''At
first they were, but when my agent saw them, she insisted
that I publish them.''

UFO publications? The covers of books about alien
abductions? ''Oh, no,'' Dorothy says. ''Most of them are
sent overseas. We've got a steady market in England for
the covers of science fiction magazines.'' She smiles
proudly. ''And they love my stuff in France. I've had
two gallery showings in Paris. I'm almost as big as
Mickey Rourke over there.''

Hidden behind the mill, encircled by a ten foot chain-
mesh fence topped with rolls of razor wire, is a large
geodesic dome. The dome contains Giddings' SHF 15-
GHz anti-aircraft radar system which constantly scans the
airspace above the town. The system was procured from
the U.S. Navy by the Astra Trust through Number One's
defense contacts.

Not far from the edge of town is a small helicopter
pad, where a French Aerospatiale SA 642 Gazelle is kept
for use by the mill's security force. Two pilots and an
observer live in a small house near the helipad. The mill's
watchers are always watching the skies over Giddings;
they've got the schedules for the commercial airliners
that regularly fly over the town, so they've learned to
ignore certain high-altitude blips on their screens. When
they spot something on radar—particularly any erratic
motion from an object that is larger than a duck or
doesn't have the V-shaped profile of a flight of migrating
Canadian geese—the pilots are called and whoever is on
duty quickly takes the Gazelle up for a look.

''I never see anything,'' says Juan Torres, the former

Brazilian Air Force captain who is one of the pilots for "Air Astra." He stands next to his aircraft, looking suave with his aviator shades and bandito mustache. "Small planes most times. Lots of stray goose . . . ah, geese. One time an ultralight. Scared the sheet out of him, never come back. But never any flying saucer. Not once. Sí?"

What would he do if he ever spotted one? Juan crooks his finger toward me, then leads me to the open side door of the Gazelle. He pulls aside a canvas tarp, revealing a pintle-mounted 7.62 mm machine gun. Two outriggers on either side of the fuselage carry four SA-7 air-to-air missiles.

"Hey, you meet any leetle green hombres, you tell 'em to come this way," he says, patting the top of the gun fondly. "Me and Pedro here, we'll really fok 'em up."

Ray Bonette greets me at the door of his log cabin with a loaded Smith & Wesson .357 revolver in his hand. He stares at me with undisguised suspicion as I identify myself, then he demands that I present my credentials. Even after I do so, Ray is still wary and hostile. Before he allows me into his house, he demands that I remove my coat, shirt, and tie.

I reluctantly strip on his front porch. It's straight-up noon; songbirds warble in the dense pines surrounding his cabin, a passenger jet moans across the blue sky. When my shirt is off, Ray tells me to raise my arms above my head and slowly turn around. As I do so, he carefully studies my back and chest; he glares at the appendectomy scar near my stomach but says nothing.

"Okay, you're clean," he mutters. "Get dressed."

Ray Bonette is a heavy-set man in his mid-50s. His hair is crew-cut and as white as his beard; he wears baggy trousers that haven't been washed in weeks and a mottled white t-shirt. He refuses to tell me much about his past. He used to live in California. He was once a master elec-

trician. He has a wife—present tense—but she's "gone
now." Ditto for two kids. That's it; the only thing he
wants to disclose publicly is the size of his arsenal.

The cabin has four rooms and in each room are loaded
weapons. There's an Ingram MAC-10 on the coffee table
in the den, a Beretta 87BB on one of the end tables next
to the couch, a Colt King Cobra on the kitchen table, and
a Heckler and Koch HK-93 assault rifle on the counter
next to the stove. Colt revolvers are on the bedside tables
in the master bedroom and the guest room, each with
spare rounds at ready. There's a night-sighted crossbow
next to the back door, a Glock 20 beneath the pillow of
his bed, and an AR-15 rifle resting in the corner next to
the toilet in the bathroom.

If that's not enough, he also hints that the property line
has been booby-trapped with explosives. "I got Clay-
mores out in the bushes," he says, "so don't let me catch
you out here in the middle of the night." He doesn't go
into detail.

Having quickly shown me around the house, he shows
me the door, still refusing to be interviewed. After he
shoves me out onto the porch, though, he gives me one
last pearl of wisdom.

"Tell that bitch Marilyn I'm ready for her and her little
friends," he snarls at me. "Tell her that I still love God
and America and Joe DiMaggio."

Then he slams the door in my face.

Charlie DuPont has been a New Hampshire resident for
the past twenty-four years and has lived in Giddings for
the past three. A native of South Carolina, he first came
to New England as a student at Dartmouth in the '60s,
but he dropped out after his sophomore year to bum
around the state before finally settling in Giddings, where
he opened MovieMania, the latest of a long string of self-
employed enterprises.

Charlie wears his hair long and lives the vegetarian,

easy-vibes lifestyle of an unreformed hippie, yet he is one of the minority in Giddings who hasn't yet been kidnapped by a UFO. "Lemme put it to you this way," he says, sipping a bottle of Evian water as he files away the videotapes that were returned in his store's overnight drop-box. "I believe in Jesus. I believe in karma. I believe that Jack and Bobby Kennedy were killed by the CIA and that James Earl Ray didn't act alone. I believe that marijuana should be legalized. I believe that women are superior to men and are better in bed besides."

He sighs and shakes his head. "But I don't believe in flying saucers, and I think all these people are up to their eyeballs in donkey flop."

Charlie had opened his video shop in Giddings less than a month before he gradually became aware that most of his regular customers were heavily into UFOs. He first discovered this when he began to get requests for obscure documentaries about the UFO phenomena, often for purchase, despite the hefty prices such tapes commanded. It wasn't long before Charlie realized, through small talk with one of the customers, that they believed that they once had gone cruising for burgers in UFOs.

"I guess, because the way I look and act, these people think I'm into all that shit," Charlie says. "What they don't know is that I've heard it all before. Yeah, when I used to drop acid, I sorta thought all that stuff was real, too, but I've been straight for a long time now, and since I got off drugs, none of that Eric von Däneken shit makes sense to me."

He cocks his thumb over his shoulder, toward the town square beyond the windows of his store. "This place, man . . . it's Weird Central Station. These people look straight, act straight. Most of 'em wouldn't know an acid tab if you put it in their hand. Y'know, half of them are Republicans. They helped keep Reagan in the White House for eight years and voted for Bush twice. Twice, for chrissakes!"

His eyes roll up. "And they think they went for rides in flying saucers. They come in here, show me their funny-looking scars and tell me long stories about big-headed guys lurking outside the bedroom windows. Hey, I voted for Jerry Brown in the last primary, and I don't believe that shit."

He pauses to open a carton of videotapes he just received via UPS from his distributor. Unsurprisingly, it contains five more copies of *Close Encounters of the Third Kind*, all special orders from his customers. Now that the video has been marked down, everyone in Giddings wants his own copy. Meanwhile, he has copies of *Europa, Europa* and *The Player* he can't rent or sell for love or money.

"I like these people, y'know," he grumbles as he unpacks the tapes. "They're nice and polite, they always rewind their tapes and pony up the late fees . . . but, shit, if I ever meet Steven Spielberg, I'm gonna rip out his lungs for making this goddamn movie."

"Tonight's quiet, least so far," Libby Reynolds says as she slowly cruises along the deserted back roads behind the wheel of one of the security trucks. "But we've got a full moon, the fog is up . . . you never know."

Libby is wearing the light blue uniform of the Astra Trust's six-person private security squad. A former New York City cop, she left the city in search of a quieter job in the country, never dreaming that she would be handling graveyard shift on what her team calls the "Spock Patrol": handling nocturnal sightings—or perhaps more accurately, "hearings"—from Giddings residents.

A thin haze has drifted off the river and into the lowlands, enveloping the road and the surrounding woods in a smokey mask. The police-band radio beneath the dashboard of the Ford Explorer chatters with crosstalk from nearby towns such as Dublin and Peterborough, but Libby has it turned down low. Her job is to listen for the occasional calls sent from the mill on the cellular transceiver. This autumn night, she hasn't gotten any calls, but there's always the possibility that something might happen.

Libby slows down and stops in front of a gravel driveway. The name ''G. W. Norton'' is spelled in reflective tape across the mailbox; the ranchhouse at the end of the drive is clearly visible from the spotlights that surround it on all sides. Even at two o'clock in the morning, light glows from all the windows. Libby taps her car horn twice, then shifts the Explorer back into first gear and moves on.

''Once, twice, sometimes three times a week, that guy calls and tells us that aliens are in his yard.'' She shakes her head. ''If racoons are going through his garbage cans, they're aliens. If our own chopper flies over the house, it's a UFO. Last winter we had a nor'easter and the town lost electricity . . . happens out here now and then. He thought it was a flying saucer, and when someone from the squad came out here to calm him down, he nearly blew his butt off with a shotgun.''

Libby glances at me, smiling in the wane light of her dashboard. ''Why did I toot the horn? Because he stays up all night with that Remington in his lap, and I want him to know it's me and not E.T.''

Nonetheless, Libby Reynolds believes in UFOs, although she has never seen one while living in Giddings. ''It's crazy,'' she says, ''but I know what fear is like. When I worked out of a precinct house in the boroughs, I used to deal with all sorts of stuff. Crack gangs, drive-by shootings, wackos with knives in their teeth . . . hey, I once opened a garbage can and found a dismembered body stuffed inside. The people who lived on my old beat in Harlem were too scared to run out even when their building was on fire. . . .''

She stops to listen to the mill radio for a moment, then she picks up the hand mike. ''Ten-four, that's a twelve-

fifty-six. Just went by there. Don't worry about it. Twelve
Ben Gay out.'' She double-clicks the mike before she
shoves it back into the holster. "Norton called again.
Thought we were the men in black or whatever.''

Libby pauses to recollect her train of thought. "I see
the same thing here," she says after a moment. "People
here are scared of something, and it's not always just
bears or the wind or whatever. I try to take it with a grain
of salt, but. . . .''

Her voice trails off and she is quiet for a few moments.
"I dunno,'' she finally says. "You tell me. Can all these
folks be nuts or what?''

Jim and Betsy Donahue live in one of the larger houses
in town, a two-hundred year old farmhouse on thirty
acres of land near a bend in the Contoocook River. Even
before he left his position as a municipal stock analyst
for a Chicago brokerage at age 65, they had considered
retirement in New England; in fact, they had previously
looked at places elsewhere in the Hillsborough County
and Chesire County not far from Giddings. Their relo-
cation to rural New England, therefore, was not wholly
unanticipated; only the circumstances are different.

The Donahues' retirement home is a big, sprawling
house with oak beams across the downstairs ceilings and
Indian shutters on the windows. The rooms are furnished
with antiques, the four-poster bed is covered with a hand-
made quilt, the kitchen walls are decorated with old iron
skillets and cats tails. The mantel over the fieldstone fire-
place holds framed photos of their children and grand-
children, and the shelves in the basement are stocked
with Ball jars containing Betsy's homemade preserves.
And there's a spaceship out in the back yard.

Jim Donahue's flying saucer is a full-scale replica of
the UFO that he and Betsy visited in 1981, while they
were driving back to Chicago from a vacation in Minnesota. Unlike most abductees, however, neither he nor

Betsy experienced the "missing time" syndrome, nor did
the aliens who took them aboard their spacecraft subject
them to painful physical examinations. As a result, both
have vivid recollections of the encounter, which later enabled Jim to rebuild the spaceship in precise detail.

The UFO is about thirty feet tall and nearly sixty feet
in diameter. It's shaped like an upside-down bowl with
a round pillbox on top, and it stands on six wide flanges,
which fold down from the flat bottom of the hull. There
are no windows in the hull. Five red-tinted glass hemi-
spheres arranged along the bottom of the ship between
the landing gear hint at the mysterious anti-gravity drive
that enabled the vessel to land silently on the lonely highway in front of their car almost thirteen years ago.

The pseudo-UFO looks as though it is made of bur-
nished aluminum, but that's an illusion produced by Jim
and Betsy's skillful use of silver enamel paint. Their re-
production is constructed almost entirely out of particle
board, with various pieces of scrap metal salvaged from
junkyards and electronics purchased from the Radio
Shack in Peterborough. Electrical lines snake across the
yard to a small port beneath the hull. Jim belonged to the
U.S. Army Corps of Engineers during World War II and
built his first house after the war; his carpentry talents
have lent themselves to making a do-it-yourself UFO.

"I did this to convince people what Betsy and I saw
was real," Jim says as he leads me up a recessed ladder
in one of the flanges to a trapdoor beneath the saucer.
"We were fortunate in that we were invited aboard, not
kidnapped like most of the others here in town. Because
of this, we figure that the aliens wanted us to spread the
word of their presence."

The trapdoor leads to a small anteroom in the center
of the ship. After Jim clicks a couple of toggle switches
next to the trapdoor that turn on the ceiling fluorescents—
"They weren't there, I just put 'em in so you could see
everything"—he points out the hatches on each of the

four walls. Although in the real saucer they had slid open automatically, he has been unable to reproduce the same effect. He has to push open the hatch that leads into the main control room: the cockpit, as he calls it.

The room is wedge-shaped, with a single wing-backed chair positioned in front of a wraparound console. "Notice the chair," he says. "It's short, isn't it? That's because the tallest of them was only four feet in height . . . but they were still humanoid in shape."

Jim gently settles down in it; the chair creaks under his weight. "See? The armrests are right where they're supposed to be."

The chair isn't what immediately attracts my attention. The console controls are evenly laid out and consist mainly of large round buttons, spaced apart from each other in unlabeled rows; I count no more than sixty in all. There are three non-functional TV monitors on the wall above the console, a panel of lights near the ceiling, and enough empty floor space behind the command chair to contain a pool table.

Contrast this with the flight deck of a NASA space shuttle—four seats, myriad control panels with dozens of tiny toggle switches jammed into every available space, two computer keyboards, and a half-dozen CRT displays, and in a craft capable of only flying to low-Earth orbit—and one comes to the realization that the aliens must have very advanced technology indeed.

Jim stands up and leads me through another hatch into the adjacent compartment. "This is the monitor room," he says. "It's where Betsy and I were shown Earth. By now, of course, we were in orbit above the Moon."

This compartment has a wall-sized TV screen, a couple of big-buttoned control panels on the walls, and little more. I press one of the buttons experimentally; nothing happens, but Jim is quick to give me an all-encompassing explanation. "They only had four fingers on each hand," he says. He holds up his right hand, his little finger crooked into his palm. "Like this. So they couldn't handle things the same as we do."

The next hatch leads to what he calls the "hibernation chamber." There are a few more panels in this compartment, but the floor is dominated by three daises, each surrounded by Plexiglass tubes. Jim launches into a long-winded treatise on how the tubes each contained the bodies of aliens who were being held in suspended animation, but by now a small memory that has been tugging at the back of my mind comes into focus.

"Excuse me, Mr. Donahue," I say softly, and he instantly falls silent, awaiting my next question. I pause reluctantly, shuffling my notebook in my hands. "But . . . did you ever see an old TV show called *The Invaders*?"

Jim stares at me, not saying anything. "A show back in the '60s? With Roy Thinnes?" I add, and his face darkens. He slowly shakes his head. "About alien invaders from space?"

His hands clench into small, tight fists as his body begins to tremble. "I don't mean to imply anything," I continue, "but everything you've shown me . . . this entire ship . . . looks like the flying saucers they used in . . ."

"Get out," he rasps, glaring at me.

"Umm . . . excuse me?"

"You heard me." He speaks in a low, barely controlled voice as he wrestles with his suppressed rage. "You son of a bitch, get out of here. Right now."

There's little more to be said between us. I leave him alone in his UFO, finding my way through another hatch into the central anteroom. As I climb down the ladder and start to walk away from the UFO, Betsy is walking into the backyard, carrying a pewter tray laden with a pitcher of iced tea and three tall glasses. She looks confused as I make a lame excuse for my hasty exit, then her face falls into a disapproving look.

"Oh, no," she says. "You didn't mention Quinn Martin Productions, did you?"

"Ummm . . . no, ma'am. All I did was mention an old TV show called . . .''

"*The Invaders*. Oh, dear. You didn't know." She tsks. "They swiped the whole idea from us. We didn't earn a dime from them. Didn't Jim tell you about that?"

I gently remind her that *The Invaders* was a show on ABC in the mid-'60s; by their own account, the Donahues didn't encounter a UFO until almost fifteen years later. Betsy Donahue brushes this aside with a motherly look of condescension. "Young man," she says sternly, "time means nothing where we're concerned."

She gazes up at the perfect blue sky over Giddings, her face becoming placid as she contemplates eternity itself. "Black holes," she murmurs. "Don't you know about them already? They bend everything, even time itself. The aliens told us this."

For a few moments, Betsy Donahue is caught in transcendental rapture, remembering alien voices that spoke to her long ago and far away. Through the open hatch of the UFO, I can hear her husband shouting curses, hurling things about. Something crashes as if it has been thrown against a bulkhead, but this doesn't seem to register on her beatitude.

She looks back down from the sky, gradually focusing on me again, her smile as sweet as the sugar cubes on her pewter platter.

"Now," she says. "Are you sure you won't stay for tea?"

INTRODUCTION:
"Jonathan Livingstone Seaslug"

If I had to pick five authors whose work has not only influenced my own writing but also profoundly affected the way I look at the world, Arthur C. Clarke would be on the list. For the record, the others would include Robert A. Heinlein, Harlan Ellison, J. Bronowski, and Mark Twain. These authors are all quite different from one another, but even so, I find myself comparing and contrasting their work with Dr. Clarke's. Although Heinlein's *Rocket Ship Galileo* was the first SF novel I read, it was Clarke whom I emulated when I started writing at age 15, and while Ellison taught me how to vent my anger onto paper, Clarke showed me how to control the rage with reason. Both Twain and Clarke showed me how to observe the world around me with tongue firmly placed in cheek, and after I read Bronowski's *The Ascent of Man* in tandem with *Childhood's End*, I was never able to view my fellow *Homo sapiens* and their works quite the same way again.

When I was thrown out of boarding school for being a pain in the ass, I was carrying a copy of *Rendezvous with Rama* under my arm when I was marched into the headmaster's office and given my walking papers. How's that for memory of a certain book?

Many years later, when I wrote my second SF novel, it seemed only fitting to pay homage to the master by titling it *Clarke County, Space*. By then, as a member of the Science Fiction Writers of America, I had a copy of its membership directory and thus knew how to write to Dr. Clarke directly. Somewhat shamefacedly, I sent a copy of my new book to his home in Sri Lanka, not really expecting to receive a reply. Much to my surprise, I received a nice note from him several weeks later, along with a few other items he had stuffed into the envelope.

And what were these items? A photocopy of an anti-space editorial from the *London Times*, at the bottom of which Dr. Clarke had written, "What do you think of this?" A magazine photo of two adjacent craters on Venus that had just been radar-imaged by the Magellan space probe ("I think they're mating," he scribbled at the bottom). A NASA internal memo ("Thought you might like to see this—Art").

After exchanging a few more letters with Dr. Clarke—I later had the privilege of addressing him as "Arthur,"—I discovered that this is the way he normally answers his mail. The letters themselves are brief and straightforward; he is a very busy man and cannot spend hours replying to correspondence. However, he makes up for this by forwarding things that he has found and believes that you, too, may be interested in seeing. Funny editorial cartoons, a laser-printed image of Olympus Mons on Mars that he has just terraformed with VistaPro, various odds and ends that have recently come to his attention . . . either Arthur has discovered a unique way of clearing his desk or he's trying to make you think.

In this instance, that's exactly what happened.

In one of his letters, he sent a copy of a wry memo he had faxed to his literary agent, regarding a movie deal that had just fallen through with a major Hollywood producer. In that memo, Arthur said that he was still interested in selling a story to said producer, and he listed a number of possible titles that might be worth developing.

The list was long and hilarious, including items such as "The Infibulator II," "That, Son Of It," "The Godmothers," and so on. And in the middle of the list was "Jonathan Livingston Seaslug."

People often ask writers where they get their ideas, only to receive a vague shrug and a mumbled reply. Beside noting that I read the *New York Times* every morning, I'm no different. Ideas come from the strangest of places and damned if I know when or where inspiration will strike next.

This is one of the few exceptions. Within minutes of reading those three words, I began pacing the living room floor.

One of my favorite road trips during my college years was to Cape Hatteras, North Carolina, which included a brief en route visit to the Woods Hole Marine Biology Institute on Cape Cod, Massachusetts. I've also wanted to write an undersea adventure story for quite some time. All this—plus disgust with the New Age movement, which substitutes understanding the natural sciences with fuzzy-headed mysticism, and the American environmental movement, which for all its good works has often been sidetracked by shamans and quacks—fell into a cerebral soup kettle, and out came a giant slug named Jonathan.

I asked Arthur if I could steal his joke as a title for a story. As it turned out, I received another letter from him, giving me permission to do so, the day before I flew down to Florida for a winter vacation. I wrote the story while staying in a beach condo. During the day I did research, including a visit to a marine science center on Sanibel Island to investigate the habits of sea slugs. At night I sat on the screen porch, writing in longhand with the sound of waves breaking as my inspiration. It drove

Linda crazy that I worked during what was supposed to be a break, but I had a wonderful time.

This story is the result. Naturally, it's dedicated to Arthur.

JONATHAN LIVINGSTONE SEASLUG

Another mystery . . . is the Great Sea Serpent. Most zoologists would be quite willing to admit that large unidentified marine creatures may exist—perhaps, as in the case of the coelacanth, even survivors from primeval times. And if they are still around, one day we should be able to prove it.

—Arthur C. Clarke

In hindsight, perhaps it shouldn't be a total surprise that we found Jonathan. Myths of sea monsters have been with us for a long time, after all: the kraken, which some marine scientists believe may be based upon sightings of giant squid—themselves once only a legend—by Scandinavian sailors, and the worm Uroboros, which the ancient Greeks said was a serpent so long that it wrapped its tail entirely around the world. Similarly, the Norse had Jormungard, which was essentially Uroboros in Viking disguise, whereas the Muslims had the zaratan, which also shows up in medieval Anglo-Saxon literature. During the last century, there was Nessie, which the Scots

held onto as a major tourist attraction even after it was
debunked as a clever hoax perpetrated by a local physi-
cian and a couple of schoolboys; meanwhile, *Jaws* continued to frighten Americans until the last of the Great
Whites was hunted into extinction.

All these creatures were great, formidable monsters
with razor-sharp teeth and insatiable appetites, who
struck without warning or provocation, assaulting hapless
vessels and taking screaming sailors in their coils to the
icy depths below. Yet the more humankind explored the
oceans, the fewer of these leviathans we tended to find,
until all that was left was half-remembered folklore and
quaint sea chanties, plus the occasional Hollywood horror
movie. Even orca finally managed to live down their rep
as killer whales—unless, of course, penguins and seals
are polled for their opinions—and humpbacks and sperm
whales elicited more sympathy than fear.

Perhaps it's only appropriate that when we did finally
discover a bona fide sea monster, it took a form appropriate for the 21st century.

You've got to remember the way things stood on April
15, 2024, when Jack Hughes and I discovered Jonathan.
Nautilus had been established only two years earlier by
AquaCorp, and already the company was losing a ton of
money. Sure, the tourist trade was good—every week,
another cruise ship sailed into harbor and deposited a few
hundred vacationers on the artificial island—but that was
the only enterprise in the colony that was making signif-
icant returns on the $10 billion investment. Our compet-
itors on the Pacific Rim were undercutting the fishing
trade by selling their catches at cost, and the Japanese
fish-farms were socking it to everyone else. The trans-
atlantic tunnel project had been postponed indefinitely
after the loss of the Grand Banks drilling platform, so
the company had just laid off a hundred and twenty-five
people from the R&D division.

Since BlueSeas was still fighting the tunnel in federal

court, trying to shut it down entirely by litigating it to death, what little profits AquaCorp earned from Nautilus were being devoured by overhead costs and lawyers. As a result, the colony wasn't generating revenue fast enough for the stockholders who had sunk billions into creating an artificial cay three miles off the coast of Cape Hatteras. Some of the major investors were already beginning to talk about jumping ship, or island, whatever.

However, the company was still squeezing marginal profits out of its undersea mining operations. Although most of AquaCorp's marine mines were located on the Continental Shelf, where teleoperated robots and manned mobile platforms dredged the metalliferous ooze six-hundred and fifty feet below the surface, this was the less profitable aspect of the company's mining operations. For each ton of nickel, iron, or silicon that the company produced from the shelf, though, about a hundred tons of organic sediment had to be dredged and filtered; this meant that the shallow-ocean operations barely broke even most of the time.

The real money lay much farther down, in the depths of the Atlantic Basin at the bottom of the Continental Slope, fourteen thousand feet below the surface. Down there, in the cold pitch darkness, lay the mother lode: manganese nodules, potato-shaped deposits of manganese veined with trace amounts of copper, nickel, cobalt, and various other heavy metals. Unlike the metalliferous ooze, the nodules could be easily scoured from the ocean floor by robotic harvesters teleoperated from Nautilus.

Did I say "easily?" Nothing was easy about deep-sea mining, particularly not at such extreme depths, where the pressure could crush a mini-sub like an empty beer can. No one ventured down there unless it was absolutely necessary. They say outer space is the most hostile environment known to man, but I'd prefer to be a lunar miner with a slow leak in his hardsuit than an aquanaut whose bathyscaphe has developed a crack in its hull. The astronaut, at least, has a half-decent chance of survival, if he or she reacts quickly enough. An aquanaut in a similar predicament beneath the Continental Slope not only doesn't have a prayer, he or she doesn't even have a chance to utter one before their vehicle implodes.

Yet, on that particular day, Jack and I took a bathyscaphe down the slope, if only because we needed to find out what had happened to Porky Pig. Porky was one of the two teleoperated harvesters that prowled the bottom, scooping up nodules and shooting them up the lift pipe to the refinery raft. The day before, Porky had suddenly stopped moving; although its drivers continued to receive telemetry, the enormous machine couldn't be budged from its last known location, and the only thing coming up the pipe was salt water—clean saltwater, which in-dicated that its scoops were no longer in contact with the sea bed.

We had no idea what could have caused Porky to cease operations abruptly. Seismometers on the shelf hadn't registered any major seaquakes—themselves unlikely in this part of the North Atlantic—and Porky's twin, Elmer Fudd, was still gobbling up nodules only a couple of miles away. Jack could have done the job himself, but it had been several months since I had last made a deep-dive, and I wanted a first-hand look at the manganese field AquaCorp was presently mining to make sure that it wasn't beginning to run dry. When something like that happens, it's always the marine geology division that gets the blame; as the department head, I was the guy wearing the noose.

Anyway, we followed Porky's tube down the slope, Jack in the pilot's chair while I lay on my belly below him behind the observation window, watching as the bathyscaphe floodlights attempted to penetrate the dark-ness. All I could see was the pale bioluminescence of tiny octopi and gape-jawed angler fish, and even they presently vanished as we reached depths where only the simplest of life forms could survive the intense pressure.

We found Porky just where the VR geeks said it would be. Incredibly, the massive machine was up-ended on one side, its caterpillar treads and trough-like scoops completely clear of the sea floor. The harvester looked as though it had run over a large object and tipped to one side, yet there were no boulders or seamounts in sight.

As Jack slowly orbited the harvester, I noticed a wide, shallow furrow running through the silt. For a few moments, I thought it had been made by Porky itself, until I realized that it was both wider and deeper than the tracks left behind by the machine, nor did it have the serrated edges of the harvester tracks. The furrow came up from behind Porky, and then it went on again, heading into the darkness on a straight line that, when I checked the compass bearing, led due west toward the slope.

I asked Jack to follow the trail. Intrigued as much as I, he readily complied, keeping a low altitude above the ocean bed as he piloted the bathyscaphe as though he were following a runway—which, indeed, the furrow vaguely resembled under the dim, greenish glow of the floodlights.

We had followed the furrow for seven and a half miles, and Jack had just warned me that we were getting close to the Slope, when the forward sonar began to ping. Jack throttled back the props; when it became apparent that something very large was just in front of us, he raised altitude until the ocean floor disappeared. Perhaps we had found a long-lost World War II U-boat, or even a small freighter that had gone down during a storm in the past few decades. In any case, he didn't want to risk ramming it, yet just as we were beginning to wonder why we hadn't spotted the debris field customary of deep-ocean wrecks, Jack hauled back hard on the yoke.

I slid backward on my stomach as the bathyscaphe nosed upward. I was still yelling obscenities when Jack leveled off again. When I looked up at him, he was hastily checking the atmosphere gauges; he later told me that he thought he was suffering nitrogen narcosis.

By then, I had scrambled back to the windows. For a moment, I saw nothing. Then the floodlights caught and held an immense hump of grey, freckled with dull orange spots, smooth and gently curved like a humongous blob of flesh that had been plopped down in front of us, featureless except for long, slender rills of skin that ran in parallel rows along the top of the curve. It seemed motionless at first, yet, despite the bathyscaphe's own forward momentum, it was soon apparent that this object was ponderously moving of its own accord.

Still unaware of what I was seeing, I triggered the still camera as Jack slowly maneuvered the bathyscaphe around the immense hump. Ten . . . twenty . . . thirty . . . forty . . . forty-seven feet passed as we followed the immense form from its tapering tail, across its vast bloated back, down to the scimitar-shaped head where a pair of long, hornlike antennae sprouted like a pair of slender prongs.

It was the size of a two-story house, and it was definitely a living organism.

"Oh, momma," Jack said when he completed our first pass over the abomination. "It's a goddamn slug."

Nobody would have believed us if we hadn't produced a picture—and even after Jack and I showed the disk to about a dozen people, most of them still refused to buy our story. Neither of us had reputations as practical jokers, though, and once the bio lab's photo analysis department returned a verdict that the pictures had definitely not been faked, the senior marine zoologist hauled Jack back to his bathyscaphe almost as soon as he had decompressed from his last dive.

Dr. Chang re-emerged from the sub some six hours later with eyes as large as the slug itself. Although this time the creature had hidden itself by squirting a cloud of ink from glands beneath its fins, Chang had managed to get a few more pictures of the mollusk. He spent his time in the decomp chamber huddled over a computer terminal, trading data over the 'net with some colleagues at Woods Hole.

Together, they reached the conclusion that the "Hughes-Sheldon Midatlantic Anomaly"—or *Gastropoda horribilis*, to use the zoological name they concocted—was indeed a giant sea slug.

Duh. I could have told them that.

Chang instructed the rest of his division and everyone else who had seen the pictures to keep a lid on the discovery, but they should have known better. Nautilus has a permanent population of just over fifteen hundred people; just as in any small town, gossip travels fast, and the satellite dishes on the arcology's roof aren't there for show. Less than twenty-four hours after Jack and I found the creature, several dozen reporters had already called Nautilus's public relations office, and another handful were stepping off the helipad.

I don't recall which journalist first came up with the name "Jonathan Livingstone Seaslug." Someone with a good memory for obscure twentieth-century pop lit and a bad taste in puns. Once dubbed, though, Hughes-Sheldon disappeared without a trace and J. S. Seaslug was born. Just as well; I didn't particularly relish having my name permanently associated with a giant slug.

Not that it mattered. As soon as the first members of the Fourth Estate stormed the concrete beaches of our artificial cay, I was subjected to a ceaseless round of interviews. Although I'm a geologist by trade, Chang didn't want to meet the press, and Jack found reasons to be absent whenever someone wanted a first-hand account of the initial discovery. The press office kept sending the news hacks my way, and I soon found myself in the role as Jonathan's ombudsman.

To be fair, many of the reporters asked reasonably in-

telligent questions. However, the majority tended to pose
queries of the "how did you feel?" variety. After the
first several descriptions of surprise and awe, I lapsed into
a prefabricated spiel until, upon the umpteenth time
someone asked me how I felt, I replied, "Like I just saw
a giant slug" and walked away. After that, the chief press
liaison answered all the questions; I told him it was time
he started earning his paycheck.

Almost every reporter wanted to go down below to
take a look at Jonathan himself; when they were refused,
two or three attempted outright bribery. Even if Jack or
I had been so inclined to fatten our bank accounts,
though, it would have been at the expense of our jobs;
Miles Van Der Horst, Nautilus's general manager, de-
clared Jonathan off-limits to all dives except those whose
orders he had personally countersigned. In addition, we
were careful not to disclose the precise coordinates of
where we had found Jonathan. This was just as well,
because there were quite a few freelance deep-ocean
prospectors on the mainland who would have been only
too willing to lease their craft to the press.

There's little point in rehashing the ten-day sensation
Jonathan caused. After the first few headline stories and
breathless TV news features, Jonathan became the perfect
timely metaphor for every pundit, talk-show host, and
standup comedian on the planet. For a while I collected
political cartoons that showed the face of one elected
official or another superimposed on Jonathan's body. The
t-shirts featuring the beast were a fad that was just as
mercifully short-lived . . . and I'll wipe the deck with the
next person who cracks an escargot joke in my presence.

The low point occurred when a pseudo-scientific crank
by the name of Peter Goudge made wild claims that Jonathan was the harbinger of an "invasion from inner
space." Trotting out that lame old horse, the Bermuda
Triangle, Goudge took the public stage to attest that Jonathan was a bioengineered juggernaut sent up from the

deepest reaches of the Atlantic by some advanced civilization bent on global conquest. Naturally, he wanted the U.S. Navy to drop nuclear depth-charges on the monster.

He was countered by a group of quasi-religious fanatics called the Church of Harmonic Convergence, who believed that Jonathan was an emissary from an aquatic species hiding out in the Caymen Trench. This undersea super-race—which, the Church carefully pointed out, bore no relationship to that undersea super-race—had sent a giant sea slug to teach the human race the error of its scientific-materialist, male-dominant, warmongering ways. They went so far as to charter a yacht out of Cape Hatteras to take them out to the edge of the shelf, where they unwittingly dropped anchor seven miles from where Jonathan had been located. According to reports, they then huddled together on the aft deck for the next two days, where they fasted, got nasty sunburns, and became seasick while they attempted to establish telepathic communion with the slug.

The only bright spot in the whole affair was that a hypertext publisher, knowing a good business opportunity when it saw one, rushed into print John Wyndam's 1952 classic *Up From the Deeps*. The novel had nothing to do with Jon, but at least a great story was rescued from oblivion; the publisher downloaded more than a million copies in less than a month.

In the midst of all the hoopla, Dr. Chang and his cohorts quietly continued to study *Gastropoda horribilis*. Safe from the limelight, they sent bathyscaphes down to the Atlantic Basin, where they watched Jonathan from a discreet distance.

At first, they were able to sneak up on Jonathan until the slug, now wise to the approach of a bathyscaphe, ejected its dense ink fog at the first sound of props. They then kept track of its progress with surface sonar, until someone noticed that the creature would remain absolutely motionless during sonar contacts; apparently, like so many other sea creatures, Jon navigated by means of its own internal sonar.

Afraid of confusing Jonathan, Chang ordered an end to sonar spying. Several days later, the next bathyscaphe to visit the slug managed to get close enough to attach an extra-low frequency homing device to its skin. In doing so, the research team discovered something new: as soft and blubbery as Jonathan's flesh appeared to be, it was actually as tough as elephant hide. Except for the usual ink-cloud, though, Jonathan barely seemed to notice the bathyscaphe's presence. It simply continued its unswerving westward crawl across the ocean floor.

The homing device in place, Chang's team set out to learn as much about Jonathan as it possibly could . . . and damned little that was indeed. Where did it come from? Somewhere deep in the Atlantic, but its trail eroded only a few miles after the creature left it behind, leaving no clues to its exact place of origin. How did it breath? Through sets of gills near its head. What did it eat? Any organic detritus on its path; it avoided manganese nodules, but greedily devoured the scum on the seafloor. What did it excrete? A long trail of slime. Was it male of female? No one could tell for sure. Did it have any natural predators? Except for a few tiny squid clinging to its flanks like remora, none to be seen; it existed in a realm far removed from that of sharks, barracuda, or giant squid, and for all anyone knew it could be hundreds of years old. Who did it think would win the World Series? The Red Sox, probably, although the Braves' outfield was looking particularly strong this season . . .

Yet the two biggest questions—where was it going, and were there any more like it back home—were not answered until Jonathan reached the edge of the Continental Shelf. Those who believed that the creature, once confronted with the mammoth bluff, would simply turn around and go back the way it came were astonished when Jonathan, without any apparent hesitation, began to climb up the steep cliff.

For one reason for another, Jonathan was heading for the submarine domain of humankind.

When Jonathan's ELF beacon showed that it was scaling the Continental Shelf, no one believed it was possible. After all, the creature was estimated to weigh in excess of ten tons, perhaps more. It was incredible that it could move in the first place, let alone climb a near-vertical wall. Surely the transmitter itself was malfunctioning— yet when Jack and I took a bathyscaphe down to check on our friend's progress, we saw Jonathan gamely clinging to the rugged slope like a snail within a tropical fish tank, inching its way upward with the same patient, inexorable progress.

Many thought that Jonathan would perish from the decreased pressure, yet as it slowly ascended from the depths, we observed that it stopped from time to time, apparently not only to rest but also to acclimate itself to the pressure differential. The rest periods would last from a few minutes to several hours, then the slug would continue upward another fifty to a hundred feet before it paused again. The gradual change in thermocline didn't seem to affect it, although we noted that the orange freckles on its hide seemed to diminish in number and size.

Jonathan's slow, meticulous journey took two days, during which time all hell was breaking loose on the surface.

Despite the news blackout, word of Jonathan's ascent soon reached the ears and pens of the news media, which wasted no time in blabbing it to the world. Naturally, the lunatic fringe claimed the latest development as proof of their pet theories; while Peter Goudge stepped up his demands for a full-scale attack upon Atlantis, the Church of Harmonic Convergence staged a press conference, stating that the day of universal peace and truth was at hand and that the slug was the new messiah come forth. Both sides made a few more bucks through calls to their 1-900 numbers; Goudge's latest tract made the online bestseller list, and Church leaders staged mass meditations across the East Coast, where dozens of believers flocked to achieve "group-mind symbiosis" with a mollusk.

Fanaticism aside, though, there was genuine concern about what might occur if and when Jonathan made it to the top of the slope and entered the Continental Shelf. It was out of the question that it would eventually make its way to dry land—Jon was strictly aquatic, as evidenced by its gills—but according to the position of its radio beacon and the beeline course it had made thus far, it seemed certain that the creature would move straight into AquaCorp's offshore mining area. There was a lot of valuable equipment scattered across the shelf, including the immobile intake ducts of the hydrothermal energy plants that supplied energy to a large portion of the eastern seaboard. We had already seen what Jon could do to a five-ton mining robot, and Porky wasn't much larger than some of the hardware that lay in its path.

That fact wasn't lost on the media. When asked about it by a reporter from the *Times,* though, Miles Van Der Horst made a serious mistake: he claimed that AquaCorp would do whatever was necessary to protect its capital investments, even if that included "warding off" the creature through unspecified means.

He was alluding to conversations he had already had with Nautilus's Barracuda squadron. Established as the colony's first-line defense team against everything from sharks to pirates, the Barracuda subs were equipped with low-yield torpedoes and electrical wands; it had been Van Der Horst's idea to send out the Barracudas if Jonathan got too close to any of the mining operations. The general manager didn't want to harm Jonathan, just deter it from wreaking havoc. In fact, because several commercial fishermen were openly discussing tuna nets to trap the creature—remember the escargot jokes?—Van Der Horst had already told the Barracudas to use force if necessary to prevent Jonathan from winding up as the catch of the day in so many French restaurants.

However, when BlueSeas read his injudicious remarks, it screamed bloody murder. Hell hath no fury like an environmental activist on a crusade. BlueSeas charged that AquaCorp intended to destroy this unique and valuable species. Within hours, one of their boats was dispatched from Cape Hatteras, its crew bound and determined to stop Jonathan from being molested by evil ecocapitalists. Because Jonathan was still some two thousand feet underwater, the *Rainbow Octopus* was only a minor nuisance, yet the organization's lawyers wasted no time in trying to get a North Carolina federal judge to place an injunction against AquaCorp, preventing any company subs from approaching within a thousand feet of the slug.

Even if the judge hadn't laughed BlueSeas out of his office, the bad publicity they created for AquaCorp was a PR nightmare. Although Van Der Horst publicly recanted by stating that the Barracudas would stay away from Jonathan, the perception was that Nautilus intended to fire torpedoes at the poor, defenseless sea creature if it so much as poked an antenna over the top of the shelf.

Once again, the press office was besieged by reporters . . . and when the press releases wouldn't work their magic, I was drafted back into being the official spokesman.

After all, I was one of the men who had found Jonathan. I was a scientist. Aren't scientists supposed to know everything? The fact that I was a geologist was lost on everyone. Reluctantly, I did another round of press conferences and interviews, during which I reiterated the company line: Jonathan would not be harmed, Jonathan would not be killed, Jonathan was a unique creature, and

AquaCorp would allow it to go unmolested wherever it damned well pleased.

After two days of renewed hysteria, though, I was beginning to wonder myself how a two-inch thick filet of escargot would taste. It wasn't like we were arguing over fishing rights to Flipper, for chrissakes. This was a goddamn slug. Didn't we have more important things to worry about? No one had paid much attention to Nautilus between the time it was built and before Jonathan appeared, even though the colony was at the vanguard of human progress. Suddenly, a sea monster appears, and everyone goes bananas.

I was beginning to resent the intrusion. Let the goddamned thing come up here and die; that was the leading theory, and I was only too willing to accept it. Let it end its natural cycle of life by dying in coastal waters; the fish could gnaw its carcass to the bones, if it had any, and then we could return to business as usual. To hell with it.

But I kept my mouth shut, because I was on company time, and finally the PR counteroffensive seemed to work. The media finally backed off . . . but just to be on the safe side, though, AquaCorp assigned me to pilot the only minisub that would be permitted to go near Jonathan once it entered the shelf. The press wanted someone on live camera to narrate Jon's grand entrance, and because I was now Mr. Trustworthy, I was picked for the job.

I was still bitching about it when, twenty hours later, Jonathan reached the edge of the Continental Shelf.

I was not alone in the sub as I followed Jonathan across the shallow sea bed. A few million people were in the vehicle with me, watching through satellite TV linkup, while I piloted the tiny vehicle at a safe distance from the creature.

I don't remember most of what I said; my concentration was wholly focused upon the controls, and I had to be prompted several times to keep up a running narrative. In any event, it happened this way:

Jonathan moved for a mile and a half along the shelf on a due West course. Most of the mining equipment had been relocated, but Jon still managed to capsize a hydrothermal plant, which in turn caused a temporary brownout in a large portion of New Jersey. For a while, I wondered if the slug would indeed attempt to beach itself on Cape Hatteras, and then. . . .

Jonathan stopped.

For the next hour and thirty minutes, it remained almost motionless. As I orbited the creature, all my sub's floodlights could pick out were the slow, labored movement of its gills, an occasional ripple that passed along its flanks, the occasional tremble of its antenna. Curious fish approached, then darted away; at one point, a distant shark pack started to home in, but it was quickly scattered by a Barracuda sub that had been covertly dispatched to the area.

Four hundred feet above, the *Rainbow Octopus* held position, its protesters waving banners for passing helicopters to see. On the shore, the Church of Harmonic Convergence sat in a circle, meditating until their brains began to boil. The TV audience channel-surfed between me, Peter Goudge, and a lot of reruns of old sitcoms; through my headset, Dr. Chang asked ceaseless questions that I could seldom answer.

But down there . . .

Down there, we were at peace, Jonathan and I, isolated from an air-breathing world that seemed to have lost its collective mind. For a few precious minutes, I switched off the comlink, and then it was just the two of us. Through the hydrophones, I thought, for a fleeting moment, I could hear it singing, like the whale songs sailors sometimes hear on the open sea.

But, of course, I could be wrong. Whales sing; sea slugs do not. . . .

In those few minutes, I forgot my resentment and remembered the wonder I had experienced the first time I had seen the creature. Yes, it was a mammoth slug—stupid, brainless, primitive, revulsive, all that and more—yet it was an alien form of life, far older than I, awesome not only in its dimensions but also in the unfathomable instincts that had driven it to this place, against all odds. It was less of an abomination than a force of nature, and for better or worse I had become its consort.

In its own way—dare I say it?—it was beautiful.

And then, abruptly, a dense cloud of ink ejected from Jonathan's dorsal area, and the creature seemed to thrash about, stirring up silt that, together with the dark purple ink, obscured my vision. I hovered nearby, reporting everything I could until the currents swept the ink away and the sand settled, and when everything was calm once more, all our questions were finally answered.

Jonathan is gone now. It—or rather, she—has returned to the trackless depths from which she came, crawling back down the Continental Slope to the depths. We have no way of knowing where she came from, because the ELF radio beacon finally failed, crushed by the extreme pressure of the nigh bottomless gulf of the Atlantic Basin.

The only thing that remains is the legacy she left behind: eight eggs, each the size of a small car, smooth and spherical, dark blue like the summer sky she never saw. They lay half-buried in a shallow trench, warmed by the subtropical currents that she instinctively sought out in her long pregnancy. Perhaps only once every century or two, she makes the arduous climb up the vast slope, searching for the single place where an intuitive compass tells her they will be safe. It matters little if her nest is now surrounded by aliens and weird machines; here the eggs will remain untouched until the time comes.

And so it will be. I'm now the guardian of Jonathan's eggs. The company has relieved me of all other duties;

the geoscience division continues to operate in my absence. Besides, AquaCorp is making a mint out of the publicity. BlueSeas has finally dropped its lawsuits, and I'm told that the TV-movie rights to my story fetched a few million bucks. Jack Hughes quit the company to become the technical advisor. I got a postcard from him last week, in fact; he's doing pretty well for himself, out in Los Angeles. I think his book will be a bestseller.

The company set up a small habitat on the ocean floor, just a few hundred feet from the nest. All the mining equipment has been cleared away from the area, and even the nearby hydrothermal plant has been permanently shut down. It's very quiet in this part of the ocean. Chang and a few other scientists come down for visits every once in a while, but otherwise I'm the only permanent resident. It's not that bad. I've got some books to read, I watch a lot of TV, and I have all the seafood I can eat.

We're down here alone, the eggs and I.

It's been ten months now, and they still haven't hatched. On the other hand, no one knows what their gestation time could be. In the meantime, I've learned to be a patient man.

When they're hatched, will eight giant slugs consider me their father?

INTRODUCTION:
"Doblin's Lecture"

So, the eternal question goes, where do you get your ideas?

From the newspaper, this author often replies.

It's no secret that Americans are fascinated with serial killers. You hate 'em, you love 'em, you can't get enough of 'em. Charles Manson wasn't the first, but he set the pace with the rampage he and his followers made through tony neighborhoods of L.A. more than twenty-five years ago; it wasn't long before two bestsellers and an oft-rerun TV mini-series followed. Thomas Harris created one of the best chain murderers in fiction with Hannibal Lecter, the featured character of *Red Dragon* and *The Silence of the Lambs*, and bestseller lists haven't suffered for lack of less accomplished imitators. It doesn't matter if it's *Psycho* or *Seven, Wait Until Dark* or *Copy Cat, The Texas Chainsaw Massacre III, Halloween V,* or hundreds of other high-or low-concept horror flicks: the man in the shadows, the glint of light on a blade, the trapped victim, that scream . . . you really like this shit, don't you?

Yet, this national obsession with society's worst creatures sometimes goes beyond filling a niche in popular culture; on occasion, people have to get a piece of the killer himself. John Wayne Gacy didn't only kill children; he also painted watercolors, a hobby he was allowed to continue in his cell on death row. Gacy's paintings, some of which featured clowns like the one he used to dress up as for kids' birthday parties, fetched enormous prices from collectors, and one appeared on the cover of a punk-rock album some years ago. Charles Manson was an aspiring songwriter before he founded the Family, and one of his songs was recorded by the Beach Boys. Guns 'N' Roses recently covered that song in their album *The Spaghetti Rebellion?* Manson himself has since released an acoustical album on a small label, recorded in the laundry room of the California state penitentiary where he's doing life.

But the weirdest revelation, the one that sparked this story, came from a small item that appeared in the *New York Times* in late 1993. According to the *Times*, Jeffery Dahmer had received nearly $30,000 after he had been sent to prison, all from private individuals who were apparently concerned for his well being. One of these contributions had been a check for $12,000; the same benefactor also sent Dahmer a Bible. The article quoted prison officials as saying that these funds had been deposited in a bank account, which Dahmer drew upon to purchase videotapes and comic books from mail-order firms.

When I read this in bed one Tuesday morning, I turned to Linda and told her that I was on the wrong track to fame and fortune, because Jeffery Dahmer was earning more money than I was. Why should I bust my ass producing science fiction stories for a measly six cents a word when I could kill a few people, get sent to prison, and write a bestseller about what I had done? Linda smiled and reminded me that New York State's "Son of Sam" law prohibits convicted felons from earning money from such publishing endeavors. "Oh, yeah, that's right,'' I said, then I stalked off to the bathroom to contemplate my current novel-in-progress in the shower.

Well, that's no longer an impediment to my career aspirations, because the New York State Supreme Court recently struck down the ''Son of Sam'' law as unconstitutional.

This is the darkest story in this collection. At first glance, it may not seem to be science fiction (and indeed, it's not hard SF, as it is usually defined); I classify it more as psychological horror than SF. Nonetheless, it's a ''what if . . .'' sort of story.

What if we gave these guys permission?

DOBLIN'S LECTURE

A crisp autumn night on a Midwestern university campus. A cool breeze, redolent of pine cones and coming winter, softly rustles bare trees and whisks dead leaves across the walkways leading to the main hall. Lights glow from within Gothic windows as a last handful of students and faculty members hurry toward the front entrance. There is to be a famous guest speaker tonight; no one wants to be late.

A handful of students pickets in the plaza outside the hall; some carry protest signs, others try to hand fliers to anyone who will take them. The yellow photocopies are taken and briefly read, then shoved into pockets or wadded up and tossed into waste cans; the signs are glanced at but largely ignored.

A poster taped above the open double doors states that absolutely no cameras, camcorders, or tape recorders are permitted inside. Just inside the doors, the crowd is funneled through a security cordon of off-duty police officers hired for the evening. They check campus IDs, open day packs, run chirping hand-held metal detectors across chests, arms, and legs. Anyone carrying metal objects larger or less innocent than key rings, eyeglasses, or ball-point pens is sent back outside. A trash can behind the guards is half filled with penknives, bottle openers, cig-arette lighters, and tear-gas dispensers, discarded by those who would rather part with them than rush them back to dorm rooms or cars and thereby risk missing the lecture. Seating is limited, and it's been announced that no one will be allowed to stand or sit in the aisles.

Two students, protesters from the campus organization opposed to tonight's presentation, are caught with cloth banners concealed under their jackets. They're escorted out the door by the cops, who dump their banners in the trash without reading them.

The auditorium holds 1,800 seats, and each one has been claimed. The stage is empty save for a podium off to one side and a stiff-backed oak armchair in its center. The chair's legs are securely bolted to the floor, its arm-rests equipped with metal shackles; loose belts dangle from its sides. Its vague resemblance to a prison electric chair is lost on no one.

Four state troopers stand quietly in the wings on either side of the stage. Several more are positioned in the back of the hall, their arms folded across their chests or their thumbs tucked into service belts carrying revolvers, tas-ers, and Mace canisters. More than a few people quietly remark that this is the first time in a long while that the auditorium has been filled to capacity without anyone smelling marijuana.

At ten minutes after eight, the house lights dim, and the room goes dark save for a pair of spotlights focused on the stage. The drone of voices fades away as the dean of the sociology department—a distinguished-looking ac-ademician in his early fifties, thin gray hair and humor-less eyes—steps from behind the curtain on stage left and quickly strides past the cops to the lectern.

The dean peeks at the index cards in his hand as he introduces himself, then spends a few moments informing the audience that tonight's speaker has been invited to the university not to provide entertainment, but primarily as a guest lecturer for Sociology 450, Sociology 510, and Sociology 525. His students, occupying treasured seats in the first six rows, try not to preen too much as they open their notebooks and click their pens. They're the chosen few, the ones who are here to learn something; the professor squelches their newfound self-importance by reminding them that their papers on tonight's lecture are due Tuesday by ten o'clock.

The professor then tells the audience that no comments or questions will be permitted during the guest speaker's opening remarks and that anyone who interrupts the lecture in any way will be escorted from the hall and possibly be placed under arrest. This causes a minor stir in the audience, which the dean smoothly placates by adding that a short question-and-answer session will be held later, during which members of the audience may be allowed to ask questions, if time and circumstances permit.

Now the dean looks uncomfortable. He glances uneasily at his cards as if it's faculty poker night and he's been dealt a bad hand. After the guest speaker has made his remarks, he adds (a little more softly now, and with no little hesitance), and once the Q & A session is over, there may be a special demonstration. If time and circumstances permit.

The background noise rises again. Murmurs, whispers, a couple of muted laughs; quick sidelong glances, raised or furrowed eyebrows, dark frowns, a few smiles hastily covered by hands. The cops on stage remain stoical, but one can detect random shifts of eyes darting this way and that.

The dean knows that he doesn't need to introduce the guest speaker, for his reputation has preceded him and any further remarks he might make would be trivial at best, foolish at worst. Instead, he simply turns and starts to walk off the stage.

Then he stops. For the briefest instant there is a look of bafflement—and indeed, naked fear—on his face as he catches a glimpse of something just past the curtains in the left wing. Then he turns and walks, more quickly now, the opposite way, until he disappears past the two police officers on stage right.

A moment of dead silence. Then Charles Gregory Doblin walks out on stage.

He's a big man—six feet and a couple of inches, with the solid build of someone who has spent most of his life doing heavy labor and only recently has put on weight—but his face, though brutal at first sight, is nonetheless kindly and oddly adolescent, like that of a grown-up who never let go of some part of his childhood. The sort of person whom one could easily imagine dressing up as Santa on Christmas Eve to take toys to a homeless shelter and who would delight in playing horsey for the kids, or on any day would help jump start your car or assist an elderly neighbor with her groceries. Indeed, when he was arrested several years ago in another city and charged with the murders of nineteen young black men, the people who lived around him in their white middle-class neighborhood believed that the police had made a serious mistake.

That was until FBI agents found the severed ears of his victims preserved in Mason jars in his basement, and his confession led them to nineteen unmarked graves.

Now here he is: Charles Gregory Doblin, walking slowly across the stage, a manila file folder tucked under his arm.

He wears a blue prison jumpsuit and is followed closely by a state trooper holding a riot stick, but otherwise he could be a sports hero, a noted scientist, a bestselling author. A few people automatically begin to clap, then apparently realize that this is one time when applause is not warranted and let their hands fall back into their laps. Some frat boys in the back whistle their approval, and one of them yells something about killing niggers, before three police officers—two of whom, not coincidentally, are black—descend on them. They've been led out the door even before Charles Gregory Doblin has taken his seat; if the killer has heard them, there is nothing in his face to show it.

Indeed, there is nothing in his face at all. If the audience had expected the dark gaze that had met a news photographer's camera when he was led into a federal courthouse on the day of his arraignment four years ago—a shot engraved in collective memory, cut lined "Eyes of a Killer"—they don't see it. If they had anticipated the beatific look of the self-ascribed born-again Christian interviewed on *60 Minutes* and *Prime Time Live* in the past year, they don't see that, either.

The killer's face is without expression. A sheet of blank paper. A calm and empty sea. A black hole in the center of a distant galaxy. Void. Cold. Vacant.

The killer takes his seat in the hard wooden chair. The state trooper hands him a cordless microphone before taking his position behind the chair. The arm restraints are left unfastened; the belts remain limp. Long moments pass as he opens the manila folder in his lap, then Charles Gregory Doblin—there is no way anyone here can think of him as Charlie Doblin, as his neighbors once did, or Chuck, as his late parents called him, or as Mr. Dobbs, as nineteen teenagers did in their last hours of life; it's the full name, as written in countless newspaper stories, or nothing else—Charles Gregory Doblin begins to speak.

His voice is very soft; it holds a slightly grating Northeastern accent, high-pitched now, with barely-concealed nervousness, but otherwise it's quite pleasant. A voice for bedtime stories or even pillow-talk with a lover, although by all accounts Charles Gregory Doblin had remained a virgin during the thirty-six years he spent as a free man. He quietly thanks the university for inviting him here to speak this evening and even earns a chuckle from the audience when he praises the cafeteria staff for the bowl of chili and the grilled cheese sandwich that he had for dinner backstage. He doesn't know that the university cafeteria is infamous for its food, and he could not possibly be aware that three cooks spat in his chili just before it was delivered to the auditorium.

Then he begins to read aloud from the six sheets of single-spaced typewritten paper in his lap. It's a fairly long speech, the delivery slightly monotone, but his diction is practiced and nearly perfect. He tells of childhood in an abusive family: an alcoholic mother who commonly referred to him as a little shit and a racist father who beat him for no real reason. He tells of often having eaten canned dog food for dinner, heated in a pan on a hibachi in the bathroom, because his parents could afford nothing better, and of going to school in a slum neighborhood where other kids made fun of him because of his size and the adolescent lisp that he didn't completely overcome until he was well into adulthood.

He describes the afternoon when he was attacked by three black teenagers who beat him without mercy only because he was a big, dumb, white kid who had the misfortune of shortcutting through their alley on the way home from school. His voice remains steady as he relates how his father gave him another, even more savage, beating that same evening, because he had allowed some niggers to get the better of him.

Charles Gregory Doblin tells of a lifelong hatred for black people that became ever more obsessive as he became an adult: the brief involvement with the Klan and the Brotherhood of Aryan Nations before bailing out of the white supremacy movement in the belief that they were all rhetoric and no action; learning how some soldiers in Vietnam used to collect the ears of the gooks they had killed; the night nine years ago when, on impulse, he pulled over on his way home from work at an electronics factory to give a lift to a sixteen-year-old black kid thumbing a ride home.

Now the audience stirs. Legs are uncrossed, crossed again over the other knee. Hands guide pens across paper. Eighteen hundred pairs of eyes peer through the darkness at the man on the stage.

The auditorium is dead silent as the killer reads the names of the nineteen teenagers that he murdered during the course of five years. Besides being black and living in black neighborhoods scattered across the same major city, there are few common denominators among his victims. Some were street punks, one was a sidewalk crack dealer, and two were homeless kids looking for handouts, but he also murdered a high school basketball star, a National Merit Scholarship winner recently accepted by Yale, a rapper wannabe who sang in his church choir, an aspiring comic book artist, and a fifteen-year-old boy supporting his family by working two jobs after school. All had the misfortune of meeting and getting into a conversation with an easygoing white dude who had money for dope, beer, or pizza; they had followed him into an alley or a parked car or some other out-of-the-way place, then made the mistake of letting Mr. Dobbs step behind them for one brief, fatal moment . . . until the night one kid managed to escape.

The audience listens as he says that he is sorry for the evil that he has done, as he explains that he was criminally insane at the time and didn't know what he was doing. They allow him to quote from the Bible, and some even bow their heads as he offers a prayer for the souls of those he has murdered.

Charles Gregory Doblin then closes the folder and sits quietly, hands folded across his stomach, ankles crossed, head slightly bowed with his eyes in shadow. After a few moments, the dean comes back out on stage; taking his position behind the lectern, he announces that it is now time for the Q & A session.

The first question comes from a nervous young girl in third row center: she timidly raises her hand and, after the dean acknowledges her, asks the killer if he has any remorse for his crimes. Yes, he says. She waits for him to continue; when he doesn't, she sits down again.

The next question is from a black student farther back in the audience. He stands and asks Charles Gregory Doblin if he killed those nineteen kids primarily because they were black or simply because they reminded him of the teenagers who had assaulted him. Again, Charles Gregory Doblin only says yes. The student asks the killer if he would have murdered him because he is black, and John Gregory Doblin replies that, yes, he probably would have. Would you kill me now? No, I would not. The student sits down and scribbles a few notes.

More hands rise from the audience; one by one, the dean lets students pose their questions. Has he seen the made-for-TV movie based on his crimes? No, he hasn't; there isn't a television in the maximum security ward of the prison, and he wasn't told about the movie until after it was aired. Did he read the book? No, he hasn't, but he's been told that it was a bestseller. Has he met any members of the families of his victims? Not personally, aside from spotting them in the courtroom during his trial. Have any of them attempted to contact him? He has received a few letters, but aside from the one from the mother who sent him a Bible, he hasn't been allowed to read any correspondence from the families. What does he do in prison? Read the Bible he was sent, paint, and pray. What does he paint? Landscapes, birds, the inside of his cell. If he could live his life all over again, what would he do differently? Become a truck driver, maybe a priest. Is he receiving a lecture fee from this visit? Yes, but most of it goes into a trust fund for the families of his victims, with the rest going to the state for travel expenses.

All this time, his gaze remains centered on a space between his knees, as if he is reading from an invisible Teleprompter. It is not until an aesthetic-looking young man in the tenth row asks him, in a rather arch voice, whether he received any homoerotic gratification when he committed the murders—an erection, perhaps? perhaps a fleeting vision of his father?—does Charles Gregory Doblin raise his eyes to meet those of his questioner. He stares silently at the pale young man for a long, long time but says nothing until the student sits down again.

An uncomfortable hush follows this final question; no more hands are raised. The dean breaks the silence by announcing that the Q & A session is now over. He then glances at one of the guards standing in the wings, who gives him a slight nod. There will be a brief fifteen-minute intermission, the dean continues, then the program will resume. He hesitates, then adds that because it will include a demonstration that may be offensive to members of the audience, this might be a good time for those people to leave.

Charles Gregory Doblin rises from his chair. Still refraining from looking directly at the crowd, he lets the state trooper escort him offstage. A few people in the auditorium clap self-consciously, then seldom-used gray curtains slide across the stage.

When the curtains part again fifteen minutes later, only a handful of seats in the auditorium are vacant. The one in the center of the stage is not.

A tall, skinny young black man is seated in the chair that Charles Gregory Doblin has kept warm for him. He wears a prison jumpsuit similar to the one worn by his predecessor, and his arms are shackled to the armrests, his body secured to the chair frame by the leather belts that had hung slack earlier. The same state trooper stands behind him, but this time his riot stick is in plain view, grasped in both hands before him.

The prisoner's eyes are cold searchlights that sweep across the audience. No one can meet his gaze without feeling revulsion. He catches sight of the young woman in the third row who had asked a question earlier in the evening; their eyes meet for a few seconds, and the prisoner's lips curl upward in a predatory smile. He starts to mutter an obscenity, but shuts up when the state trooper places the end of his stick on his shoulder. The girl squirms in her seat and looks away.

The dean returns to the lectern and introduces the young black man. His name is Curtis Henry Blum; he is twenty-two years old, born and raised in this same city. Blum committed his first felony offense when he was twelve years old, when he was arrested for selling crack in the school playground; he was already a gang member by then. Since then, he has been in and out of juvenile detention centers, halfway houses, and medium security prisons, and has been busted for mugging, narcotics, car jacking, breaking and entering, armed robbery, rape, attempted murder. Sometimes he was convicted and sent to one house of corrections or another; sometimes he was sentenced on lesser charges and served a shorter term; sometimes he was just let go for lack of evidence. Each occasion he was sent up, he spent no more than eighteen months before being paroled or furloughed and thrown back on the street.

Nineteen months ago, Curtis Blum held up a convenience store on the city's north side, one owned and operated by a South Korean immigrant family. Blum held mother, father, and teenage daughter at gun point while he cleaned out the cash register and tucked two bottles of fortified wine into his pockets. The family knelt on the floor and begged him to be merciful and just leave, but he shot them anyway, along with an eleven-year-old kid from the hood who had been sent out by his mother to buy some cat food and beer and had the misfortune of walking through the door just as Blum was going out. He didn't want to leave any witnesses, or maybe he simply felt like killing people tonight.

A police SWAT team found Blum at his grandmother's house two days later. He wasn't hard to find; although by then he had bragged to everyone he knew about how he had capped three slants the night before, it was his grandmother who had called the cops. She also testified at her grandson's trial six months later, saying that he regularly robbed and beat her.

Curtis Blum was convicted on four counts of second-degree murder. This time, he faced a judge who didn't believe in second chances; he sentenced Blum to death. Since then, he has been filling in time on death row in the state's maximum security prison.

The dean steps from behind the lectern and walks over to where the prisoner is seated. He asks Blum if he has any questions. Blum asks him if the girl in the third row wants to fuck. The dean says nothing. He simply turns and walks away, vanishing once again behind the curtains on stage left.

Curtis laughs out loud, then looks again at the woman in the third row and asks her directly if she wants to fuck. She starts to get up to leave, which Blum misinterprets as willingness to conjugate; even as he assails her with more obscenities, though, another female student grasps her arm and whispers something to her. The girl stops, glances again at the stage, and then sits back down. This time, she has a slight smile on her face, for now she sees something that Blum doesn't.

Curtis is about to shout something else at the girl when a shadow falls over him. He glances up, and finds himself looking into the face of Charles Gregory Doblin.

Killing a man is actually a very easy thing to do, if you know how. There're several simple ways that this can be accomplished that don't require knives or guns, or even garrote wires or sharp objects. You don't even have to be very strong.

All you need are your bare hands and a little bit of hate.

The dry crack of Curtis Blum's neck being snapped follows the students as they shuffle out of the auditorium. It's a cold wind, harsher than the one that blows dry leaves across the plaza outside the main hall, that drives them back to dormitories and apartments.

No one will sleep very well tonight. More than a few will waken from nightmares to find their sheets clammy with sweat, the sound of Blum's final scream still resonating in their ears. Wherever they may go for the rest of their lives, whatever they may do, they will never forget what they have witnessed this evening.

Fifteen years later, a sociology post-grad student at this same university, in the course of researching her doctoral thesis, will discover an interesting fact. Upon tracking down the students who were present at Charles Gregory Doblin's lecture and interviewing them or their surviving relatives, she will find that virtually none of them has ever been arrested on a felony offense, and not one was ever investigated or charged with spousal or child abuse, statistics far below the national average for a population of similar age and social background.

Yet that is still in the future. This is the present:

In a small dressing room behind the stage, Charlie Doblin—no longer Charles Gregory Doblin, but simply Charlie Doblin, Inmate #7891—sits in a chair before a makeup counter, hunched over the dog-eared Bible the mother of one his victims sent him several years ago. His lips move soundlessly as he reads words he does not fully comprehend but which help to give his life some meaning.

Behind him, a couple of state troopers smoke cigarettes

and quietly discuss tonight's lecture. Their guns and batons are holstered and ignored, for they know that the man in the room is utterly harmless. They wonder aloud how much vomit will have to be cleaned off the auditorium floor and whether the girl in the third row will later remember what she yelled when the big moment came. She sounded kinda happy, one cop says, and the other one shakes his head. No, he replies, I think she was pissed because she missed out on a great date.

They both chuckle, then notice that Charlie Doblin is silently peering over his shoulder at them. Shut up, asshole, one of them says, and Doblin returns his attention to his Bible.

A radio crackles. A trooper plucks the handset off his jacket epaulet, murmurs into it, listens for a moment. The van is waiting out back. The local cops are ready to escort them to the interstate. He nods to his companion, who turns to tell Charlie that it's time to go. The killer nods his head; he carefully marks his place in the Bible, then picks it up along with the speech that he read tonight.

He didn't write this speech, but he has dutifully read it many times already, and will read it again tomorrow night in another college auditorium, to a different audience in a different city. And, as always, he will end his lecture by becoming a public executioner.

Somewhere else tonight, another death-row inmate unwittingly awaits judgment for his crimes. He sits alone in his cell, playing solitaire or watching a sitcom on a TV on the other side of the bars, and perhaps smiles at the notion that, this time tomorrow, he will be taken out of the prison to some college campus to make a speech to a bunch of kids, unaware that what awaits him are the eyes and hands of Charles Gregory Doblin.

It's a role that Charlie Doblin once savored, then found morally repugnant, and finally accepted as predestination. He has no say over what he does; this is his fate, and, indeed, it could be said that this is his true calling. He is very good at what he does, and his services are always in demand.

He has become a teacher.

Charles Gregory Doblin scoots back his chair, stands up and turns around, and lets the state troopers attach manacles to his wrists and ankles. Then he lets them take him to the van, and his next lesson.

INTRODUCTION:
"A Letter From St. Louis"

When I started reading science fiction back in grade school, many of the classics that hooked earlier generations were the same ones I first discovered: Heinlein's *Rocket Ship Galileo*, Asimov's *I, Robot*, Wylie and Balmer's *When Worlds Collide*, Verne's *20,000 Leagues Under the Sea*. But the one that really gave me the chills was the first invasion-from-space story ever written and, in my humble opinion, still the best—*The War of the Worlds*, by H. G. Wells.

I read this novel in the hallway of Robertson Academy outside my sixth grade classroom, after the teacher threw me out for the umpteenth time for the umpteenth reason (What was I like as a kid? Picture a well-read Bart Simpson . . .). I devoured about half of the Golden Books edition while sitting out there, until Mrs. Harris told me I could come back if I promised to be good. I kept my promise, all right; quiet as a kitten, I was. In fact, I was so quiet that Mrs. Harris threw me out again when I refused to put away the book I was reading to participate in math lessons. Some people are never satisfied.

I loved *The War of the Worlds*, but because I was also

reading every SF novel and story collection I could get my hands on, I never went back to reread it. If anyone asked me if I had read *The War of the Worlds*, I would say, sure, of course, it was one of the very first SF books I picked up . . .

And yet, I hadn't really read *The War of the Worlds* after all.

I didn't realize this until twenty-five years later, when my friend and colleague Kevin A. Anderson invited me to submit a story to an anthology he was editing, *War of the Worlds: Global Dispatches*. Kevin's brainstorm was to invite a whole bunch of SF authors to create mini-sequels to the original Wells novel, each one relating a different aspect of the great Martian invasion of 1900, as told or witnessed by contemporary figures of the time: Rudyard Kipling, Jack London, Albert Einstein, Jules Verne, Leo Tolstoy, and various others.

By now, I had written five short stories and one novel set in St. Louis, and I felt as though this literary period had run its course; however, because I couldn't resist having Wells' Martians invade my fair city, I decided to do one more St. Louis SF story. Missouri's most famous literary figure is, of course, Mark Twain, which made him the perfect raconteur, but when I asked Kevin if I could do Mr. Clemens, he informed me that Daniel Keys Moran already had dibs on Twain. Besides, Kevin had rather hoped that I would write about Percival Lowell, the astronomer whose turn-of-the-century popscience books about Mars and its ''canals'' had inspired the original Wells novel.

I knew a lot about Lowell, but I really wasn't crazy about treating him as a viewpoint character; I was much more interested in writing about St. Louis during the Martian invasion. Yet, because Mark Twain, the most logical choice for this story, was already spoken for, who would be its focal character? I delayed giving Kevin a definite yea-or-nay answer to his invitation while I pondered this problem.

Skip forward several months to Labor Day weekend, 1994. The 52nd World Science Fiction Convention was being held in Winnipeg, Canada; I flew up that Friday morning, making a noontime connection in Minneapolis. The travel agent who sold me my tickets neglected to send me a boarding pass for the Minneapolis-Winnipeg leg of the trip, and the jet from St. Louis was delayed on the runway, so by the time I got to Minneapolis and sprinted to the Northwestern Airlines gate from which the plane to Winnipeg was scheduled to depart, the flight was already overbooked and anyone without a boarding pass had been placed on the waiting list. A long waiting list.

Not only that, but nearly everyone sitting and standing in the crowded gate was heading for the WorldCon, because all of the domestic flights from the U.S. to Winnipeg were being funneled through Minneapolis. So, it looked like a little SF convention was being held right then and there. Over here were Ken Moore, John Hollis, and Charlie and Anita Williams, my hometown friends from the Nashville Science Fiction Club; over there were Dick and Nicki Lynch, the editors of the fanzine *Mimosa*. Fellow authors Harry and Laura Turtledove were there, as were Connie Willis and Dan Marcus . . . and, lo and behold, Kevin and Rebecca Anderson.

It was nice to see all my friends again, but the jet was due to leave in less than an hour, and I was at the bottom of the pecking order. The gate agent assured me and the other standbys, including Dan, that we would be bumped to the next Winnipeg flight, about five hours from now, arriving in Canada shortly after six o'clock. Normally, this wouldn't faze me—Northwestern was even offering to shuttle all the standbys over to the Mall of America—but I was scheduled to participate in two panel discussions that afternoon, one at five o'clock and another at seven. And I really wanted to make those panels. At one point, Dan and I discussed the possibility of renting a car and driving the rest of the way north, until we added up the mileage, did a little mental arithmetic, and realized that, by the time we made the haul, cleared Canadian customs at the border, and arrived at our destination, the next plane out would have beaten us to Winnipeg by an hour at the very least.

Then Rebecca Anderson did me one of the nicest favors anyone ever has done for me in my life. Even as the flight was being boarded, she had quick, whispered conversation with her husband; then, she turned to me and offered to trade tickets. She would wait in Minneapolis and use the time to dictate a chapter of her next *Star Wars* young adult novel into her pocket recorder, while I took her seat on the plane.

I hemmed and hawed and tried to talk her out of it, but Rebecca cast me one of her patented this-is-my-rock-and-I-shall-not-be-budged-from-it looks and shoved her ticket and boarding pass in my hand. Feeling like I was catching the last chopper flight out of Saigon, I hauled my carry-on bag over my shoulder, gave Rebecca a quick kiss on the cheek, then dashed down the jetway to the plane, where I tucked myself into the seat next to Kevin's just minutes before the stewardess closed the hatch.

And what did Kevin and I talk about during our ride to Winnipeg? *The War of the Worlds* anthology, of course, and the stories we would write for it . . .

To make a long story short, Kevin and I decided that he would do Percival Lowell, and I would do my St. Louis story from the perspective of another famous St. Louisian: Joseph Pulitzer, the founder of the *St. Louis Post-Dispatch* and the Pulitzer newspaper chain. I knew next to nothing about Joe Pulitzer, but we were both journalists, we were both from St. Louis . . . what else did I want? And there was no question I would now write a story for Kevin's anthology, even if I had to crawl through rusty nails to do so. After all, I had a karmic debt to fulfill. But when I came home from the WorldCon and began researching for this story, I discovered two disturbing facts.

First, Joseph Pulitzer didn't live in St. Louis in 1900. He had unofficially moved to New York City by then; not only that, but he was almost totally blind by that time. Neither fact made him a good eyewitness for events in St. Louis.

Second—and this was even more surprising—the Golden Books edition of *The War of the Worlds* I had read in the hallway of Robertson Academy wasn't the same book that H. G. Wells had written.

That edition had been bowdlerized, its most horrific scenes either downplayed or outright censored, much the same way George Pal's 1953 film adaptation, as wonderful as it was, updated the book from the England of 1900 to contemporary America and cut out the parts regarding poison gas, red vines, and Martians eating humans. Reading this novel—for the first time, really— made me realize what a masterpiece it truly is and that I couldn't trivialize it by writing a sequel that was either a parody or a takeoff.

A knotty problem. To remain faithful to both Wells' novel and historical fact and also fulfill my promise to Kevin that I would deliver a story about Joseph Pulitzer in St. Louis, I had to do something a bit different than what I myself had expected.

So, I cast myself in the lead role. No, he doesn't bear my name, and Arthur Barnett's biography is different from my own, but, nonetheless, this is how I reimagined myself: a young journalist for the *Post-Dispatch* in 1900, writing a letter to one of my sisters during the alien invasion.

This story is for Kevin, Rebecca, H. G. Wells . . . and Mrs. Harris, wherever you are.

A LETTER FROM ST. LOUIS

The following is an annotated letter from Arthur Barnett, a staff reporter for the *St. Louis Post-Dispatch*, to his elder sister, Rachel Barnett Simpson, a resident of San Francisco. The original handwritten letter now resides in the archives of the St. Louis Historical Society, which has graciously permitted it to be reprinted here with the approval of Mrs. Simpson's estate.

July the 24th, 1900

My dearest Rachel,

I wish that this note could be written on a happier occasion, because I have seldom found time to write to you during the past few years. Because I know not for certain whether you will receive this correspondence at all, considering the current dire state of affairs, it is one more reason to regret failing to reply to the many letters you have sent me following your marriage to Chet.[1]

---

[1]St. Louis native Rachel Barnett married San Francisco financier Chester J. Simpson on April 20, 1897. They moved to San Francisco shortly thereafter.

By whatever means and time this letter finally reaches you, the good Lord willing. I hope you will forgive my lassitude. I always thought that there would be time for correspondence, once the work was done and there were not so many pressing engagements. Now, my labors are at last complete, but I seem to have run out of time as well.

You know of the Martians, of course. I shan't repeat the story of their coming to our world, for if they bothered striking at Saint Louis, then there is little doubt that you witnessed their wrath in San Francisco as well. I can only pray that you and Chet have escaped without harm and that this missive finds you in good health and spirits. Yet, it is necessary for me to relate to you the dire fate that has befallen your native city. As Father used to say (with some scorn, as I recall) I'm a ''tattler'' by nature . . . although I far prefer to use Mr. Pulitzer's favored term, a ''newspaper man.''

I finally had the opportunity to meet Mr. Pulitzer, by the way. It occurred only a few days ago, as I write, during which he gave me the greatest compliment of my professional career. Yet, I'm getting ahead of myself, and there is much to be told as prelude to this chance encounter.

The first Martian shell in these parts arrived on the evening of July the 5th, as a fireball that crashed to the Earth a few miles from East Saint Louis.[2] Although several people witnessed its descent and reported it to the newspaper, the newsroom staff dismissed it as a remnant of the Independence Day fireworks—perhaps a final Chinese rocket sent aloft by some boys who had stolen it from the Veiled Prophet Society parade.

It was not until the following morning that we received a reliable report of what seemed to be a large ballistic

---

[2]East St. Louis is a small city in southwestern Illinois, on the opposite side of the Mississippi River from St. Louis, Missouri.

shell, half buried in a crater that it had carved in a cow pasture not far from the Indian mounds. A small crowd had already gathered around the fallen shell, we were told, and, although its surface was much too hot to approach, witnesses claimed to have heard muted sounds from within the thing, along with great puffs of green smoke that rose from the crater.

By this time, we had already received the first telegraph reports of similar occurrences elsewhere in the world, beginning with the landing of a shell in Woking, England, courtesy of the international desk at the *World*.[3] I begged the city room editor to be allowed to cover this story, but he reminded me that I was still facing a deadline for another story involving the repainting of the Four Courts Building, and he sent McPherson to the scene instead.

I was left at my typewriter, murmuring unseemly oaths beneath my breath. In hindsight, though, it is most fortunate that I was hampered with this trivial assignment, else I might not have survived to write these words. On the other hand, I almost envy McPherson now, for at least his death was quick, and he did not have to witness the terrifying events yet to come.

The next word we received from Illinois was in the middle of the afternoon, when a young farmhand who had ridden his horse in a great hurry across the Eads Bridge dashed into the city room with a breathless tale on his lips. At first we were incredulous. Monstrous grey creatures emerging from the shell? A tentacle holding a rotating mirror, which in turn sent forth beams that put everything ablaze? Dozens of bystanders disintegrating within moments? Absurd!

Yet, within the hour, we received more reports from bystanders who, like the lad, had narrowly escaped death. McPherson himself never returned to our offices. We

---

[3]*The New York World*, sister newspaper to the *Post-Dispatch*.

were finally left with the cold realization that some unearthly horror was indeed upon us.

Nor was East Saint Louis alone. As the afternoon wore on, the telegraph operator received a flurry of dispatches from elsewhere in the country, telling of similar landings throughout the country. Another shell had crashed in Grovers Mill, New Jersey, followed by a similar slaughter of hapless civilians. Local militias were being mobilized in Massachusetts, Pennsylvania, Ohio, Tennessee, Virginia, and Texas, where other shells had crashed, usually in rural areas not far from major cities. Later, there came disjointed reports of great machines—sometimes described as "walking milk stools" or "three-legged boilers"—that were seen emerging from the craters that the shells had formed upon impact.

We were still attempting to make coherent sense of these reports when the editor was informed that he had a long-distance telephone call awaiting him. He promptly adjourned to his office and closed the door, yet, through the glass walls, I was able to see him speaking into the instrument. He seemed considerably agitated, and, when he returned a few minutes later with a pronouncement, the staff learned the reason why. He had just spoken with Mr. Pulitzer himself,[4] who had instructed him to compile whatever reports were available into an extra edition, which was to be printed as quickly as it could be set in hot type and rushed onto the street before the ink was dry on the pages.

By late afternoon, newsboys were hawking the extra on every street corner, where they were instantly snatched from their hands by the citizenry. I imagine that many of our readers initially thought we were engaged

---

[4]By 1900, Joseph Pulitzer no longer lived in St. Louis. After the scandal that resulted from the killing of a local attorney by the previous editor of the *Post-Dispatch*, he had taken permanent residence in New York City.

in another bout of "yellow press" warmongering. Memory of the accusations that Mr. Pulitzer had deliberately fostered the Cuban conflict as part of his rivalry with Mr. Hearst was still fresh, and I must confess that the thought crossed my mind that we were making too much smoke out of too little heat. Yet even though we did not have Stephen Crane's sterling prose as eyewitness testimony, there seemed little doubt that something of dire importance was indeed occurring.[5]

Once the extra was on the street, I barely had time to hastily consume half of a grocery sandwich at my desk before the city editor approached me. "Arthur," he said, "we've received word that the Army is mobilizing, and a defensive line is being established at the levee. I need a good man to cover this for as long as it takes, even if he has to remain there all night. Can you do this?"

I told him that I could, but before I could rise from my chair, he put a hand on my shoulder. "There is one more thing," he continued, dropping his voice to a near whisper. "If this is indeed an invasion of sorts, there may be just cause for you not returning to the office."

I raised an eyebrow at this stark admission, yet, before I could inquire further, he went on. "If this is the case, you are to go straight to Union Station, where you will search for a private Pullman coach called 'Newport.' If it is there, tell the porter that you wish to speak with Andes. Do you understand? Ask for Andes."

Although mystified, I dutifully repeated the word, and he sent me off, with little more than pen, notebook, and the other half of my sandwich to sustain me.

I hastened to the levee, where I discovered the riverfront already crowded with soldiers from the Jefferson

[5]Barnett alludes here to the Spanish-American War, which was largely incited by the *World* and William Randolph Hearst's *New York Journal*. The novelist Stephen Crane was the Pulitzer Newspapers' correspondent during the war.

Barracks. Wagons bearing munitions had just arrived from the city armory, and heavy artillery pieces were being set up in a row along the top of the levee. Army officers were engaged in heated arguments with river boat captains, trying to get them to move their craft away from the piers so that the guns would be assured of a direct line of fire across the river, while troops positioned Gatling guns upon the floating wharfs. It was rumored that ironclads would soon be arriving, but I was told by a lieutenant that all available gunboats had already been sent farther downriver, although for what purpose, no one seemed to know for certain.

Yet, despite the high state of anxiety, there was no sign of enemy movement from the other side of the Mississippi. Some of the soldiers with whom I spoke were convinced that this was an elaborate hoax. Once they were in position behind sand bags and gun emplacements, many settled down to roll cigarettes and enjoy a casual meal from their dinner pails. After a time, curious civilians began to gather along the levee, and several industrious vendors pushed their carts down from Market Street to hawk their wares.

Westbound trains continued to rumble across the Eads Bridge, apparently unscathed from their journey through Illinois, and, although most of the river traffic had been cleared away, a few packet steamers and barges continued to cruise down the broad, muddy expanse. If this was the prelude to war, then it was oddly peaceful.

Nonetheless, I remained on the riverfront all night, composing a quick story in longhand that was sent back to the paper with the copy boy who was sent down to check on me. Although he told me that the telegraph operator had been unable to receive news from anywhere east of Saint Louis, and I spied intermittent flashes of what seemed to be heat lightning from across the eastern horizon, all seemed to be calm. Around midnight, I curled up behind a row of barrels and napped for a few hours.

The peace was only temporary, though, and not to last. In hindsight, it is obvious that the Martians were awaiting dawn to make their move.

The eastern sky had just been painted pale red with first light when we were awakened by a string of fires that spontaneously erupted among the buildings of East Saint Louis. As the soldiers, most of whom had been dozing behind their barricades, stumbled to their feet in bleary-eyed confusion, a cry rose from a young sergeant standing watch atop one of the wharfs: "Enemy sighted! Enemy sighted!"

It was then that the first of the Martian war machines strode into view. If you have not seen one of these "tripods" yourself, Rachel, there is little I can say that fully describes the dreadful enormity of this unholy creation. Fully a hundred feet tall, it somewhat resembles a railway water tower, except that its jointed legs move at a fast gait that belies their cumbersome arrangement. Beneath its saucer-like cab, slender tentacles whipped about, swatting aside brick chimneys as if they were stacks of children's blocks.

No sooner had the first tripod appeared than another machine joined it several hundred yards away to the left. Then a third, the same distance to the right, then a fourth following behind it. Finally, there was a fifth machine, bringing up the left rear leg of this star-shaped figuration.

As they marched through East Saint Louis, blazes broke out on all sides as buildings exploded into flame. Although we could not see what ignited these fires, they were the work of the awesome "heat rays" caused by the spinning mirrors carried by the tripods. Despite their invisibility, whatever the heat rays touched was instantaneously destroyed as the tripods carved their way through the Illinois town.

Above the roar of flames, unearthly sirens wailed from

the machines as some sort of signal from one to another. This made the soldiers even more afraid; there was the crack of rifle shots as some opened fire with their carbines, until their commanding officers shouted for them to hold their fire until the tripods were within range.

For a few minutes, the tripods disappeared from view within the dense smoke of the burning town. I took the opportunity to dash up to the top of the levee behind the artillery guns, both to obtain a better view of the coming battle and to escape from being caught by the crossfire. In retrospect, that prudent decision may have saved my life.

A few moments later, the foremost tripod lurched out of the smoke and onto the Illinois levee, its massive legs reaching the edge of the river. If anyone thought it would be daunted by the mighty Mississippi, they were proven wrong, for without any apparent hesitation it walked straight into the curling brown water.

At this instant, the army colonel who had previously urged restraint gave the order to open fire, and the gates of Hades swung fully open.

The thunder of a score of artillery guns letting loose was the most deafening sound I ever heard. It was as if all the world's supply of TNT was being let go at once. Huge gouts of water kicked up as shells impacted the water all around the first tripod; the buildings around its companions to the left and right were ripped asunder as more shells slammed into them. At the same instant, the battery of Gatling guns let loose with all their chattering fury, while individual sharpshooters sought to train their rifles through the fog of combat.

For a few moments, it seemed as if the assault would have no effect. Strange as it seems, it appeared that artillery shells detonated in midair only a few feet from their mark, as if they struck an invisible shield. Then, a shell exploded within the hood of the leading war machine. There was a mighty blast, and the tripod staggered.

Then, with a slow grind of tortured metal, its legs succumbed to the Mississippi's relentless tide and the tripod toppled into the river.

A great shout rose from the defending army. The damned things weren't invulnerable after all! With great haste, the artillerymen made to reload their guns while the battery gunners shouted for fresh belts, even as the four remaining tripods seemingly hesitated just as they reached the river's edge.

I had just ducked into the open doorway of a warehouse behind me and was reaching for my notebook and pen when the true horror began.

Although I'm a writer by trade, I still cannot find words to describe all that happened next. It almost seems like a madman's hallucination, such was the insane extent of the violence that occurred around me. If I tried to describe all that I saw, I fear that I might go mad myself.

Within the next minute, I watched hundreds of men die, although they courageously . . .

No . . . this is a lie. This was no charge of the light brigade, and I am no Lord Tennyson. There was no honor or glory in the way that they fought, for the massacre was so swift that it left no room for such human qualities.

The truth of the matter, dear Rachel, is that these brave men were burned alive, screaming and writhing in mortal agony as their weapons exploded in their hands. Even those who sought refuge behind sandbags perished, for the heat rays spared nothing and no one. Boats and wharfs went up as massive funeral pyres, incinerating all that stood on their decks, while gun carriages and ammunition stacks detonated before they could be used. The air was filled with the stench of burning gunpowder, wood, and flesh.

Realizing that I was in peril, I dashed from the doorway in which I was hiding and ran down the levee until I reached the corner of Market Street. Already the avenue was crowded with soldiers and civilians. Hearing an ex-

plosion from close behind me, I glanced around just in
time to see a waterfront building go up in flames as one
of the tripods leveled its heat ray upon it. Even as brick
and plaster rained down around the crowd, I ran as hard
as I could, narrowly escaping my own destruction.

Nor did it cease there. One by one, warehouses and
factories burst into flames as the beam swept across them.
Within minutes, the entire river district had become a
raging inferno. As if to spite God Himself, the spire of
the Catholic cathedral crumbled beneath the heat rays,
causing debris to rain down upon screaming pedestrians.

I ran straight down Market, pushing my way through
mobs of panic-stricken men and women who had filled
the street, knocking each other down in their haste, while
behind us more buildings were being set afire by the advancing tripods. Although fire companies rushed to the
scene, their wagons could not penetrate the crowds; finally, even the firemen were forced to abandon their
equipment and flee for their lives.

I finally managed to leap aboard a trolley as it careened
down Market Street, jammed with men and women clinging to every seat and railing. Safe for the moment, I
briefly considered returning to the office but realized that
this was ludicrous; the newsroom would not protect me,
and it was much too close to the waterfront. Besides,
what would I do there? I laughed bitterly at the very
thought. No, there would not be an extra published this
morning!

It was then that I remembered my editor's final words
to me the evening before, and I realized that I had one
last duty to perform.

I rode the trolley until it reached Union Station, where
I jumped off. The crowds were thinner here, but when I
looked back I saw now that the downtown business district had become a vast wall of flame that already had
reached the courthouse dome. I couldn't see the tripods,
but I knew that they were coming; if the mighty currents

of the Mississippi River didn't stop them, then they would soon be marching across the Eads Bridge.

The train shed was packed with citizens, all attempting to force their way aboard coaches. Even the freight cars were packed with refugees; I saw several men wrestling with each other as they tried to struggle on top of a coal carrier. What few policemen were present had already given up attempting to control the mob.

I savaged my way through the mob until I suddenly located a short train parked on a siding. Armed Pinkertons surrounded the four cars, firing rounds into the air to ward off those who attempted to board without presenting identification. Through the windows, I caught a glimpse of faces pressed against the glass while the train's nervous driver watched the confusion from within his cab.

The last car on the train was an ornate private coach, with the word "Newport" inscribed in gold filigree above the curtained windows. One of the Pinkertons leveled his Winchester at me as I approached and told me to back away, but when I told him that I was here to see Mr. Andes, he relented and stood aside, allowing me to climb up the coach's rear steps and push open the door.

The interior of the coach was dimly illuminated by only a couple of gas lamps, but, once my eyes adjusted to the gloom, I saw that it was as lavishly furnished as a club drawing room. In the quiet of the coach, I saw a handsome woman sitting on a plush settee. She clutched a crying child to her bosom, and she looked up at me in fear when I entered, but, before either one of us could say a word, a European-accented voice spoke from farther within the car.

"Yes?" the man inquired. "Who is it?"

I cleared my throat. "Arthur Barnett, from the *Post-Dispatch*. I'm here to see Mr. Andes."

There was a low chuckle. From its location, I was finally able to discern its source. I saw a tall gaunt man in his middle years, whose bushy beard had grown silver with age and whose eyes were shadowed by tinted spectacles. He sat alone in an armchair at the far end of the compartment.

"Just Andes, Mr. Barnett," he said. "Like the mountain range.[6] Please, be seated. I'm Joseph Pulitzer."

Mrs. Pulitzer stood up and guided me to a chair next to her husband. As exhausted and fearful as I was, I found myself humbled by the proximity to the great man, yet, when I sat down, I noticed that he did not look straight at me until I spoke again.

"Have you visited your newspaper?" he asked.

"No, sir, I haven't," I replied. "I was told that I was to come straight here if I believed . . ."

I hesitated, suddenly unwilling to explain my reasons. It was then that Mr. Pulitzer's face turned in my direction.

"If you believed what, young man?" he demanded. "Why haven't you returned to your office? We've got an evening edition to publish, haven't we?"

I swallowed what felt like a lump of dry lint. "I believe that this is no longer possible, sir," I said. "I don't think the *Post-Dispatch* will be published today."

Mr. Pulitzer frowned as he considered that statement for a moment. As he did, he reached down with his left hand and groped along the carpeted floor until he found a silver-headed cane. He picked it up and set it upright on the floor, clasping his hands together atop its crook.

"Tell me everything you have seen," he said.

I began to stammer out the events of the last half hour, but he interrupted me with an impatient shake of his head. "You're a reporter, Mr. Barnett," he said. "Pre-

---

[6]To insure privacy, the Pulitzer organization used in-house code words to designate various individuals. "Andes" was Joseph Pulitzer's code name.

tend as if I'm your reader and know nothing of the facts. Now, from the beginning . . .''

From outside the coach, I could hear shouting and more gunshots. It all seemed surreal; our world was collapsing under the heel of an unearthly invader, and I was being told to deliver a journalistic report. Nonetheless, I did so. Plucking my notebook from my jacket pocket, I quickly delivered the facts as I had witnessed them, beginning with the arrival of the Martian shell the previous morning and ending, finally, with the destruction of the U.S. Army troops on the levee and the torching of the business district.

Throughout it all, Mr. Pulitzer sat quietly and listened, occasionally nodding or shaking his nod but otherwise rarely displaying any outward emotion. When I was done, he asked a couple of minor questions, which I answered as honestly as I could. Then he nodded again in apparent satisfaction.

''You've done well, Mr. Barnett,'' he said. ''If I were able to see, I would want your eyes as my own.''

I almost gasped at this admission. Of all the things I had heard about Mr. Pulitzer, the one thing I did not know was that he had lost his eyesight. He must have picked up on my astonishment, for he smiled. ''The curse of all my years of hard work,'' he said quietly. ''I gained great wealth from the newspaper business but at a sacrifice.''

The smile faded, replaced again by the dark frown. ''They say I helped instigate a war,'' he murmured bitterly, more to himself than to me, ''and, in that, they may be right. Hearst and I sold many copies by trumping up charges against the Spaniards. Now, we have a real war on our hands, one whose devastation far exceeds that of Havana Harbor and San Juan Hill . . . and the irony of it is that I have no newspapers left to publish the story.''

''*The World?*'' I asked, quite astonished. ''It's gone, too?''

He slowly nodded his head. "*The World*, yes, and New York with it." He pointed toward the front of the train. "If you go up front, you'll find a few of my friends. Morgan, Vanderbilt . . . even Bill himself, damn him! . . . plus assorted sycophants who begged their way aboard at the last moment . . ."

He emitted a great sigh. "Not that it matters. I had rather hoped Saint Louis would fare better, but now, it turns out that its fate will be the same, if only delayed. No more editions. No more stories . . ."

Another gunshot from outside. It seemed to awaken the great man. He abruptly stood, using his cane to push himself to his feet. "Time is short," he said, "We must be getting off." He thrust out his hand. "Thank you, Mr. Barnett. You're a first-class journalist. I'm proud to have had you on my staff."

I thought of begging for sanctuary aboard his coach, but that was clearly out of the question. There was no place for me on his train, compliments notwithstanding; only the wealthy and important would ride with Mr. Pulitzer on his westward flight. I shook his hand, then I made my leave from his rail car.

A freight train was beginning to leave the station just then, and I managed to pull myself onto the rear platform of its caboose before it worked up steam. By then, the skies above Saint Louis were turning dark black with a dense smoke that masked even the flames devouring the city. Even without realizing the poisonous nature of those Martian fumes, I intuitively knew that nothing lived beneath that hideous cloud.

I write these words from a farmhouse basement just outside Springfield, where I have sought refuge for the last two days. I thought that I would be safe here, but yesterday, yet another shell landed only a few miles distant. The evening light is fading now, and, because I dare not strike a torch, I cannot spend more time with this letter. I will hide here for as long as I can, but I fear that this will be my final dispatch.

If these pages find their way to your hands, please know that I love you and that you have never been far from my mind. And, if you remember me for anything, please may it be as a good newspaper man.

—Arthur

This letter was found on Arthur Barnett's body shortly after the fall of the Martian invaders. It is the only known account of the destruction of St. Louis. The letter was delivered to Mrs. Chester Simpson, whose children donated it to the St. Louis Historical Society after her death in 1947.

More than 35,000 people perished during the siege of St. Louis. Joseph Pulitzer, his family, and his entourage were among those listed as missing.

INTRODUCTION:
"The Good Rat"

Several years ago, a couple of friends of mine shared an apartment in Nashville. They've since gone on to bigger and better things, but while they were living together, they had a hard time making ends meet. Only one of them was employed, and even then as a waiter; the other guy was constantly getting fired or laid off because of his attitude, so he was out of work most of the time.

Besides the fact that they had rent and utility bills that had to be paid, though, they both shared an expensive habit. Not drugs or alcohol; indeed, they were two of the most clean-living dudes I've ever met. But they collected comic books, and read every new title Marvel, DC, and the various independent publishers produced. If you think that's a cheap fix, drop by your nearest comic book shop and check out what the latest issue of *The Uncanny X-Men* costs these days.

So, once a month, they caught a bus downtown and went to the blood plasma donator center, where they would sit for several hours with needles stuck in their arms, reading paperbacks and waiting for the bottles to fill. When they were done, someone would write them a check, which they would immediately have cashed at the bank. . . .

And then they'd take the money straight to their favorite comics shop, where they'd buy a couple of hundred dollars worth of comic books.

They also signed up for lab experiments at Vanderbilt University. Nothing grotesque. Mostly psych stuff being done by grad students. One of them talked me into volunteering for one of these experiments, and I went along with it just for grins. I watched photo slides for a couple of hours, filled out a questionnaire, and walked out with a check for fifty bucks. Easy money, but nothing I particularly cared to do again. Altogether, it reminded me too much of winos selling their bodies to medical schools to buy another bottle of Wild Irish Rose.

I recently stumbled upon a book called *Sell Yourself to Science*, by Jim Hogshire (Loompanics Unlimited, 1993). Reading it, I discovered that blood plasma donations or the occasional slide show is only half of it. With a little ingenuity, it's possible for a healthy individual to make a half-decent living not only from volunteering for lab experiments but by donating his or her organs. If you know where to look, you can even sell your hair or blood vessels.

At this time, selling your organs outright is illegal in the United States. However, these laws could be changed, especially when you realize that there is an acute shortage of many essential organs and far too few donors. Not so many people are signing those organ donor blanks on the backs of their driver's licenses. In time, it's conceivable that the laws may be adjusted to make it possible for someone to mortgage a liver, heart, or eyeball. Sort of a layaway plan, if you're into it.

At the same time, the need for subjects for human experimentation may increase along with the outcry against animal testing. I'm somewhat opposed to animal experimentation; a couple of years ago, two of my dogs were almost grabbed by a couple of sleazeballs while I was running them in a park. When those guys were eventually busted, it turned out that they had been selling "stray" dogs to hospitals all over St. Louis County. However, if laws are passed that protect all animal species—rats, rabbits, cats, monkeys, and so on—from scientific experimentation, then this leaves very little recourse for commercial labs. They'll have to recruit human volunteers and be prepared to pay them pretty damned well.

So it comes down to this: would you allow yourself to be subjected to the same sort of treatment that you wouldn't want your pet to endure? Would you be willing to go to the grave without all your organs in your body? If so, what kind of money would someone have to pay you to do so?

I've saved this story for last because, in many ways, it's the most optimistic story in this collection. Everything the main character does is out of a free mind and conscience, and that's more choice than many of us are allowed to have in this day and age. For this, I actually envy him.

It also brings to closure the thematic arc that was begun five years ago, when I moved out of a small cabin beside a New Hampshire lake and went in search of America, or at least a few good stories to tell. I still haven't found America, but I've got a wife, a home, a job, and a clue. I've found some stories, and I hope they've pleased you.

Thank you for your indulgence, and good night.

THE GOOD RAT

Get home from spending two weeks in Thailand and Nepal. Nice tan from lying on the beach at Koh Samui, duffle bag full of stuff picked up cheap on the street in Kathmandu. Good vacation, but broke now. Money from mortgaging kidneys almost gone, mailbox full of bills and disconnect notices. Time to find work again.

Call agent, leave a message on her machine. She calls back that afternoon. We talk about the trip a little bit; tell her that I'm sending her a wooden mask. Likes that, but says she's busy trying to broker another couple of rats for experiments at Proctor & Gamble. Asks why I'm calling.

Tell her I'm busted. Need work soon. Got bills to pay. She says, I'll work on it, get back to you soon, ciao, then hangs up on me. Figure I'll send her the ugliest mask in my bag.

Jet-lagged from spending last twenty-four hours on airplanes. Sleep a lot next two days, watch a lot of TV in between. Mom calls on Tuesday, asks me where I've been for the last month. Says she's been trying to find me. Don't tell her about Koh Samui and Kathmandu. Tell her I'm in night school at local college. Remedial English and basic computer programming. Learning how to do stuff with computers and how to read. She likes that. Asks if I got a job yet. About to lie some more when phone clicks. Got another call coming in, I say. Gotta go, bye. Just as well. Hate lying to Mom.

Agent on the phone. Asks if my legs are in good shape. Hell yeah, I say. Just spent ten days hiking through the Annapurna region, you bet my legs are in good shape. What's the scoop?

She says, private test facility in Boston needs a rat for Phase One experiments. Some company developing over-the-counter ointment for foot blisters. Need someone in good physical condition to do treadmill stuff. Two-week gig. Think you can handle it?

Dunno, I say. Got a few bruises on thighs from falling down on rocks a lot. How much they pay? A hundred bucks a day, she says, minus her fifteen percent commission. Not bad. Not great, but not bad either. Ask if they're buying the airplane ticket. She says, yeah, tourist class on Continental. I say, gee, I dunno, those bruises really hurt. First class on TWA would make them feel better. Says she'll get back to me, ciao, and hangs up.

Turn on TV, channel surf until I find some toons. Dumb coyote just fell off cliff again when agent calls back. She says, business class on TWA okay? Think about trying to score box-seat ticket for a Red Sox game, but decide not to push my luck. Bruises feel much better, I say. When do they want me?

She says two days, I say okay. Tickets coming by American Express tomorrow, she says, but don't tell them about bruises, all right? Got no bruises, I say. Just wanted to get decent seat on the plane.

Calls me a name and hangs up again. Doesn't even say ciao this time. Decide not to send her a mask at all. Let her go to Kathmandu and buy one herself.

• •

Two days later. Get off plane at airport in Beantown. Been here before two years ago, when some other lab hired me to drink pink stuff for three days so scientists could look at what I pissed and puked. Like Boston. Nice city. Never figured out why they call it Beantown, though.

Skinny college kid at gate, holding cardboard sign with some word on it and my name below it. Walk up to him, ask if he's looking for me. Gives me funny look. He says, is this your name on the sign? I say, no, I'm Elmer Fudd, is he from the test facility?

Gets pissed. Asks for ID. Show him my Sam's Club card. Got my picture on it, but he's still being a turd about it. Asks if I got a driver's license. Drop my duffel bag on his shoes, tell him I'm a busy man, so let's get going.

Takes me to garage where his Volvo is parked. No limo service this time. Must be cheap lab. Got limo service last time I did a job in Boston. Kid looks mad, though, so don't make Supreme Court case out of it.

Get stuck in tunnel traffic after leaving airport. Want to grab a nap in back seat, but the kid decides to make small talk. Asks me how it feels to be a rat.

Know what he's getting at. Heard it before. Say hey, dude, they pay me to get stuck with needles fifteen times a day, walk on treadmills, eat this, drink that, crap in a kidney tray and whizz in a bottle. It's a living, y'know?

Smiles. Thinks he's superior. Got a college degree that says so. He says, y'know, they used to do the same thing to dogs, monkeys, and rabbits before it got outlawed. How does it feel to be treated like an animal?

No problem, I say. You gotta dog at home you really like? Maybe a cat? Then bring him over to your lab, make him do the stuff I do, and half as well. Then you tell me.

Then he goes and starts telling me about Nazi concentration camp experiments. Heard that before too, usually from guys who march and wave signs in front of labs. Same guys who got upset about dogs, monkeys, and rabbits being used in experiments are now angry that people are being used instead. Sort of makes me wonder why he's working for a company that does human experiments if he thinks they're wrong. Maybe a college education isn't such a great thing after all, if you have to do something you don't believe in.

Hey, the Nazis didn't ask for volunteers, I say, and they didn't pay them either. There's a difference. Just got back from spending two weeks in Nepal, hiking the lower Himalayas. Where'd you spend your last vacation?

Gets bent out of shape over that. Tells me how much he makes each year, before taxes. Tell him how much I make each year, after taxes. Free medical care and all the vacation time I want, too.

That shuts him up. Make the rest of the trip in peace.

Kid drives me to big old brick building overlooking the Charles River. Looks like it might have once been a factory. Usual bunch of demonstrators hanging out in the parking lot. Raining now, so they look cold and wet. Courts say they have to stay fifty feet away from the entrance. Can't read their signs. Wouldn't mean diddly to me even if I could. That's my job they're protesting, so if they catch the flu, they better not come crying to me, because I'm probably the guy who tested the medicine they'll have to take.

Stop at front desk to present ID, get name badge. Leave my bags with security guard. Ride up elevator to sixth floor. Place looks better on the inside. Plaster walls, tile floors, glass doors, everything painted white and grey. Offices have carpets, new furniture, hanging plants, computers on every desk.

First stop is the clinic. Woman doctor tests my reflexes, looks in my ears, checks my eyes, takes a blood sample, gives me a little bottle and points to the bathroom. Give her a full bottle a few minutes later, smile, ask what she's doing two weeks from now. Doesn't smile back. Thanks me for my urine.

Kid takes me down the hall to another office. Chief scientist waiting for me. Skinny guy with glasses, bald head, and long bushy beard. Stands up and sticks out his hand, tells me his name. Can't remember it five minutes later. Think of him as Dr. Bighead. Just another guy in a white coat. Doesn't matter what his name is, so long as he writes it at the bottom of my paycheck.

Dr. Bighead offers me coffee. Ask for water instead. Kid goes to get me a glass of water, and Dr. Bighead starts telling me about the experiment.

Don't understand half the shit he says. It's scientific. Goes right over my head. Listen politely and nod my head at the right times, like a good rat.

Comes down to this. Some drug company hired his lab to do Phase One tests for its new product. It's a lotion to relieve foot blisters. No brand-name for it yet. Experiment calls for me to walk a treadmill for eight hours the first day with a one-hour break for lunch, or at least until I collect a nice bunch of blisters on the soles of my feet. Then they'll apply an ointment to my aching doggies, let me rest for twelve hours, but put me on the treadmill again the next day. This will be repeated every other day for the next two weeks.

Do I get paid for the days I'm not on the treadmill?

Of course, he says, but you have to stay here at the test facility. Got a private room in the dorm for you upstairs. Private cafeteria and rec room, too.

Does it have a pool table?

Got a really nice pool table, he says. Also a VCR and a library. Computer, too, but no fax or modem. Company has strict policy against test participants being permitted open contact with outside world. Phone calls allowed, but they're monitored by security operators. Can receive forwarded mail, but all outgoing mail has to be read by a staff member first.

Nod. Been through this before. Most test facilities work this way. Sounds reasonable, I say.

When you're not on the treadmill, he says, you have to be in bed or in a wheelchair. No standing or walking, except when you're in the shower or going to the bathroom.

Shrug. Not a big deal. Once lay in bed for three days, doing nothing but watch old Flintstones cartoons on closed-circuit TV. Some kind of psychiatric experiment for UCLA. Ready to shout yabba-dabba-do and hump Betty Rubble by the time it was over. After that, there's nothing I can't do.

Dr. Bighead stops smiling now. Folds hands together on desk. Time for the serious stuff now.

The ointment we put on your feet may not be the final product, he says. May have to try different variations on the same formula. Side-effects may include persistent itching, reddening or flaking of the skin, minor swelling. Computer simulations of the product have produced none of these results, but this is the first time the product has undergone Phase One testing.

Nod. Been there, done that.

Goes on. Tells me that there's another three volunteers doing the same experiment. Three of us will be the test subjects, the other one the control subject who receives a placebo. We won't know in advance who gets the product and who gets the placebo. Do I understand?

Test subjects, control subjects, placebos, and my feet may rot and fall off before this is all over. Got it, doc. Sounds cool.

Dr. Bighead goes on. If any of this bothers me, I can leave now, and his company will pay me a hundred dollars for one day of my time and supply me with airfare back home. However, if I chicken out during the test period, or if I'm caught trying to wash off the ointment, they'll throw me out of the experiment and I won't be paid anything.

Yeah, uh-huh. He has to tell me this because of the way the laws are written. Never chickened out before, I say. Sounds great to me. When do we get started?

Dr. Bighead grins. Likes a nice, cooperative rat. Tomorrow morning, he says. Eight o'clock sharp.

Ask if I can go catch a little night-life tonight. Frowns. Tells me I may have to submit another urine sample if I do so. Nod my head. No problem. He shrugs. Sure, so long as you're back by midnight. After that, you're in here until we're through with the experiment.

No problem.

Spend another hour with contracts and release forms. Dr. Bighead not surprised that I don't read very well. Must have seen the file my agent faxed his company. Make him read everything aloud, while I get it all on the little CD recorder I brought with me. Agent taught me to do that. Means we can sue his company if it pulls any funny stuff. Maybe this rat can't read, but he's still got rights.

Everything sounds cool. Sign all the legal stuff. Dr. Bighead gives me plastic wristband and watches me put it around my left wrist, then lets me go. Notice that he doesn't shake hands again. Maybe afraid he'll catch functional illiteracy.

Same kid waiting outside. Takes me up to dorm on the seventh floor.

Looks like a hospital ward. No windows. Six private rooms surrounding a rec area. Small cafeteria off to one side. Couple of tables, some chairs and sofas. Bookshelf full of old paperbacks and magazines. 52-inch flatscreen TV, loads of videos on the rack above it. Pay phone in the corner. Pool table, though it looks like a cheap one. Look up, spot fish-eye camera lens hidden in the ceiling.

Same as usual. Could be better, could be worse.

Room is small. Single bed, desk, closet. No windows

here either, but at least it's got a private bathroom. Count my blessings. No roommate this time. Last one snored, and the one before that went nuts six days into the experiment and was punted.

My bag is on the bed. Notice zipper is partly open. Been searched to make sure I didn't bring in any booze, dope, butts, or cellular phones.

Kid tells me he's got to go. Reminds me not to leave without my badge. See you tomorrow, I say.

Unpack bag, leave room. Want to get a bite to eat and check out the night life.

Two people sitting in the rec room now, watching TV news. A guy and a woman. Guy looks like he's about thirty. Thin, long-haired, sparse beard. Paperback book spread open on his lap. Barely glances my way.

The woman is different. Another rat, but the most beautiful rat I've seen in a while. Long brown hair. Slender but got some muscles. Good-looking. My type.

Catch her eye as I walk past. Give her a nod. She nods back, smiles a little. Doesn't say anything. Just a nod and smile.

Think about that nod and smile all the way to the elevator.

Found a good hangout last time I was in Boston, over in Dorchester. Catch a rickshaw over there now.

Sign above the door says "No * Allowed." First time I was here, someone had to read the name to me, then explain that the symbol in the middle is an asterisk. What part of your body looks like an asterisk. Still don't get it, I say. Laughs and says, bend over, stick your head between your legs, and look harder. Get it now, I say.

Can smoke a butt inside wherever you want, if you can find a butt to smoke these days. Fifty-six brands of beer. Not served only in the basement, but at your table if you want. Hamburgers, hot dogs, chicken-fried steak and onion rings on the menu. No tofu pizza or lentil soup.

Framed nude photos of Madonna, Keith Moon, Cindy Crawford, and Sylvester Stallone on the walls. Antique Wurlitzer jukebox loaded with stuff that can't be sold without a parental warning sticker on the cover.

No screaming kids, either.

Cops would shut down this place if most people knew it existed. Or maybe not. Several guys hanging out at the bar look like off-duty cops. Cops need a place to have a smoke and drink, too, y'know.

Good bar. Should be a place like this in every city. Once there was, before everyone took offense to everything and no one could stay out of other people's business. Laws got passed to make sure that you had to live in smoke-free, low-cholesterol, non-alcoholic, child-safe environments. Now you have to go slumming to find a place where no *s are allowed.

Cover charge, tonight, though. Can't have everything.

Find seat near the stage, order ginger ale, watch some nuevo-punk band ruin old Romantics and Clash numbers. It's Boston, so they're obligated to do something by the Cars. Probably toddlers when Ric Ocasek was blowing speakers.

Usually have a blowout the night before an experiment. Never binge, but have good fun anyway. Lots of babes here tonight, most of them with guys who look like they should be home wanking off on Internet. A couple of their girlfriends throw gimme looks in my direction.

Should do something about it. Still early. Can always get a hotel room for a few hours. Use the line about being a biomedical research expert in town for an important conference. Babes love sleeping with doctors.

Heart not into it. Keep thinking about the girl in the rec room. Don't know why. Just another rat.

Find myself looking around every time the door opens, hoping she'll walk in.

Leave before eleven o'clock, alone for once. Tell myself it's because the band was dick. Know better.

Wonder if Mom's not right. Maybe time to get a job. Learn how to read, too.

Bet she knows how to read.

Eight o'clock next morning. Come downstairs wearing my rat gear. Gym shorts, football jersey, sneaks. Time to go to work for the advancement of science and all mankind.

Dr. Bighead is waiting for me. Not as friendly as he was yesterday. Takes me to clinic and waits while I fill another bottle for the doctor. Escorts me to the lab.

Four power treadmills set next to each other on one side of the room, with a TV hanging from the ceiling above them. Stupid purple dinosaur show on the tube. Sound turned down low. College kids wearing white coats sitting in front of computers on other end of the room. One of them is the guy who picked me up at the airport. Glances up for a second when I come in. Doesn't wave back. Just looks at his screen again, taps fingers on his keyboard. Too cool to talk to rats now.

Two other rats sitting in plastic chairs. Already wired up, watching Barney, waiting to go. Walk over to meet them. One is the skinny longhair I saw last night. Wearing old Lollapolooza shirt. Name's Doug. Other guy looks like he works out a lot. Big dude. Shaved head, nose ring, truckstop tattoo on right forearm. Says his name is Phil.

Doug looks bored, Phil nervous. Everyone swats hands. We're the rat patrol, cruising for a bruising.

Time to get wired. Sit on table, take off shirt, let one of the kids tape electrodes all over me. Head, neck, chest, back, thighs, ankles. So much as twitch and lines jump all over the computer screens. Somebody asks what I had for breakfast, when was the last time I went to the bathroom. Writes it all down on a clipboard.

Phil asks if the TV has cable. Please change the channel, he says, it's giving me a headache. No one pays attention to him. Finally gets up and switches over to *The Today Show*. Dr. Bighead gives him the eye. Wonder if this is the first time Phil has ever been on the rat patrol. If the scientists want you to watch Barney, then you do it, no questions asked. Could be part of the experiment for all you know.

Don't mess with the scientists. Everyone knows that.

Last rat finally arrives. No surprise, it's the girl I saw last night. Wearing one-piece workout suit. Thank you, Lord, for giving us the guy who invented Spandex. Phil and Doug look ready to swallow their tongues when they see her. Guy who tapes electrodes to her gets a woody under his lab coat when he goes to work on her chest and thighs.

She ignores his hands, just like she ignores everyone else, including me and the boys. She's a true-blue, all-American, professional rat.

Time to mount the treadmills. Dr. Bighead makes a performance about us getting on the proper machines, as if it makes a difference. The girl is put on the machine to my left, with Doug on my right and Phil next to him.

Grasp the metal bar in front of me. Dr. Bighead checks to make sure that the computers are up and running, then he switches on the treadmills. Smooth rubber mat beneath my feet begins to roll at a slow pace, only about a foot or so every few seconds. My grandmother could walk faster than this.

Look over at the girl. She's watching Willard Scott talking to some guy dressed like a turkey. Asks Dr. Bighead if he'd turn up the volume. He says, no, it would just distract his team. Think he's pissed because Phil switched off the purple dinosaur.

Just as well. Gives us a chance to get acquainted.

She starts first. Asks me my name. Tell her. She nods, tells me hers. Sylvie Simms. Hi, Sylvie, I say, nice to meet you.

Scientists murmur to each other behind our backs. Sylvie asks me where I'm from. She tells me she's from Columbus, Ohio.

C'mon, man, Phil says. Turn up the volume. Can't hear what he's saying about the weather.

Dr. Bighead ignores him.

Look over at Doug. Got a Walkman strapped to his waist. Eyes closed, head bobbing up and down. Grooving to something in his headphones as he keeps on trucking.

Been to Columbus, I say. Nice city. Got a great barbecue place downtown, right across the street from the civic center.

Sylvie laughs. Got a nice laugh. Asks if it's a restaurant with an Irish name. Yeah, I say, that's the one. Serves ribs with a sweet sauce. She knows the place, been there many times.

And so we're off and running. Or walking. Whatever.

Doug listens to rock bands on his Walkman, getting someone to change CDs for him every now and then. Phil stares at the TV, supplying his own dialogue for the stuff he can't hear, bitching about not being able to change the channel. A kid walks by every now and then with a bottle of water, letting us grab a quick sip through a plastic straw.

Sylvie and I talk to each other.

Learn a lot about Sylvie while waiting for the blisters to form. Single. Twenty-seven years old. Got a B.A. in elementary education from the same university where I got my start as a rat, but couldn't get a decent job. Public schools aren't hiring anyone who doesn't have a military service record, the privates only take people with master's degrees. Became a rat instead, been running for two years now. Still wishes she could teach school, but at least this way she's paying the rent.

Tell her about myself. Born here. Live there. Leave out part about not being able to read very well, but truthful about everything else. Four years as a rat after doing

a stint in the Army. Tell her about other Phase One tests
I've done, go on to talking about places I've gone hiking.

Gets interested in the last part. Asks me where I've
been. Tell her about recent trek through Nepal, about the
beach at Koh Samui where you can go swimming without running into floating garbage. About hiking to the
glacier in New Zealand and the moors in Scotland and
rain forest trails in Brazil.

You like to travel, she says.

Love to travel, I say. Not first class, not like a tourist,
but better this way. Get to see places I've never been
before.

Asks what I do there. Just walk, I say. Walk and take
pictures. Look at birds and animals. Just to be there,
that's all.

Asks how I've been able to afford to do all this. Tell
her about mortgaging my organs to organ banks.

Looks away. You sell your organs?

No, I say, I don't sell them. Mortgage them. Liver to
a cloner in Tennessee, heart to an organ bank in Oregon,
both lungs to a hospital in Texas. One kidney to Idaho,
the other to Minnesota . . .

Almost stops walking when she hears that. You'd sell
them your whole body?

Shrug. Haven't sold everything yet, I say. Still haven't
mortgaged corneas, skin, or veins. Saving them for last,
when I'm too old to do rat duty and can't sell plasma,
bone marrow, or sperm anymore.

She blushes when I mention sperm. Pretend not to notice. She asks if I know what they're going to do with
my organs when I'm dead.

Sure, I say. Someone at the morgue runs a scanner
over the bar-code tatoo on my left arm. That tells them
to put my body in a fridge and contact the nearest organ
donor info center. All the mortgage holders will be no-
tified, and they'll fly in to claim whatever my agent ne-
gotiated to give them. Anything left over afterwards, the

morgue puts it in the incinerator. Ashes to ashes and all that happy stuff.

Sylvie takes a deep breath. And that doesn't bother you?

Shrug. Naw, I say. Rather have somebody else get a second chance at life from my organs than have them rot in a coffin in the ground. While they're still mine, I can use the dough to go places I've never been before.

Treadmill is beginning to run just a little faster now. No longer walking at a granny pace. Dr. Bighead must be getting impatient. Wants to get some nice blisters on our feet by the end of the day.

Phil sweats heavily now. Complains about having to watch Sally Jesse instead of Oprah. Don't wanna watch that white whore, he says. C'mon, gimme that black bitch instead. Doug sweating hard, too, but just keeps walking. Asks for Smashing Pumpkins CD, please. One of the kids changes his CD for him, but doesn't switch channels on the TV.

Couldn't do that, Sylvie says. Body too precious to me.

Body precious to me, too, I say, but it ain't me. Gone somewhere else when I'm dead. Just meat after that. Why not sell this and that while you're still around?

She's quiet for a long while. Stares at the TV instead. Sally Jesse is talking to someone who looks like a man dressed as a woman but looks like a woman trying to resemble a man, or something like that.

Maybe I shouldn't have told her what I think about organ mortgages. Being a rat is one thing, but putting your innards on the layaway plan is another. Some people don't get it, and some of the ones who get it don't like it.

Sylvie must know this stuff. All rats do. Most of us sign mortgages. So what's her problem?

Bell dings somewhere behind us. Time for lunch. Didn't even notice that it was noon yet. Dr. Bighead comes back in, turns off treadmills. Gets us to sit on examination tables and take off shoes. No blisters on our feet yet, but he still puts us in wheelchairs. Okay, he says, be back here by one o'clock.

Can't wait, Phil says.

Lunch ready for us in rec room. Chicken soup, grilled cheese sandwiches, tuna salad. Push our way down the service line, carrying trays on our laps, reaching up to get everything. Been in a wheelchair before, so has Doug and Sylvie, but Phil not used to it. Spills hot soup all over his lap, screams bloody murder.

Share a table with Sylvie. Newspapers on table for us to read. Intern brings us mail forwarded from home. Bills and junk for me, but Sylvie gets a postcard. Picture of tropical beach on the front.

Ask who it came from. Her brother, she says. Ask where her brother lives, and she passes me the postcard.

Pretend to read it. Only big word I know is Mexico. Always wanted to visit Mexico, I say. What does he do down there?

Hesitates. Business, she says.

Should shut up now, but don't. What kind of business? Looks at me funny. Didn't you read the card?

Sure, sure, I say. Just asking.

Thinks about it a moment, then she tells me. Younger brother used to live in Minneapolis, but was busted by the feds early last year. Sold cartons of cigarettes smuggled from Mexico out of the back of his car. Smoking illegal in Minneapolis. Felony charge, his third for selling butts on the street. Three-strikes law means he goes to jail for life. For selling cigarettes.

Judge set bail at seven grand. Sylvie came up with the cash. Brother jumped bail, as she knew he would. Fled south, sought amnesty, went to work for Mexican tobacco company. Sends her postcard now and then, but hasn't seen him in almost two years.

That's tough, I say. She nods. Think about it a little. Question comes to mind. How did you come up with seven grand so fast?

Doesn't say anything for a minute, then she tells me.

Got it from mortgaging her corneas.

Five is the usual price, but she got seven on the overseas black market. When she dies, her eyes go to India. At least it kept my brother from going to prison, she says, but I can tell that isn't the point.

Sylvie doesn't want to be buried without her eyes.

She takes back the postcard, turns it over to look at the beach on the front. Kind of makes you want to visit Tijuana, doesn't it?

Tijuana looks like a great place, I say. Always wanted to go there. At least he's found a nice place to live.

Gives me long, hard look. Card wasn't sent from Tijuana, she says. It's from Mexico City, where he's living now. That's in the letter. Didn't you read it?

Oh, I say. Yeah, sure. Just forgot.

Doesn't say anything for a moment. Pulls over the newspaper, looks at the front page. Points at a headline. Says, isn't that a shame?

Look at picture next to it. Shows African woman with a dead baby in her arms, screaming at camera. Yeah, I say, that's tough. Hate it when I read news like that.

Sylvie taps a finger on the headline. Says here that the unemployment rate in Massachusetts is lowest in fifteen years, she says.

Oh yeah, I say. That's not what I meant. That's good news, yeah.

Pushes newspaper aside. Looks around to see if anyone is listening. Drops her voice to a whisper. You can't read, can you?

Face turns warm. No point in lying to her. She knows now.

Only a little, I say. Just enough to get by, like a menu

or a plane ticket. Not enough to read her brother's post-card or a newspaper.

Feel stupid now. Want to get up and leave. Forget that I'm supposed to stay in the wheelchair, start to rise to my feet. Sylvie puts her hand on top of mine, makes me stay put.

It's okay, she says. Doesn't matter. Kind of suspected, but didn't know for sure until you asked me about what my brother said in his letter.

Still want to leave. Grab rubber wheels, start to push back from table.

C'mon, don't go away, she says. Didn't mean to embarrass you. Stay here.

Feel like an idiot, I say.

Sylvie shakes her head. Gives me that smile again. No, she says, you're not an idiot. You're just as smart as anyone else.

Look at her. She doesn't look away. Her eyes are owned by some company in India, but for a moment they belong only to me.

You can learn how to read, she says. You've just never had a teacher like me.

Get blisters on my feet by end of first day. Same for the other guys. Dr. Bighead very pleased. Never seen someone get so excited about blisters. Wonder if he's got a thing for feet.

Scientists take pictures of our feet, make notes on clip-board, then spread lotion on our soles. Pale green stuff. Feels like snot from a bad head cold, smells like a Christmas tree soaked in kerosene. Use eyedroppers to carefully measure the exact amount. Should have used paintbrushes instead.

Everyone gets theirs from different bottles. No idea if I got the test product or the placebo, but blisters feel a little better after they put it on.

Doesn't last long. Skin begins to itch after dinner. Not bad itch, but can't resist scratching at the bottom of my feet. Sort of like having chigger bites from walking in tall grass. Sylvie and Phil have the same thing, but Doug doesn't. Sits in corner of rec room, reading paperback book, never once touching his feet. Rest of us are watch the tube and paw at our tootsies.

Guess we know who got the placebo.

No treadmill work the next day, but we go back down to the lab after breakfast and let the scientists examine us some more. Tell them about the itching while they draw blood samples. They nod, listen, take more pictures, make more notes, then put more green stuff on our feet.

Different formula this time. Now it's Extra Strength Green Stuff. Must be made out of fire ants. Nearly jump off the table. Sylvie hisses and screws up her eyes when they put it on her. Phil yells obscenities. Two guys have to grab him before he decks the kid who put it on his feet.

Feet still burning when we go back upstairs. Sylvie goes to her room. Doug picks up his book and reads. Phil mad as hell, pissing and moaning about Dr. Bighead. Says he only did this to get a little extra dough, didn't know they were going to put him in jail and torture him to death. Says he wants to go put his feet in a sink.

Don't do it, I say, it'll screw up the test. Tell him that trying to punch out a scientist is way uncool. Calm down, dude. Let's play some eight-ball. Get your mind off it.

Mumbles something under his breath, but says, yeah, okay, whatever.

Hard to shoot pool sitting in wheelchairs, but we manage for a while. Phil can't get into it. Blows easy shots, scratches the cue ball twice. Sinks eight-ball when I've still got four stripes on the table. Loses temper. Slams his stick down on table, turns chair around and rolls off to his room. Slams the door.

Look up at lens in the ceiling. Know someone must be catching all this.

Go over to TV, turn it on, start watching Oprah. Sylvie

comes over a little while later. Asks if I want to begin reading lessons.

Not much into it, I say. Wanna watch Oprah instead.

Gives me a look that could give a woody to a monk. C'mon, she says. Please. I'd really like it if you would.

Think maybe I can score some points with her this way, so I go along with it. What the hell. Maybe I might learn something. Okay, I say.

Turns off TV, wheels over to bookshelf, starts poking through it. Think she's going to grab a book or a magazine. Can't even read the titles of most of them. If she brings back Shakespeare or something like that, I'm outta here.

Picks up a bunch of newspapers from the bottom shelf. Puts them in her lap, hauls them over to a table, tells me to come over next to her.

Finds the funny pages. Asks me if I like comic strips. Naw, I say. Never really looked at them. Smiles and says she reads the funnies every morning. Best part of her day. She points to the one at the top of the first page. Here's one I like, she says. Tell me what this little kid is saying to the tiger.

That's how I start to learn how to read. Seeing what Calvin and Hobbs did today.

After lunch, we go down to the lab again for another checkup. Feet no longer burning, but the itch is back. Feet a little red. More blood samples, more photos, more notes. More ointment on our feet. Doesn't burn so much this time. Looks a little different, too. Must be New Improved Extra Strength Green Stuff.

Scientists notice something different when they look at Phil's feet. Spend a lot of time with him. Compare them to photos they took earlier. One of them takes a scalpel, scrapes a little bit of dead skin off the bottom of each foot, puts it in a dish, takes it out of the room.

Phil keeps saying, what's going on? What's the big deal? Gotta right to know.

Scientists say nothing to him. Examine Sylvie and Doug, spread more ointment on their feet, then let the three of us go back to the dorm. Tell Phil he has to stay behind. Say they want to conduct a more thorough examination.

Dr. Bighead walks past us while we're waiting for the elevator. Just says hi, nothing else. Goes straight to the lab, closes door behind him.

Phil screwed up, I say to Doug and Sylvie when we're alone in the elevator. Don't know how, but I think he screwed up.

Just nod. Know the score. Seen it before, too. People go crazy sometimes during a long test. Happens to new guys all the time. Every now and then, some dumb rat gets washed down the gutter.

Return to rec room. Doug picks up his paperback, Sylvie and I go back to reading the funnies. Trying to figure out why Sarge just kicked Beetle in the butt when door opens and Phil comes in. Not riding a wheelchair now. Dr. Bighead and a security guard are right behind him.

Doesn't say much to us, just goes straight to his room and collects his bag. Leaves without saying goodbye or anything.

Dr. Bighead stays behind. Says that Phil was dismissed from the experiment because he scrubbed off the product. Also displayed lack of proper attitude. Won't be replaced because it's too late to do so without beginning the tests again.

We nod, say nothing. No point in telling him that we were expecting this. Warns us not to do the same thing. Phil isn't being paid for his time, he says, because he violated the terms of his contract.

Nod. No sir. We're good rats.

Apologizes for the inconvenience. Asks us if we need anything.

Sylvie raises her hand. Asks for some comic books. Dr. Bighead gives her a weird look, but nods his head. Promises to have some comic books sent up here by tomorrow. Then he leaves.

Doug looks up from his book as the door shuts behind him. Good, he says. Leaves more green stuff for us.

Two weeks go by fast.

Phase One tests sometimes take forever. Drives everyone crazy. This one should, because we're not on the treadmills every single day and have lots of time on our hands, but it doesn't.

For once, I'm doing something else besides staring at the tube. Usually spend hours lying on a couch in the rec room, watching one video after another, killing time until I go to the lab again.

But not now.

After work and on the off-days, I sit at a table with Sylvie, fighting my way through the funny pages.

Sometimes Doug helps, when Sylvie needs to sleep or when her feet are aching too much. Both are patient. Don't treat me like a kid or a retard or laugh when I can't figure out a long word, and help me pronounce it over and over again until I get it right. If it's something difficult, Sylvie describes what it means in plain English, or even draws a little picture. Take notes on stationery paper and study them at night until I fall asleep.

Able to get through the funny pages without much help after the first few days, then we start on the comic books Dr. Bighead got for us. *Archie* and *Jughead* at first, because they're simple. When Sylvie isn't around, Doug and I get into discussing who we'd rather shag, Betty or Veronica, but pretty soon I'm tackling *Batman* and *The X-Men*. Find out that the comics are much better than the movies.

Doug is a good teacher, but I prefer to be with Sylvie. Funny thing happens. Start to make sense of the newspaper headlines. They're no longer alien to me. Discover that they actually mean something. Stuff in them that isn't on TV.

Then start to figure out titles on the covers of Doug's books. Know now that he likes science fiction and spy novels. Better than movies, he says, and I believe him when he tells me what they're about. Still can't read what's on the pages, because I still need pictures to help me understand the words, but for the first time I actually want to know what's in a book.

Hard to describe. Sort of like hiking through dense rain forest, where you can't see anything except shadows and you think it's night, and you try to stay on the trail because you don't know what's out there. Then you get above the treeline and there's a clearing. Sun is right over your head and it's warm and you can see for miles, mountains and ranges and plains all spread out before you, and it's so beautiful you want to spend the rest of your life here.

That's what it's like. All of a sudden, I'm not as stupid as I once thought I was.

One night, after everyone else has gone to bed and the lights are turned off, I find myself crying. Don't cry easily, because that's not the way I was brought up. Dad beat the crap out of me if he caught me doing so, called me a faggot and a little girlie-boy. No short or easy way to explain it, but that's sort of why he took me out of school, made me go to work in his garage. Said he wanted me to be a man, that he didn't want no godless liberals messing up my brain with books and ideas.

When he dropped dead with a socket wrench in his hand, I was eighteen. Only thing in my wallet was a draft card I couldn't read. Time in the army showed me the rest of the world and made me want to see more, but by then was too late to go back to school. After that, only choice I had to stay alive and see the world was to become a rat. A rat whose body didn't belong to himself.

Something wrong when the law lets a human be a rat, because a rat has more respect than a human. Rats can't learn to read, but a human can. No one wants to spend money on schools, though. Rather spend it on building prisons, then putting people in there who sell cigarettes. Meanwhile, teachers have to go do things that they won't let rats do anymore.

Didn't cry that night for Sylvie or her brother, even though that was part of it. Cried for all the lost years of my life.

Spend few days trying to learn as much as I can, but can't get past one thing.

Sylvie.

Started to learn how to read because I wanted to shag her. Going along with her seemed like the easiest way of getting her into bed.

Can't do that during an experiment, because sex with other rats is a strict no-no in the standard contract. Seen other rats get punted for just being caught in someone else's room, even when both persons had their pants on. When tests are over and everyone's paid, though, there's nothing wrong with a little party time at the nearest no-tell motel.

Still want to sleep with her. Get a Jackson sometimes just sitting next to her in the rec room, while she's helping me get through some word I haven't seen before. Can't take my eyes off her when she's running the treadmill next to me.

Different situation now, though. Isn't just about getting Sylvie in some cheap motel for some hoy-hoy. Not even about learning how to read. Got some scary feelings about her.

Two days before the end of the tests. Alone together in the rec room, reading *Spider-Man* to each other. Ask her straight. Say, hey, why are you helping me like this?

Keeps looking at comic book, but flips back her hair

and smiles a little. Because I'm a teacher, she says, and this is what I do. You're the first pupil I've had since college.

Plenty of winos in the park who don't know how to read, I say. Could always teach them. Why bother with me?

Gives me long look. Not angry, not cold. Can't quite make it out.

Because, she says, I've always wanted to visit Kathmandu, and maybe I've found someone who can take me there.

Can take you there, I say. Can take you to Nepal, Brazil, Ireland. Mexico to visit your brother, if you want.

Blushes. Looks away for a second, then back at me. Maybe you just want to take me to nearest hotel when we're done here, she says. I've done that. Wouldn't mind doing it again, either.

Shake my head. Like Kathmandu better, I say. Sunrise over Annapurna is incredible. Would love you to see it with me.

Love? Thought I was just teaching you how to read.

Look around to see if anyone is watching. No one there, but there must be someone behind the lens in the ceiling.

Hell with them. Put my hand under the table and find hers. One more word you've taught me, I say.

She smiles. Doesn't take her hand away. Finds a pen in her pocket, hands it to me, pushes some paper in front of me.

If you can write it, she says, I'll believe you.

Phase One test of the product pronounced a success on the final day. Last batch of Brand New Improved Green Stuff doesn't smell, doesn't itch, doesn't burn, and heals the blisters on our feet. Doesn't do a thing for our leg cramps, but that's beside the point.

Dr. Bighead thanks us, writes his name on the bottom

of our checks. Tells us we've been wonderful test subjects. Hopes to work with us again soon. In fact, are you
available next March? Scheduled test of new anti-
depressant drug. Looking for subjects now. How about
it?

Look at Sylvie. She's sitting next to me. Doesn't say
anything. Look at the check. It's written on an account
at the First Bank of Boston, and it's signed by Dr. Leon-
ard Whyte, M.D.

Thank you, Dr. Whyte, I say. My agent will be in
touch with you. Ciao.

A cab is waiting for us at the front door. We tell the
driver to take us to the nearest hotel.

Three years have passed since Sylvie and I met in Boston. A few things are different now.

She finally managed to get me to use proper grammar
instead of street talk. I'm still learning, but personal pro-
nouns are no longer foreign to me, and it's no longer
necessary to refer to all events in the present tense. To
those of you who have patiently suffered through my
broken English during this chronicle, I sincerely apologize. This was an attempt to portray the person I once
was, before Sylvie came into my life.

We used the money earned during the Boston tests for
a trip to Mexico City, where Sylvie got to see her brother
for the first time in two years. Six months later, we flew
to Nepal and made a trek through the Annapurna region,
where I showed her a sunrise over the Himalayas. Since
then we have gone on a safari in Kenya and rafted down
the Amazon. Now we're planning a spring trip to northern Canada, above the Arctic circle. A little too cold for
my taste, but she wants to see the Northern Lights.

Anything for my baby.

The first night in Kathmandu, I promised to give her
the world that I knew in exchange for hers. She made
good by her promise, and I'm making good by mine.

Nonetheless, we're still rats.

We can't marry, because the labs that supply our income won't accept married couples as test subjects. Although we've been living together for almost three years now, we keep addresses in different cities, file separate tax returns and maintain our own bank accounts. Her mail is forwarded to my place, and only our agents know the difference. We'll probably never have children, or at least until we decide to surrender this strange freedom that we've found.

This freedom is not without a price. I've mortgaged the last usable tissue in my body. Sylvie hasn't repossessed the rights to her corneas, despite her attempts to find a legal loophole that will allow her to do so, and although the time may come when she has to give up an organ or two, she insists that her body is her own.

More painful is the fact that, every so often, we have to spend several weeks each year participating in the Phase One tests. Sometimes they're often the very same experiments, conducted simultaneously at the same test facility, and we have to pretend to be strangers.

I haven't quite become used to that, but it can't be helped.

But the money is good, the airfare is free, and we sometimes get to see old friends. We spent a week with Doug a couple of months ago, while doing hypothermia experiments in Colorado. He and I discussed favorite Jules Verne novels while sitting in tubs of ice water.

For all of that, though, I lead a satisfactory life. Sylvie and I have enough money to pay the bills, and we visit the most interesting places around the world. I have a woman I love, my mother has stopped bothering me about getting a job, and I've learned how to read.

Not only that, but we can always say that we've done our part for the advancement of science and all mankind.

For what more can a good rat ask?